Love
Happens

Annabelle Howard

FOR MY MOTHER

Peggy Stevens (née Evans), with love and gratitude

CONTENTS

ACKNOWLEDGMENTS

I would like to acknowledge a nonprofit, Big Fun Education, for funding my adaptation of Hamlet and allowing me to make free audio plays available to schools everywhere. Google also merits acknowledgement for giving Big Fun Education a marketing grant via AdWords.

1 EXACT CHANGE

"You hungry?" Holly asked Danah from the passenger seat.

"Trying not to be." Danah smiled, gripping the steering wheel. The traffic light blinked green. She held her breath and eased her foot off the brake, grateful to have a distracting adventure with Holly. "Dunkin Donuts OK?"

A nod from Holly and Danah turned left. They settled into a drive-through line with four cars ahead of them.

"Thanks for coming with me today, Danah. This woman is amazing. She says things that jolt you out of your skin. Last time — I already told you this, didn't I — she saw my grandfather and gave me a message from him!"

A photo Danah had come across last night flashed in her mind, a faded image of her glamorous mother standing in front of curtains patterned with elves. She held a baby that was reaching towards a man. He held the curtain tight against his cheek. The baby and the man scrutinized each other, somehow knowing the peekaboo game was no laughing matter. That must be me, Danah had thought, running her finger from the baby's face to the man's and back. He wore a tweed sports coat with leather buttons and a cravat. She hadn't recognized his profile at first, but now it was unmistakable: We have the same chin. This must be me with my father! She had not said those words out loud. She did not speak about her father. Once, I was all he saw. Tears invited themselves into her eyes as she tried in vain to see through the baby's eyes and to feel her father's gaze directly on her. She knew very little about her father aside from the fact he had been famous a long time ago, in England, as an actor. And yet, only this morning at breakfast, Danah's teenage daughter, Elsie, had asked, "Do I have a great grandfather, Mom?" and while Danah was soothing her daughter by insisting everyone has great grandfathers and grandfathers – whether they get the chance to meet them or not – a magical thing happened: Danah believed her own words.

"She literally *saw* the ghost of your grandfather?" Danah

asked, studying her friend's face as if she could scan for truth.

"I hadn't been able to go to his funeral. I'd always felt bad about it, but hadn't told a soul. There I am, in a normal room in a normal house and suddenly, a woman tells me a ghost wants to speak to me. She describes the birthmark on his left hand: It was him. Then she says he loves me and understands why I couldn't be there at the end. Danah released the brake and the car pulled forward a few feet. "By the way, she doesn't remember anything she says during a reading. You'll want to record your session. Is your phone charged?" Holly checked Danah's phone and plugged it into the dashboard.

"I want a ghost to speak to *me*." Danah stared at an American Robin hopping along a dirty wooden fence and wondered why it chose not to fly. "I haven't told Bob we're doing this. He thinks I'm too sensible to see a psychic. This stays between us. What do you want, Holly?"

"I don't know," Holly said, twirling her wide wedding band around her finger.

"Muffins, Holly. What kind of muffin?" The cloud passed from Holly's face when she saw the drive-through-lady smiling down at her.

"Regular coffee and a fat-free orange cranberry, please. Here: I have exact change."

Some minutes later, as they merged onto I-95, Danah said: "Exact change . . . is that even possible?"

"What d'you mean?" mumbled Holly, through muffin.

"Change is so *unreliable*. You want to change. You try to change. You think maybe you have changed, but have you really?"

"You're in a strange mood! What are you trying to change?"

"I don't know. Something, something feels wrong. Something needs to change, maybe something is about to change. I don't know. I have a strong hunch, but I don't know what about."

They drove in silence until the next exit, when Holly said, "It took me ages to decide what to wear this morning. People say psychics read everything: your clothes, body language, wedding ring, all of it. So, I asked the computer. I said, 'OK, Google, what to wear to a psychic reading? You can ask Google anything. It has never told me I'm crazy. It said: Yellow helps you find the clearest direction for your life. And wearing something wooden increases your ability to see the future."

"I'm wearing a yellow cardigan with wooden buttons!"

screamed Danah.

"Now that *is* crazy!" said Holly.

"Holly, are you allergic to your wedding ring? Why are you playing with it so much?"

"Paul's wedding ring was sitting on the side of the hand basin this morning, after he left for the health club. He *never* takes it off. Something is very off with him."

"My guess is he forgot to put it back on after washing his hands. If you'd found it in his jacket pocket that would be different."

"You're a good friend," Holly sighed, and a few silent miles slid by.

"So you want the psychic to somehow improve your marriage? Why don't you just talk to Paul directly?"

"Oh, come on, Danah. You know why: men don't talk! I've tried. He won't talk. He said nothing is going on and that's that: End of story. But I know. I know something *is* going on. Did I tell you that you can ask questions at the end of your reading? By the way, what makes me crazy about Paul is that he's so unbelievably out of touch with how I'm feeling. He was so upbeat last night, literally singing along with some stupid song. Meanwhile, I'm silent. So, after he left this morning, I checked out his underwear drawer and he had two bags of new boxers. Isn't that what they do when they have affairs – buy new boxers?"

"Well . . . that's not all they do, but yes, that is one of the classic tell-tale signs. The man goes for a decade wearing whatever you throw at him, and then suddenly he's fussy about his underwear, and goes out there somewhere to buy his own."

"I went to bed early last night. Paul couldn't have cared less. I came downstairs for some water just after midnight, and there he was -- on the computer. He said he'd found a website that let him draw architectural plans for our health club. He's been talking about building an addition, or renovating. But I knew he was lying, covering. He had definitely been chatting with *her*, whoever the hell *she* is. Oh God! I never thought I'd be talking like this. We were high-school sweethearts!"

"Why don't you install Spyware on his computer? It'll tell you everything he says and everywhere he goes."

"I've heard of that. But there is such a thing as anti-spyware, you know. He could totally wipe out his traces and go incognito. I want to stay married to Paul. I'm hoping she'll reassure me. She was great last time. She calls what she does psychic healing. A computer report just wouldn't do it for me."

A red Miata passed by. Danah entertained a brief fantasy of living a sports-car life. "I'm really sorry you feel bad, Holly. But these are your worst fears you're talking about. You mustn't start believing them and acting like your marriage is over. It's the next exit, right? Then a right off the ramp. We're almost there."

Holly fished in her bag and offered Danah some tropical-flavored TUMS.

"I honestly think you have psychic powers. Two please." Holly bumped two tablets out of the bottle, and served them on the palm of her hand.

"Take this exit. Right off the ramp. Go straight till we see a liquor store. There. Now, right onto Long Hill Road. It's number 148. See it?"

"How could a psychic live in a raised ranch with a bunch of broken-down cars in the driveway?" Danah said. The women gave each other a we-came-all-this-way-so-we-might-as-well-go-see look and carefully walked the wavy line of cracked paving stones to the front door before pressing the plastic doorbell. A pot-bellied man answered the door wearing a thin white undershirt and navy pants splattered with beige paint.

"You girls come far? Come in." Danah bristled at being called 'girls.' She drew her lips into the smiling position but her eyes failed to smile. Both women nodded while looking around. The man exited through a door under the stairs. They sat on a small couch draped with a multi-colored, hand-crocheted blanket.

"Maybe he was a Greek god in a past life?" Danah offered.

"Stop it!" Holly whispered, sucking down laughter. "Stop! For this to work we have to take it seriously."

A door opened and out came a quiet conversation. Litany was approaching with a client. The woman was thanking Litany. She seemed flustered, and was clearly in no state to exchange pleasantries with strangers. Litany reminded the lady how to get back to the highway. Then she closed her front door and smiled.

"Holly?" she inquired. Litany looked like grandma from a children's picture book. She was small, rotund in a cozy way, and moved slowly. She wore a gathered skirt, a white blouse, purple slippers, and a pink, chenille shawl which she held tightly across her shoulders. "It gets cold talking with the other side, you know," she said, feeling their eyes on her. "Now, who's first?"

"I'm first," Holly replied, jumping up. "This is my friend, Danah."

"Yes, I know. Well, dear. Can you wait here while I read Holly?"

"No problem," said Danah, rethinking the word *read*.

As Danah sat there daydreaming, she thought she could smell gingerbread cookies. She couldn't, but the imaginary smell sent her back to her mother's kitchen table and afternoons spent baking, stealing tastes of cookie dough, and arranging tea parties for her Chinese doll, Ming Lee.

After what felt like only a few seconds to Danah, Holly reappeared. She gave Danah two emphatic thumbs-up without Litany seeing.

"Come to the back room when you're ready, dear. I must blow my nose," said Litany, disappearing into a bathroom.

"She's seriously good," Holly whispered. They heard the toilet flush. Danah was not convinced that anything mystical was about to take place. She walked down the narrow hallway, past the bathroom, and entered a winterized, screened-in porch complete with

Native American wall-hangings, a picnic bench, and a wood-burning stove.

"They are telling me it's too hot for you," said Litany, who had followed Danah into the back room. Danah laughed nervously. She *was* too hot, but she thought this could easily be Litany's standard opening to make customers into believers. Litany cracked open a window and they sat down at the table—the kind of simple wooden picnic table found in a park.

"I am not a fortune teller," said Litany, in a sharper voice than she had used when talking about blowing her nose. "God gave you free choice in this school of life. Are you recording this?" Danah placed her phone on the table and tapped the icon of a microphone. With this simple action, she abandoned her comfort zone. It occurred to Danah that she would never describe this moment to Bob. Never.

Litany pressed her puffy hands together and mouthed a prayer. Danah rested her forearms on the table, clasped her hands, and looked at the multi-colored, braided, cotton rug on the floor. The women sat opposite each other in silence until Litany said:

"I am surrounding us with pure, white light, Danah, so that

only good spirits will come to us. You understand about mediumship. They tell me you understand. I'll forget everything when the reading is over. You have the tape. It's your business, not mine. Ask questions at the end. If I bring a name to you from the spirit world, you can play back the tape, figure it out later. Do not interrupt me.

"As I come into your vibration your grandmother is dancing to get in. She is stocky, from your mother's side, and she was a medium. She comes in with a lot of love. She had trouble walking before she passed.

"You can relax, please. Don't try so hard."

Danah unclench her teeth, place her feet flat on the ground, and breathed in deeply to the silent count of six. She didn't have the nerve to look Litany in the face, so she studied the wood grain in the table.

"I see a male vibration who resembles you very much," Litany continued. "You two are so similar in the way you are, your feelings, everything. There is pain between you." Litany abruptly turned away to look over her right shoulder and spoke as if she could see someone. "Give it to me so I can understand it and give it out. You've walked this path in life with a weight around your neck.

You've been badly hurt by your family over and over again. But you accomplish a lot. Your grandmother tells me, 'She hasn't done so bad!' You have considered other people's feelings before your own, but having a child changed that. Can you place this?"

"Yes." Danah instantly thought of how she had restricted Elsie's contact with her alcoholic step-grandfather, Bernard, never mind how much that hurt her mother.

"You are a powerful soul. Your spiritual self is emerging. You were loved as a baby. You were wanted. But something happened. Relatives who never saw you because of the circumstances prayed for you. There has been much sadness for you." Litany suddenly looked restless: she rocked from side to side. She tugged at the sides of her skirt, rearranging the folds of fabric.

"Ask me a question so I can hear your voice, dear."

"Is my father there?"

"The tall, thin man has a face like yours. He lost a lot of weight before he crossed over. I'm drawing blanks here. No message. Is your father still in the living?"

"No."

"You have many unanswered questions because of a lack of

communication with your family. I'm seeing a handsome man with a full head of hair. The same man who was flesh on bone when he went. He looks so much like you. He had a good life. He was well known and then he was suddenly ill. He passed so quickly." Litany went silent. She nodded and waved her hand as if to call someone forward. "Your father is saying there was a . . . speak clearly, 'a strange eruption.' Can you place this?"

"No."

"You are waking up to your spirituality and the nature of things. This is all your father can give you -- an answer without an answer. The spirits are pulling your shoulders back. Stand proud. How they love you! Remember to ask for help. You are not used to asking for help. Ask for their help. Let them guide you." Litany mouthed a closing prayer and then slumped a little. Danah felt dazed as she picked up her phone. She placed a hundred dollars in the small basket marked for donations, and wondered what she had done. Then, she rejoined Holly and left the house feeling unnerved and light-headed.

With the car doors slammed shut, Holly asked Danah what she thought of the experience.

"I don't know yet. That was a lot to take in. She definitely has some kind of gift." Danah's mood was plummeting, but she could see how happy Holly looked, and so she shut off her own thoughts. "How about you, Holly?"

"Well, I am so glad we came. It's incredible how much better I feel." Danah wondered if there was a law of emotional physics that gave best friends a combined happiness quotient – when one is really happy, the other has to be miserable.

"What did she say exactly?"

"Let's see. Well, basically, she said: I have nothing to worry about because I have love. I mean, she said a lot more than that, but that was the basic take-away. She said I was so lucky to have a loving husband and that I need to trust his love."

"That's exactly what you wanted to hear!"

"I know. And to hear that from a stranger, it feels so healing. I can't explain it, but I feel so comforted, calmer than I've felt in months. What did she say to you?"

"That's the funny thing. I can't remember much,' Danah said.

"You recorded it, right?"

"I did."

"What's the matter?"

"She's left me feeling off-balance. Sad, I guess. I don't know why. It seemed exciting at the time. She said my father's mother had always sent her love to me, stuff like that. That was nice to hear. My dad was there, but he didn't speak to me. I didn't even know I wanted him to speak to me until now. I've been fine without him my whole life, and now I suddenly feel like I need him to talk. So weird." Danah fixated on an exit sign fast approaching.

"Maybe he did say something, but you couldn't take it in? Litany told me to listen to the tape because I'd be surprised at what I'd hear the second time. She immediately knew it was my marriage that brought me to her. I didn't say a word about Paul. She said there is always a dormant time right before you see growth. And the dormant stage can be disturbing because it seems like something has gone wrong, so that's what I'm going through."

"I'm glad you heard what you wanted to hear. I'm really sorry, but do you mind if we don't speak for a while? I'm getting spikes of migraine."

"No. Of course. Do you want me to drive?"

"It's good for me to drive, to focus on something . . . real; but my head hurts. I just can't talk any more right now. Sorry, Holly."

Upon returning to Danah's house, Holly jumped in her own car and went straight home. Danah immediately felt better alone, and her muddled thinking lifted like morning mist. "A strange eruption, a strange eruption," she repeated aloud and then, as if watching theater curtains opening, she suddenly settled down. My dad wants to tell me something, and I'm going to ask Litany for help.

2 GETTING THE LOAN

The next morning, Danah felt more alive: the exact change she had wished for had happened. Instead of feeling uneasy and restless, she now had an urgent mission and a secret plan to construct.

"More coffee?" her husband called from downstairs.

"Please. Yes." She had decided to wear a fitted black corduroy dress with a full skirt to the bank this morning. It had occurred to her to ask Google what to wear when signing a construction loan, but then she caught sight of this dress that her mother had bought her a few Christmases ago. She lifted the sides of her skirt as if she were about to curtsy, then dropped the soft, black fabric and stared deep into her own eyes to see if she could see the enormous emotional change she felt. She had grown up watching her mother inventing herself in the mirror. Vera never let a day go by without 'putting on her face.' Danah assumed, in retrospect, this was a hangover from her mother's theater days. Somehow, Vera could always manufacture an upbeat persona with a little sponge and foundation. However, Danah sensed at a young age that makeup wasn't going to save her. With or without makeup, her feelings always showed, and that meant she had a melancholy look. About a month ago, she heard a woman on N.P.R. say: "Until a person hits forty they have the face they were born with, and after forty they've got the face they made themselves." This alarmed Danah. She did not want people thinking her sadness was of her own making. That would be shameful. After all, she was so lucky having a loving husband, a beautiful daughter, a flexible job, great friends, her health, and more.

"Is that new? Looks good," her husband said, coming up behind her, and kissing her cheek in passing. Bob wore navy suit pants, a white shirt laundered by the dry cleaner, and black socks. Danah thanked him for bringing her a coffee and watched him finger his way across his rack of ties on the back of his closet door. He picked out a jaunty Save-the-Children design showing strings of yellow, red, and green children holding hands.

"I don't look like me when I wear a dress." She turned her back to the mirror as you might to a liar, and sipped strong Columbian coffee with a dash of chocolate soy milk. She watched her husband take his blue suit jacket from its Brooks Brothers' hanger: always a finger to the bridge of his glasses to push them up his nose before putting his arm into the jacket; and always the right arm first. Bob's contented nature comforted and stabilized Danah. She watched her well-dressed husband leave the bedroom. "What time do we have to be at the bank?" She slipped off a heavy, gold bracelet and left it on her bedside table. She didn't want the bank person to think this was her big outing for the week, because it wasn't. Going to the psychic had been the big one.

"Ten," Bob called, from downstairs. She glanced at her phone. It wasn't even nine. Danah entered her pale grey bathroom and rummaged in her transparent makeup bag, hoping some stick or another would jump into her hand and give her a photo finish. She backed out and wandered into Elsie's bathroom instead, for no good reason. *Apparently, I'm on a tour of the bathrooms.* Bending over to pick up a damp towel made her feel queasy. *I'm nervous, not sick, nervous, everyone feels nervous before taking out a loan.* But she knew that wasn't it. The psychic's words were curdling her insides: *A strange eruption. Can you place that?* She felt guilty about dabbling in the occult. *Perhaps I should tell Bob everything?* She felt briefly comforted by the certainty that if she did tell him, she would never see Litany again, and the power of those words would surely fade.

She crossed the hallway into Elsie's bedroom, which stood as a testament to the adorability of each and every stuffed creature in creation, especially pandas. She spotted Tiny Panda stranded on the old, stained white carpet. Why do people love pandas so much? Maybe it's something about the black-and-white of them, holding Tiny Panda in the palm of her hand. It's impossible to resist the clear-cut confidence of a black-and-white animal. The length of Elsie's bed was pushed up against the wall. She straightened up the clutter on the bedside table, smiled to see *Now We Are Six* by A.A. Milne, and longed for a poem called "Now We Are Forty-Six."

"Danah! It's your mother!" shouted Bob. How can my mother be here? She lives in Florida, panicked Danah; and as if Bob could hear her thoughts, he added, "On the landline."

"OK!" she yelled, feeling a gush of the mixed feelings she always felt at the onset of her mother. She seized a breath. "Hi, mom. You don't usually call during the day. Everything OK?"

"Bernard's out, so I thought I'd give you a call."

"Everything's fine here, except I'm sort of nervous today.

We're just about to sign for the construction loan."

"Why are you nervous about that? Bob wouldn't do it if it weren't a good thing. He's good like that. It must be something else you're nervous about, darling." She knows me too well.

"Maybe it's something else then? Let's think. What's the date?" Bob appeared tapping his watch. Danah raised her index finger like a wand, while giving him three quick nods of her head: he disappeared.

"February 18th. Stewart's death date," Vera answered with the optimism of a game show contestant.

"Of course," said Danah, gripping the phone far harder than needed.

"Yes. Fifteen years. Fancy that!" Danah wished she had missed this call.

"I've got to go, mother."

"Now, don't get down about your father's death, darling. Everyone dies, Danah. Try to remember that. Hello, Bernard. Why are you back so soon?" Danah heard her stepfather yelling about the cost of long-distance calls. There's no distance long enough between you and me, you horrible little man, feeling as if a grenade of venom had exploded in her belly.

"OK, mom, we mustn't be late for our appointment at the bank. Bye."

"Good luck today. Remember what I said, darling."

"Everyone dies. I'll remember that. Bye now."

"We're going to be late," said Bob.

"No, we're not going to be late. We'll be on time instead of early. It'll be OK." Danah ran downstairs and stood in the foyer gazing at a sea of shoes. Bob picked up his brown leather briefcase. She had one sneaker on before she remembered she was wearing a dress.

"I'll be right back. I've got to get my ankle boots," and ran back up the flight of floating stairs that she knew were no longer up to code because at least three carpenters had pointed this out when she was asking them to give her bids on removing a sagging skylight. Danah had been looking at her house with the eyes of an appraiser for some time now. It pained her to know her home had been classified as a split-level. She was silently hoping this renovation would transform the house into a contemporary. On her way back down to the front door, she imagined persuading the bank to reclassify the house on psychological grounds.

There's a new study out. It was in *The New York Times* today. It says adult children of divorced parents have a very hard time living in the present and that living in a "split" house prolongs the absence of healing. It says that issues come up when such children reach their mid-forties and that living in a contemporary is recommended.

"I really want to drive. Do you mind?" she asked Bob.

"But my car's ready to go." A concatenation of garden furniture occupied the space in the garage where Danah's car should have sheltered itself from the ice that now caked her windscreen. Danah never drove Bob's car.

"Please? I've imagined us going in my car."

"OK. Let's not be late." He locked the front door to the house. They stepped cautiously over the icy, cracked flagstones between the front door and her minivan.

"We need to reset these flagstones," said Danah. Bob set to work scraping ice off the windscreen. Meanwhile, Danah sat in the driver's seat, running the heater and the defrosters. It was bitterly cold. She regretted wearing the stupid dress. She deeply appreciated how Bob always accommodated her wishes, once she made them clear. It's rare we tell each other what we want. Her eyes wandered the rock garden on her right. She noticed the cylindrical, red birdfeeder, and then her eyes traveled the breezeway through to the soft, golden tones of marshland on the horizon. She had an imaginary conversation with a nonexistent loan officer.

"Do you offer loans for renovating a marriage?"

The loan officer leans towards us, trying to bridge the gap between his comfy leather chair and our metal folding chairs. He says, "It's a little-known fact, but yes, we do offer loans for marital renovations. What size loan do you have in mind?"

"I'm thinking Extra Large, sir, Jumbo perhaps. What sizes do they come in?"

"What is the principal reason for the loan?"

"He doesn't talk to me. We don't say anything to each other that we wouldn't say to any of our friends." The loan officer acquires a sharp intake of breath, and extradites a stray hair from the arm of his charcoal gray suit jacket.

"So that's what women mean by 'talking?'"

"That's a big part of it. If he's telling me something he told someone else earlier, well, I don't really consider it 'talking.'"

Through the rearview mirror, Danah saw Bob jabbing the blue, plastic ice scraper across her rear window. Her eyes kept track of him, while her mind continued to converse with her imaginary loan officer.

"My wife says I don't talk. But since I talk all day, I always tell her she's being ridiculous. But you think she might be right, don't you?" I shrug, not wanting to ruin my chances of getting the loan.

"Have you thought of applying for a marital renovation loan for the two of you?" I venture, gently.

"I probably shouldn't be telling you this, but yes, we did apply. But this bank is extremely rigorous about looking into loan applications by employees." He looks up and smiles very quickly at a suited woman entering the glassed-in office next door. Suddenly, he looks like he isn't going to talk.

"What happened?" I prompt.

"She failed the spousal inspection."

"They inspect the spouse?"

"Of course, madam," he says, suddenly sitting abnormally upright. "The application procedure requires the completion of a detailed checklist. Did you think the bank just gives out loans willy-nilly?"

"No, no, of course not, but a spousal inspection?"

Bob was coughing. Danah coughed, unconsciously trying to clear Bob's throat for him. Meanwhile, Bob caught hold of his dangling grey scarf, pulled it tight across his chest, and tucked the ends inside his navy overcoat.

"My wife was a bad risk," says the loan officer. I stare at him. I refuse to let it go at this. His eyes sweep the listening distance. "She named too many girlfriends. They said she would never truly confide in me." I adjust my position in the chair and attend to folds in my skirt, hoping that my apparent inattention will trick him into revealing more than he should. "And, well, she agreed that ideally she would like us to talk more, but that it was true she did have one girlfriend or another to go to with all the types of thoughts she tended to have. She said it was unlikely she would cut out her girlfriends and talk to me instead. So they denied the loan."

"I'm very sorry," I say, reeling from the fact that I thought this would be a simple story about him and it turned out to be a parable about me not confiding in my husband.

Bob swung into the passenger seat with a waft of cold air. He blew hot air into his cupped hands. Bob had a thing about not wearing gloves. He'd rather have cold hands, even if his wife had bought him a soft, brown leather pair, and popped them into his stocking on Christmas morning. Today, Danah admired him for doing things his own way and ignoring the naysayers.

"Thanks for doing that," Danah said. "Is your throat OK?"

"It's a bit scratchy. I swallowed the wrong way and it set me off. Have you got any cough drops in here?"

"There are some in my bag, I think." Bob rummaged while Danah eased the car onto the coastal road in reverse.

The bank was a few minutes north. Danah approached a 4-way stop. A car, so big it looked like the U.S. army needed it back, pulled to a stop directly across from them.

"At the risk of irritating you, dear, why did you turn left back there? The bank was straight over."

"I know." She slid into her favorite gas station.

"We have a quarter of a tank of gas!"

"Fill her up," she said to the young gas guy. "You're asking me why I'm getting gas right now, even though we clearly have enough to get to the bank?"

"It's a fair question."

"Well," she explained, pulling on the edge of an American Express card that was passively resisting her from its tight sleeve in her black leather wallet. "So many people have said renovating a house is a nightmare and that we don't know what we're getting ourselves into." The twenty-something guy leaned towards Danah as he washed her windscreen, and she did not remove her eyes. "And you know how people go on about all the pitfalls of renovating: the stress of writing check after check, how it can tear a marriage apart, on and on, you know. Well, I got the idea of going to the bank on a full tank of gas." Bob looked at her as if she hadn't finished the explanation. "I took some other precautions, too. Look in the glove compartment." Bob glanced at it the way he might if she had booby-trapped it.

"There's a full deck of cards in there. As in, we are working with a full deck." Danah handed her credit card to the gas guy and when he was at a safe distance, she whispered to Bob, "And I've got balls, Bob!" She glanced over her shoulder, hoping to prove her point.

"What?" he said, all high-pitched and happy.

"I've got 5 juggling balls on the back seat somewhere. I wanted to be *prepared*. I wanted to go into this with the proverbial full deck. You know, hit it with a full tank of gas? And I wanted to be proud of us having the balls to ignore the common wisdom." She paused. "We got balls, Bob!" They were both laughing as she signed for the gas and took her credit card back.

Bob pushed open the heavy glass door to the bank and held it for Danah, who was struggling to walk – her corduroy skirt clung to her legs like a toddler.

"Can I help you?" said a woman standing at a booth in the center of the hall. Danah noted how comfortable the woman seemed to be with her dress, belt, jacket, bangles, bracelet watch, rings, necklace, and earrings.

"We have a ten o'clock with Mrs. O'Shea." Bob's voice was broadcast-quality.

"You're the principal of Island Elementary, I believe!" said the woman with a wink. Danah's face didn't perform such acrobatics. She felt as if she had accidentally strayed beyond her own planetary system. "My daughter's in the high school now, but not so long ago I was picking her up at your school. How time flies! Is Mrs. Keener still there? My Bonnie loved being a Keener Kid!"

"Yes, Mrs. Keener is teaching second grade. What's Bonnie's last name?"

"Munroe. Bonnie Munroe."

"An excellent reader, I recall," said Bob, at which Mrs. Munroe flushed with pride.

"Yes, Bonnie does love to read. Always has." She glanced into the offices to her left. "Mrs. O'Shea is off the phone now," she added, smiling at Mrs. O'Shea, who wore a bright red suit and an entire shopping channel of jewelry. The resonance of her high heels on the marble-tiled floor impressed Danah, who felt like a little girl wearing a school uniform.

Mrs. O'Shea shook Danah's hand and said: "How nice to see you again."

"This is my wife, Danah," said Bob, insisting the women enter the office before him.

"Oh, of course!"

Danah felt zero connection with financial people, and so her eyes darted around the office for clues into the banker's personal life. No husband picture in sight, just one large frame on the wall with multiple openings occupied by babies and kids. Danah decided to believe Mrs. O'Shea was widowed at a young age. That way she instantly generated compassion toward her and stifled the hostility she often felt towards women who wore bright red in daylight hours.

"I have the additional documentation required," said Bob, reaching into his briefcase. "This is the information about our car payments. And this provides you with a record of my pension plan." He placed two clumps of papers on her desk and spun them around to face her.

"Well," said Mrs. O'Shea, after giving the new papers a cursory going-over, "I believe you have satisfied our requirements at this point in the game." Something Mrs. O'Shea saw on the new papers sent her fingers into a flurry of clacking on her calculator. Danah felt a nervous pang because she couldn't work that fast with numbers. Mrs. O'Shea removed her gold-rimmed glasses and let them hang on her chest by a string of miniature pearls. She turned to a page tagged with a pink Post-It. "Allow me to fill in a few basics that seem to have been overlooked. Where were you born, dear?"

"Um . . . London, England.

Mrs. O'Shea smiled.

"But no trace of an accent!"

"No, I'm afraid not, well, I came to America when I was two." Danah's aggravation was now turning on herself. For God's sake, stop being apologetic about not sounding British, she told herself, and then said, "My mother still sounds British."

"And, let me see," Mrs. O'Shea said, walking her red nails through the stack of printed pages. "Somewhere we have . . . yes, the Department of Immigration and Naturalization! These must be your naturalization papers."

Danah lost herself in a prolonged internal cringe. How she hated playing the clichéd wife without a financial clue. At the first meeting, a few months ago, Mrs. O'Shea had begun by politely addressing financial questions to both parties signing the loan, but a few minutes later she dropped that formality like a dirty diaper. Bob had answered every question. Mrs. O'Shea hadn't even looked at Danah again until it was time to say goodbye, and today she hadn't even remembered her name. Danah rarely spoke in a mathematical conversation.

". . . naturalization?" she heard Mrs. O'Shea say, looking directly at her.

"Yes, she did," said Bob. Danah yearned for her cue to exit. She loathed the smugness she sensed around the term "naturalization." *Would I have been a poor unfortunate "*un*natural"* *if I had remained a British subject?*

"And how old are you?" smiled Mrs. O'Shea. *As old as my tongue and a little older than my teeth,* came the silent answer. Her mother had drilled into Danah at a young age how rude it was to ask an adult his or her age. So now the rudeness about age on top of the agony she felt around numbers affected Danah so she could barely function. Her mouth opened and hung there, waiting for her brain to send a message that never arrived. Mrs. O'Shea did not hide her amazement at having to refer the question of Danah's age to Bob.

"Forty-six," he said, amused.

"That's why I married him," said Danah, abruptly back in action now that the number had been spoken. "We're the same age." Danah had intended to be funny, but had hit upon some truth by mistake. It wasn't true that she'd married Bob because they were both born in the same year, but she had come to rely on him to take care of all the numbers in her life, and to remember the things they had definitely done. However, to discover that she had let it go this far was embarrassing. "I've never been good with numbers, and they do say age is a number, don't they?" No one laughed, and Danah was ready for the mortician to lay her out right there on the banker's desk.

"Danah's written a wonderful children's picture book about math phobia. What was it called, Danah?"

"*The Magic Paint Box*," replied Danah, all neutrality now, as if the all-clear sirens had sounded. There will be no more air raids today. Rest assured everyone.

"Have you picked everything out for the renovation?" asked Mrs. O'Shea. Please God, make this woman shut up, prayed Danah, and Danah rarely asked God for anything.

"Yes, pretty much," responded Bob, looking proudly at Danah who was doing her very best to vaporize. "My wife has some terrific ideas. She's very good with color." Mrs. O'Shea nodded and Danah believed Mrs. O'Shea was thinking what an idiot Bob was to trust her with the checkbook.

"I hope I haven't jeopardized our chances of securing the loan!" Danah said. Bob and Mrs. O'Shea laughed.

"No, no. I'm sure your home will be delightful. You really

can't go wrong on Beach Road. I think we're all making a solid investment."

"Have you financed other renovations on Beach Road," asked Bob.

"Oh yes! Many, many over the twenty-six years I've worked here. The loan-to-value ratio is excellent on beachfront properties. Property overlooking the water always increases in value."

"Unless there's a hurricane, or an earthquake, or something, and then the value would drop off pretty sharply, I'd imagine," said Danah, unable to resist that one. Mrs. O'Shea and Bob laughed in unison, and Danah took this as her cue to exit. She scraped back her chair and stood up.

"So, Mrs. O'Shea," said Bob, "the next step for us is to get a closing date from our attorney?"

"Yes, that's right. He may receive the go-ahead as early as next week."

"And how do we get the money?" inquired Danah, regretting how naïve she sounded.

"That's a good question," laughed Mrs. O'Shea. "You'll be contacted by the Disbursement Officer. The loan is usually broken down into four draws. At the closing, you'll receive a schedule of work that has to be completed before the first draw can be released. The renovation must be completed within eleven months from the date of the closing." Bob stood up slowly. "But the good news is that you pay no interest on a construction loan until it is paid out in full and you've had the mini-closing to consolidate your pre-existing mortgage with the converted construction loan." Mrs. O'Shea shook hands with them both and claimed it had been a real pleasure doing business.

"I am so glad that is over," said Danah to Bob in the car on the way home. "Bank people make me feel like a spoiled kid. And why do bank women wear so much jewelry? Why gold? I don't think there's another single profession where the women wear so much gold jewelry, except maybe the jewelry profession itself."

They rode in silence for a few minutes. Bob drove.

"Well, we got balls and a construction loan, now!" said Bob.

3 GETTING CONCRETE

Thank god it's Monday, thought Danah. She had managed to stay home for five days straight. Ever since the psychic reading she had become increasingly reluctant to go out. She had a feeling that if she left the house she might find herself at Litany's door, begging for another reading. Part of her wanted nothing more and yet she was deeply afraid of being told anything that contradicted the stories Vera had told her about her childhood. All through the weekend, snatches and phrases from the reading had tormented Danah. She hadn't dared to listen to the session yet. Again, she was afraid it might inspire her to take action she would regret. I'll make a transcript as soon as Elsie and Bob leave the house this morning. Bob had already left and Elsie had about fifteen minutes before the bus would arrive.

"Mom!" Elsie yelled.

"Coming," Danah called. She padded upstairs in her white slippers and yellow dressing gown, holding out a fresh mug of coffee before her like a compass. Elsie's room was the warmest in the house since the furnace was directly below and this made it an excellent place to sit on a cold March morning.

"Where are my black vest and my long, black shorts?" Elsie

stood with one arm leaning against her built-in closet. She was an inch or so taller than Danah, although this had yet to be acknowledged by both parties. She was dressed head-to-toe in baggy black.

"I put them away, honey."

"Mom, I need them."

"They are forecasting snow again, Elsie. I've put all the thin things away. Spring isn't here yet."

"Where did you put them?" Elsie's hands were now on her hips.

"What's the big deal?"

"There's an audition today."

"Oh Elsie! Are you going to audition?"

"If I get my black vest and shorts."

"You didn't tell me."

"I'm telling you now."

"OK, I'll dig it out again. But I only just put it all away. I thought I'd make more room in your closet because they really are spring clothes."

"I don't need the backstory, Mom. I've got to go." Danah

smiled at her child for using the word backstory, and then, in the time it took for Elsie to clean her teeth, Danah found the clothes and laid them out on Elsie's bed. Elsie packed the long shorts in her backpack and put the vest on over her black polo neck.

"What's the play? Anything I've heard of?"

"*Hamlet.*"

"*Hamlet?* I'm amazed they're doing *Hamlet.*"

"Why? It sounds like a cool story, you know, a kid wondering if he'll kill his step father or not." Elsie tilted her head to the right and grinned.

"It's a difficult play. That's all."

"Yes," said Elsie, swinging her transparent, soft plastic backpack over her shoulder and leaving the bedroom door, "And can I have some lunch money? Is Dad still here?"

"I'll see what money I've got. No, your father left early. He had a meeting in Hartford." Danah remembered finding a five-dollar bill in the pocket of her black jeans yesterday while doing the laundry. She had momentarily considered ironing it, what with the iron being right there, but she had resisted the temptation, believing that sort of compulsion a shortcut to a very public insanity. People in stores would notice immediately if the money had been ironed. No, if I'm going to be eccentric, I'd prefer to cultivate a private madness, she had decided.

Elsie reappeared wearing a broad-rimmed felt hat of her father's.

"Really, Elsie?"

"Why? What does it make me look like?"

"Well, a man, I suppose."

"Thank you!"

"Don't you want to look all floaty like Ophelia?"

"Mrs. V. will give Ophelia to Janet. No, I want to be Hamlet."

"You can't *be* Hamlet, honey."

"Why?" asked Elsie.

"No woman has ever played Hamlet as far as I know. Although, with all that hesitating he does, I can see it being a female role, well, that's if Hamlet were middle-aged and female. Is that sexist of me?

Elsie had one hand on the front door handle. "Wish me luck in this weary, stale, flat and unprofitable world today!" She turned the handle and had the door open when Danah added,

"No, I mean . . . *why* do you want to be Hamlet? Are you sure girls can audition for the role of a Prince?"

"Mrs. V. said we can audition for what we want."

"OK. Well, break a leg!" Elsie waved goodbye from the other side of the glass door. Danah watched her daughter jog down the short driveway to catch the school bus. The tall collar on her coat hid her long blond hair. Her black coat swung from side to side in time with her bouncing backpack.

The school bus pushed along Beach Road, absorbing the neighborhood kids like a giant, yellow sponge. She turned and ran up the half-flight of badly scarred wooden, soon-to-be refinished stairs, and she marveled at how 'refinished' is a positive when applied to a wooden surface. You wouldn't dream of a person wanting to be refinished. No, a person wants a makeover.

Danah sat at her kitchen island, surveying the kingdom. She loved her house for sheltering her, for making her life seem easy and safe. She loved the light from the untreated windows. When Bob had once suggested *treating* the windows, she had squinted at them, saying, "Why would we *treat* them? Treat them for *what?*" and so they had remained untreated. The kitchen, sitting room, and dining room flowed into each other around a central fireplace that had counted as two fireplaces in the appraisal. The wall to the left of the kitchen consisted of three sets of oversized glass sliders and there was a row of four square windows resting above the sliders, and above those, two stained glass skylights. From late morning until late afternoon direct rays of sunlight penetrated the colored glass, throwing splashes of intense color onto the walls and floor: yellow, red, and blue. During the course of the decade they had lived on Beach Road, Danah and Bob had been given a fine collection of blue glass bottles and vases which they displayed on the deep sills of the untreated windows, thus increasing the glow of the room. Recently, Danah had decided to add red glass to the mix. This impulse had surprised her, because apart from the red coat and hat she had liked when she was in elementary school, red was a color she avoided. She had thought it too loud. Now, she had growing respect for people who spoke up and out.

Danah wandered upstairs and was vaguely on her way to getting dressed when she heard a truck pull up and the doorbell ring. She lived a brief version of the actor's nightmare in which the curtain goes up and you are totally unprepared to go onstage. She grabbed yesterday's clothes, which were conveniently piled on the floor on her side of the bed—black sweatpants and sweatshirt. Seconds later, she opened the door to Norm, her carpenter, who stood with a semi-amused expression and half a cup of coffee.

"Forgotten all about me, eh?" he said. "What's the saying . . . out of sight, out of mind?" He stood on the doorstep hunched around his paper coffee cup.

"You got the 'out of mind' part right! Come in, come in. Is it really cold out today?"

"You got the permits, then?" he asked. Danah marched triumphantly to a drawer at the end of her twelve-foot, soon-to-be-refinished kitchen island, and pulled out three envelopes.

"We got a demolition permit! And, ta-dah! We got two building permits!"

"Hot dog! What do you know? The building department came through."

Danah handed the permits to Norm, and the pure, positive power of them seemed to warm his hands. He put down his coffee cup on the island and looked them over. Danah was a little embarrassed by how proud she felt of having her name on these papers.

"Got any tape?" Norm asked. "We should stick them up on the front door. Just in case. Let's show Bob we're playing his game."

"Bob? Why are we proving anything to Bob?"

"Building-inspector Bob. I heard another story about him."

"Oh, I thought you meant my husband Bob. Go on, what?"

"Once, on a job on the north side of town, he shot a woman's dog dead."

"He what?"

"He was there to inspect something. He got out of his truck, and this dog came at him. He pulled out his 9 millimeter. Shot the animal to death." Norm drained his coffee cup.

"Oh, my god!"

"And guess who I'm calling now?"

"Dead-dog Bob?"

Norm nodded while grinning.

"Oh great, let's invite him over!" she said.

"Yes, this is Norm Lewis. I'm working on the Beach Road property. Sure, I can wait." Norm covered the mouthpiece and whispered to Danah, "Never hurts using a fancy address." The mother of a child Elsie had liked in fifth grade had recommended Norm to Danah. That and the fact that he was reliable was all she knew about him. "Right, OK," said Norm. "I have some questions about footings and a frost wall. Right. Rest of the day, yeah. OK. Thanks."

"Dead-dog Bob's coming over?"

"Yup. We're on his schedule now." Norm handed back the permits.

"I'm guessing this is a guy we should take seriously, right?"

"Just pay attention to what he doesn't say," Norm said.

"What are you going to do today?"

"I think you should stick these permits on the front door. It says they should be posted. I'll get started on the deck." Norm went outside. Danah had visions of Dead-dog Bob shooting out the glass in the front door if he didn't see these permits displayed. As Danah measured off lengths of tape, she realized she had grown fond of the demolition permit. She hoped she could work demolition permits into a few conversations; for example — Well, I'd be careful with your tone of voice if I were you, buddy, 'cos I got a permit to demolish. It's got my name on it and yesterday's date. Norm knocked on the door as she continued to stare at the three posted permits. She stepped back, and he poked his head in.

"Did you call Ed yet?"

"Ed?" said Danah, as if it were a vocabulary word she had forgotten to study.

"The landscaper. He'll make dump runs. It'll be cheaper than a dumpster."

"Right. Yes. Yes, I called Ed. He can come at the end of the week if we're ready for him by then."

"We'll be ready. I'm going to start taking out the deck and the porch right now."

"OK. Great." Danah felt a surge of energy at the thought of her plans being put into action. It had been her idea to redesign the deck and convert the screened-in porch into an insulated office space. I'd much rather have a real office than be screened-in, she had said to Bob, who saw her point immediately, and added that the office would be an ongoing tax deduction.

The phone rang. It was an Ed, who was at a job a few streets away, who knew Norm, and who wanted to come and look at the job. It took a few direct questions to discover what exactly Ed did. Apparently, Ed was a mason who had worked with Norm. Norm knows me, he kept repeating. He couldn't come over now, but he wanted to know how long Norm would be there. She told Ed he must come before four and hung up.

Danah stood in the kitchen, leaning with her back against the counter, and watched Norm who was smoking in the screen-in porch. She wished he didn't, and was grateful that she had never had to ask him not to smoke in the house. He didn't look like a smoker. He looked strong. His teeth were extremely white. But he did smell like a smoker. He was able to work and smoke at the same time, which was good, because he was on the clock. So, with cigarette in mouth and no gloves, he carried off a large chunk of splintery deck railing, and this left Danah feeling a little sad despite the fact that she had cursed at that wood for ten years. When Elsie was a toddler, she had received some nasty splinters from that railing.

Danah secluded herself in her bathroom and changed into a more presentable outfit—black jeans and a couple of sweaters. She kept the heat pretty low in the house during the day.

She came downstairs and put an aluminum kettle on to boil

on the glass stovetop. She wanted tea. She checked on Norm's whereabouts. He was on the far side of the screened-in porch with his electric saw blazing. While she watched the kettle gradually work its way up to producing a wisp of steam, she decided to transcribe Litany's session today. *A strange eruption.* Danah drew a blank over and over again. Maybe when I make the transcript and see it in context again, something will come to me. Danah proceeded to make a cup of orange tea with a teaspoon of honey and take it upstairs to the computer. She connected her phone to the charger and tapped the recording app. The sound of Litany's voice spooked her, making the experience very real again and impossible to ignore. Danah typed as fast as Litany spoke: *I feel you are at a place now where you're tired of second-guessing, tired of putting up with not knowing. You have held yourself back for the sake of others.*

Danah went downstairs for a break. She suddenly became aware of an enormous man at the front door. The side of his fist thudded on the glass, and she knew in an instant that it was Dead-dog Bob. Her impulse was to hide: she was in no mood for an inspection. However, she played her part and went to greet him. He did, after all, have the power to condemn her house as uninhabitable, shut down all work on the house until he changed his mind, or to knock off a domestic pet.

"Need some exploratory drilling!" he said for openers. She was afraid he was going to call her 'little lady' and equally afraid she was going to take it.

"Thank you for coming by at such short notice. Yes, I think we will need to do some exploratory drilling. Where do you suggest we start?"

Dead-dog put out a steak of a hand, saying, "My name is Bob. It's not your fault. That's my name." Danah's hand disappeared inside Bob's for a moment while she said, "Danah Reynolds." She thought better of telling him that her husband was also named Bob.

"This your contractor?" continued Bob, giving Norm, who was walking towards his truck, the once-over.

"Yes," hesitated Danah. Norm was named as the general contractor on the town's paperwork because he had a license number, but, in fact, she was hiring everyone and paying them herself. Norm walked over with a slight swagger, something she hadn't seen before. Must be the walk he does for dog shooters. Norm and Dead-dog shook hands. They had met once before, at the

Building Department offices in the Town Hall when Norm had filed for the permits.

"These pavers?" said Bob.

"We're filling in the breezeway. Taking ten feet of the garage and making a recreation room," said Norm. Danah didn't think Norm had answered Bob's question, but Bob had a steady gaze on the paving stones and seemed content.

"Need some exploratory drilling to see what's under there, how deep it goes," insisted Bob. Danah marveled at him. Proposing to go beneath the surface of anything struck her as hugely courageous. "House built on a slab?" Dead-dog fired at Norm.

"Yep."

Danah winced. She did not like to think of her house as being on a slab.

"No basement? No crawl space?" He over-shook his head as if he were an amateur actor in a death scene. Danah wanted to tell Dead-dog that she didn't care for crawling, that having a "crawl space" had never been a dream of hers. "Might be all right, then. Might be able to get away with pouring concrete into molds. But you'll need to drill here, here, and here," Dead-dog said, sliding heavy-duty boots into three different places. "Don't want it to heave," he said to Danah in particular.

"God no! I hate heaving," she said, instantly regretting it, but Dead-dog liked her guts and Danah shared a bonding moment with Dead-dog in spite of herself.

"If you don't go deep enough into the ground with foundation in New England, it rises up at you," Dead-dog added. Danah was honestly grateful to have this explained so clearly. "You don't want some kind of strange eruption now do you?" Danah gasped at his words, but neither man noticed her reaction. "Well now, you see," Dead-dog Bob continued, "you have to look into these things."

"Maybe the slab under the house continues under the breezeway," said Danah, determined to stay in this conversation.

"Won't know till we drill," Dead-dog said. "Otherwise, we're talking forty-two inches." Danah wondered if the subject had been changed.

"I'll get the mason to drill," she said.

"Can you take a look at this?" Norm led him through the breezeway to the back of the house. Danah sank onto the doorstep and waited for them to return. It amazed her how quickly the Inspector had decided on a course of action. *Taking action is a way of life for these men. Need to see what's under there, how deep it goes.* His words would not leave her alone. And on top of that, she was still reeling from the shock of hearing him say *strange eruption.* *It's as if I'm being told not to give up, to go on exploring.*

"You're the boss!" she heard her carpenter say to Dead-dog. She smelled unforeseen labor costs. They rounded the corner. Dead-dog had his back to her and she threw an imploring look at Norm.

"How 'bout that trailer, Bob. D'yer sell it yet?" Bob swung around, walked across the spots marked for expensive, noisy drilling and faced both Norm and Danah. He smiled so deeply into Norm's eyes that Danah wondered for a second if he'd fallen in love with him.

"Sold!" proclaimed Bob and he strode crisply towards his red Dodge Ram. "Gone!" he yelled out his window, triumphantly. Norm and Danah watched him hang his right arm over the back of the passenger's seat and reverse onto Beach Road without a hint of caution.

"There *is* some good news," Norm said slowly. "He didn't say he needed to come back and inspect the drilling." Danah felt grateful for Norm, and it occurred to her that Norm could be short for Normal.

"He's OK."

"He is? He shoots dogs."

"Yeah, but he likes me!"

"I noticed!"

"He'll be OK. Don't worry about him. You've got other things to worry about." Norm's toothy grin appeared.

"Like what?" Danah snapped, quasi-alarmed.

"Getting a mason locked in, for one."

"Ed's coming over today. He called this morning," said Danah, hoping desperately that she was competent enough to pull this renovation off.

"Oh yes, there's always Ed."

"And what does that mean?"

"Let me put it this way. Once, when we were in high school, I saw Ed bite a beer can open with his teeth and suck the can dry. And all this with his hands tied behind his back." Norm looked ecstatic with this recollection.

"Why would someone do that?"

"Insane, I guess."

"So should I hire an insane mason?" Norm laughed. "No, seriously, Norm, is this the man I want to see coming at my house with a pneumatic drill and a truck load of cement?"

"If you can get him. Last thing I heard, he and his dad were building a seawall in Norwalk. Someone said it wasn't going well. It was taking longer than they thought."

"Well, when I spoke to him this morning, he was on a job near here. He said he'd come over this afternoon."

"Good enough."

Danah entered the house and took in a deep breath to the beat of six silent counts. She told herself if Ed could build a wall that kept back an ocean he could surely build her a twenty-foot stretch of foundation that wouldn't heave. She reached for the comfort of some tea and realized her mug of tea had gone deadly cold. *I want a teapot, a pretty teapot with a cozy.*

She took the mug of cold, peppermint tea to the leather couch and stared into it. *Why didn't my father speak to me? He was a performer, for Christ sakes. You'd think he could rise to the* occasion. The man was an actor: He gave speeches to strangers who sat in the dark, unable to talk back.

The high-pitched rasp of Norm's saw started up. She walked over to the stove to look at the digital clock. She went upstairs to check e-mail on the desktop computer. There was one from Bob. "Meeting this morning went well, but means I'll be home late. Don't wait for me."

The words 'Don't wait' pushed towards her, elbowing the other words out of her way. *Don't wait.* Everything felt like a mysterious message to her now. Danah instinctively put on some white headphones and continued making a transcript of Litany's reading. *You have many unanswered questions because of a lack of communication with your family. I'm seeing a handsome man with a full head of hair. The same man who was flesh on bone when he went. He looks so much like you. He had a good life. He was well known, and then he was suddenly ill. He passed so quickly. Your father is saying there was a . . . speak clearly, 'a strange eruption.' Can you place this?*

Was a strange eruption, Danah repeated. She released herself from the headphones and leaned back. So, the strange eruption has already happened. But aren't ghosts supposed to warn you of things *about* to happen? Why must I care about something that's over? What was so strange about this eruption? What am I supposed to do?

Danah went downstairs, sat on the couch and wrapped herself in a bright blue fleece blanket. She sat for a good long time digging a mental tunnel that led nowhere.

She heard voices: Norman and someone. She went to the front door and saw a white, windowless truck. I hope it's the mason, she thought, and slipped on a white down vest and black boots before joining the three men standing in the breezeway: Norman, an old man, and a younger man. Norm was smoking. No one acknowledged Danah. After listening to them talk for a few minutes, she interrupted.

"Did I speak with you on the phone this morning?" she said, smiling at the younger man.

"I'm Ed. Norm knows me. This is my father." Ed's father looked like a random garden gnome: knees buckled, no red hat, motionless.

"Yes, we did speak this morning." Danah took the liberty of answering her own question and wondered why Ed fixated on the idea of being known by Norm. "Norm, did you tell Ed what the inspector told us about drilling?"

"Yep."

"Bob still got that red Mustang?" Ed asked.

"Mustang? No. He's driving a Dodge Ram."

"A red one," added Danah. No one spoke and Danah wondered if she had suddenly been given the power to end conversations. When she couldn't take the strain of silence any longer, she asked the older man who hadn't said a word yet, "So, you work with Ed?"

"Best in the business at laying forms," said the younger man, Ed, grinning at his father sweetly. Danah panicked at the sight of his pointy, yellow teeth. She could picture him biting through an aluminum can.

"So what do you think?" Danah asked younger Ed, masking her own doubts. Ed missed his cue. "This'll only take a couple of days, right?" she said, looking intently at Ed who ought to be looking at an orthodontist. "I mean, it's not a . . ." she hesitated. She didn't want to say "big job." Bob and Danah had used those words when potty-training Elsie. Danah used to applaud big jobs. Ed scratched his head with a grimy hand and followed this up by studying the dirt under his nails. Danah snatched a look at the old man, the mason's father. The poor man was horribly pale and didn't look at all well.

"I don't know," proclaimed Ed, finally.

Danah was determined to make something positive out of his statement. This is the man I am looking to for a foundation, after all, a foundation, a basis upon which all else will follow. "We have a construction loan. I'm not relying on the stock market to pay for any of this."

The mason turned to his father who now looked like he was trying to remember which medication he forgot to take today. Perhaps it is unfair of me to ask how long this job will take. I wonder how much insurance they carry for on-the-job accidents.

"Remember that big job we got, Sid?" said the younger mason said to his father. Danah was at once relieved to hear someone speak and to get the words "big job" out of the way. The air had been cleared. She shifted her position and looked at the old man for a response. Not a flicker. He stared down at something that wasn't there. "Remember that sea wall, Dad? That old guy?"

Suddenly, all eyes were on her. It felt like a pivotal moment. She nodded, thinking that perhaps her role was that of a conversational go-between, that somehow she must supply the gestures and dialogue missing from the father. Perhaps they only choose to work with clients who can do this, who can channel the father's thoughts and convey them to the son? She continued nodding and hoped the son understood that his father did indeed remember the sea wall and the old guy.

"He died," Ed confided to Danah. She stopped nodding. She felt bad for the old man who died and for the old man listening to the fact that old guys die. "He was coming back from New York on the train. They told us he didn't have much money. He needed a sea wall. I got the price down about fifteen thousand. Then he died. Like that. On the train." Sharing this with her seemed to have been cathartic for the masons. They began showing interest in her house. Ed kicked a broken flagstone.

However, Danah's thoughts remained on that train. Was the old guy traveling alone? Did anyone notice and stop the train? Or, did no one notice until they got to New Haven and found the body slumped with a one-way ticket? She hated to waste the mason's time, but she needed some sort of closure on the story. "So he just died? Just like that?" she said.

"Yup. So we have a gap in our schedule, right, Sid?" The father miraculously took full responsibility for his own nodding.

"That's great," she said, feeling a bit queasy about taking the dead man's spot so readily. "What happened to the old guy, then? I mean, did they have to stop the train?"

"Don't know," said her foundation man, tugging at the waistline of his navy pants.

Danah's cell phone rang. She held up the index finger on her right hand. "I'll be right back!" she said to no one. Sid and Ed were already inside the garage with Norm. "Hello!" she said sauntering down her driveway.

"This is Ed." It could have been Plumber-Ed, Landscaper-Ed, Ed the silent electrician, or maybe another Ed entirely. Judging by the silence, she assumed it was the electrician.

"Hi, Ed. Thanks for calling back. Now, when can we schedule you to look at the office?" She paused, knowing that she hadn't spoken for long enough. She felt that with Silent-Ed she had to slosh words around in his ears when she first spoke to him, that she sort of cleaned his ears out with the sound of her voice first, and, after a while, he could hear her. "Have you been busy, Ed? I suppose all this rain even affects the electricians, right? Because you can't do what you do until the sheet rock is up and everything, right?"

"It's OK," said Ed.

"Good. That's good, Ed. So when can you come to look at the office?" Silence. "OK, well, let's see, it's Monday today, right? So you could come Tuesday, Wednesday, Thursday, or Friday." She tried to get him to catch a verbal wave.

"Wednesday."

"Great, Ed! That'll work great. I'll see you Wednesday then. Oh, any rough idea about *when* on Wednesday?"

"8:30." So far, Ed had always said he'd come at 8:30 and arrived sometime between 9 and 10.

"OK, Ed. That's great. I'll see you Wednesday."

She turned and walked back towards the house. Ed and Sid were both kicking loose stones on the driveway. Taking a cue from Ed, she walked over and said nothing. It worked like a charm: he looked up and made his first direct eye contact with her, so she smiled.

"You need retaining walls," Ed said. Danah wondered if he was being personal and telling her to lose weight. I think *you* look like you need retaining walls, she wanted to tell him as she watched him appear to shrink, walking away from her, down a slope that led to her neighbor's yard. She held her ground. By the time he'd walked back up the slope she had thought of something to say.

"Why?"

"Soil's gonna wash down."

"But this is a twenty-year old house and the hill hasn't washed away yet, has it?"

"That's what I'd do," Ed said.

"Build retaining walls?"

"Yeah."

"Of course, it's a nice idea, but I'm on a budget. Let's just get the foundation done first." Sid had sat himself in the driver's seat of the dirty white truck by this time. "So, there's a gap in your schedule, right?" Ed nodded while looking down. Danah held her breath by way of controlling the situation.

"I'm going to give you the number of my concrete guy."

"Thank you." She tried not to gush. The masons left.

Danah returned to her desktop computer and finished transcribing Litany's reading: *You are a very intuitive person. When you*

decide to tune into the Spirit World you will have no trouble hearing the messages.
She lifted off the headset and slumped back. Dead-dog's words came
to her: *You don't want some kind of strange eruption do you? You have to look
into these things.* Danah felt bone tired. She got up and hid the
transcript. Elsie was due back.

Over the course of the next few days Danah left the concrete
guy three messages. His name was Johnny Zito, and he had a New
Haven number. So, for the past three days she had been irritable. She
couldn't settle. Added to that, she hadn't seen the masons all week
and they had assured her they'd be back before the end of the week.

Now it was Friday. If they didn't pull up in the driveway by
ten o'clock, she told herself, she'd call them. At ten o'clock, she
walked to the front door and there they were: father and son,
standing in the breezeway, examining the ground. Danah slipped into
soft leather clogs and joined them. This time she knew talking was
not required and she managed to enjoy a few moments of silence in
which she felt no compulsion to speak.

She watched Sid light a cigarette with such methodical
pleasure it made her want one herself. She had smoked every summer
of her twenties.

"How you doin'?" inquired Ed. It had been a while since someone had asked her how she was and she had to fight a strong impulse to spill.

"I called the concrete guy, Johnny, a few times, but he hasn't called me back."

"He's here tomorrow."

"He is? Saturday?" It alarmed her to think of the concrete arriving so soon.

"Or Monday," said Ed.

Danah's shoulders dropped with relief. She was accustomed to uncertainty. Action, even if it was good action, tended to frighten her with its high-definition.

"We're not really ready for him yet, are we?"

"Yep," replied Ed. She liked his answer. It was positive and yet full to the brim with ambiguity. This gave her the satisfaction of having asked a tough question. She had asked. Whether or not he had understood the question was not on her.

Meanwhile, Sid was unloading rather beautiful and weathered old planks from their truck and setting them down in the breezeway. The antique wood had metal buckles attached on one end. The men didn't seem in the least bit conscious of her, so she stood by, watching father and son very nimbly set a series of the planks upright on their narrow ends and lock the planks together into a miniature maze. Two lines of planks ran parallel, about four inches apart. In what seemed like a matter of minutes, Danah could see these little wooden passageways define her foundation. She saw that they would act as molds for the concrete and keep dampness from entering her new room.

"So, if Johnny comes tomorrow, will he be here early?"

"He'll get here after me. I have to be here when he's here," Ed informed her. Sid gave one of the wooden forms a gentle kick. Then he ducked down and tugged at a strip of metal lying under the short, wooden wall. Danah realized with perverse pleasure that she had a mold for some alleged concrete that would be poured at an unspecified time. She could see how construction workers might drive most homeowners crazy, but their rather fatalistic way of working intrigued her.

"So we don't have to do that drilling the inspector was talking about, then?"

"No," Ed confirmed.

"Well, that's good then," said Danah out loud to herself, and then, needing more reassurance, she added, "I suppose it's obvious that the breezeway is on the same slab as the house and the garage."

"Bob was only talking. He does that."

As she entered the house, her cell vibrated – a text message from Little Books, her newest client. Danah was a social media consultant. She texted back that she would call tomorrow with an answer. Norm's electric gun shooting nails into the office framework allowed for no thinking. She put her feet up on the couch and tried to relax.

The phone vibrated again: "What's going on? Call me." It was Holly. Danah stared critically at the wooden ceiling eighteen feet above her—one surface that required no repair. And soon there will be a new room in the house, where now there is a wet and windy passageway. I shall witness concrete being poured into the molds, into the openings that now sit patiently waiting. It's possible to dream something into existence, but first you have to have the dream. Her eyes dropped from the ceiling to the coffee table, landing on her white cell phone. She thought of the photos she had taken before Norm started work on the house. I must remember to show those pictures to Norm, she thought, as she continued to drift and doze.

Minutes later, she jolted awake as if an alarm had sounded. She swung into an upright position, ran her fingers through her hair and stumbled away from the couch feeling guilty.

Glancing outside, she saw the masons going towards their truck. Their day of honest work was over. She panicked at the sound of the truck doors sliding shut, like prison doors. She wished, somehow, she could detain them. When the workmen left, so did her feeling of living in a purposeful world. She stifled the impulse to wave goodbye for fear of appearing childish. She listened for Norm. Not a sound. She felt abandoned and she cursed herself for being so ridiculous.

4 MURDER?

"Oh, Holly! I can't. I'm sorry. I'm so busy this week. My deadlines are out of control," Danah lied, fearing that if she saw Holly, she would say too much, start planning to see Litany again, and she did not feel ready.

"Are the new rooms looking good or is it still at the messy stage? Is it like growing out a hairstyle?"

"Yeah. It is like that. It takes patience to live with the mess. Norm's calling me, Holly, I've got to go, OK? Sorry." Danah tapped "end call."

Norm was out buying wood and cedar siding, Bob was at his office, Elsie was on a field trip to the Yale Rep to see *Much Ado About Nothing*, and she had no urgent work deadlines. Maybe I should start refinishing the wood trim in the kitchen. Can I tolerate more dust and disruption right now? Then she remembered Electric Ed had said he was stopping by this morning to look at the office.

Danah began straightening up the house in case Ed needed to look at wiring everywhere. She started in the master bedroom and felt drawn to look at the two photos on her bedside table --two old photographs suspended in glass frames, edged in black wrought iron. Closest to her pillow was a black-and-white picture of herself as a child—perhaps eight years old—sitting next to her straight-backed grandmother on a stone wall in Cornwall. Her grandmother's sister lived in Truro and her mother's side of the family had reunited there for a few weeks one summer. Danah wore a checkered dress, newly bought by granny, and her legs and hands were placed exactly the same way as her grandmother's. She liked to think of herself taking after her grandmother. *Your grandmother was a medium.* Litany had said this and Danah wondered if her grandmother had known. A memory flashed across Danah's mind: Her grandmother had promised that if she could, she would contact her after she died. The other photograph was much older and showed her grandmother sitting outdoors with her Victorian husband at a small, round table set for a formal tea. Granny looked dutiful. I ought to have a picture of my father's parents. These pictures only tell half the story of where I came from. Litany's words came floating—*The spirits are pulling your shoulders back. Stand proud. How they love you. Ask for their help. Let them guide you.*

Asking for help was not something Danah did. As a child, she had soon learned that her main job at home was to maintain her mother's emotional equilibrium. Asking questions about her father's family history was not done, and, on the few occasions she had persisted, it had sent her mother helter-skelter into a darkened bedroom. So she never complained when they moved again and again. After the move to America, Vera had warned Danah not to talk about her actor-father in England to anyone. No one needs to know about that, she had said, implying with a pointed look that the "no one" included Danah. Vera had drilled into Danah that they were Americans who lived in the present. Until now, Danah had accepted this as normal and assumed her mother gave nothing but good advice. Even now, Danah wouldn't dare to challenge her mother on this score for fear of upsetting her. And every time we moved to a new town, Vera made no effort whatsoever to keep in touch with anyone. She behaved as if all these people weren't real at all, as if they were all actors in a repertory company. She severed ties the way actors do after the run of a show. These people were "family" for a while. "There is no shortage of characters in this world, darling. We'll soon meet some new ones," Vera was born an actress.

How they love you. Ask for their help. Danah found it miraculous and comforting to learn, after all this time, that perhaps her father's side of the family had prayed for her and loved her despite never having known her.

Danah placed the photo she had found recently between these two photos of her granny, taking a step backwards to look at them, as if she couldn't take them all in otherwise. She no longer had to look for family from so few. Her family had grown, if she could believe it. The newness of this idea shocked her because, as a child, she could only look to her mother. Upsetting the only relative I had in the world was never an option. However, if I can trust Litany, there are other spirits on my side. Help me to connect with you, she prayed, looking at the photo of her father playing peekaboo. Help me to see you in myself and in Elsie. And let us know that you are watching over us. The prayer-thoughts came quickly and surprised Danah, who was not accustomed to praying.

When Bob entered the house at six, carrying pizza, she asked, "Did you remember the milk?"

"Oh! The groceries are in the car! Elsie, would you mind getting them for me, dear?" Elsie dutifully brought in the bags, and

Danah's spirits were lifted by the sight of there being more than just milk.

After placing the pizza box on the counter, Bob put the newspaper on the counter, and began fanning out the day's mail as if he were playing Gin Rummy.

"Anything good?" She turned to rinse a drinking glass at the kitchen sink.

"Bills and junk," said he, over the running tap.

"Bills and junk. Junk and bills."

Elsie approached the kitchen with two brown paper bags filled to the jagged edges with groceries. Danah took them from her and unpacked them with the attention Red Cross packages usually receive. She tried to estimate how many days she could make these supplies last.

"Red?" Bob presented her with a glass of wine.

"Mmm. Thank you. Just what I needed."

"Tough day?" asked Bob.

"Oh! I don't know. It's Friday, I guess." She sipped Merlot.

"Do you like it?"

"I do. What is it?"

"It's from a vineyard owned by Francis Coppola."

"Francis *Ford?*"

"Do we know another?"

"I had no idea."

"He invested in a vineyard. Rick, at the wine shop, told me this was good." Danah cleared some counter space for the pizza lid to remain open. Elsie was on her second slice before Danah started her first.

"Elsie, don't eat standing up, dear. Let's all sit at the dining table," said Bob, transferring his own plate and wine glass to the head of the dining table.

"I can't, Dad. I'm going out," said Elsie, through warm cheese and dough.

"How was the play?" asked Danah, staying at the counter with Elsie.

"It was OK."

"OK-good or OK-OK?"

"It was a bit over the top. A couple of them tried to do British accents and they shouldn't have bothered. Grandmother would have died laughing."

"What happened with the audition? Did Elsie tell you, Bob, she auditioned for the role of Hamlet." Bob inhaled pizza in his surprise and spent a moment coughing, breathing, and drinking water.

"No. I didn't know," he got out, finally.

"Weren't you in *Hamlet* once, Dad?" asked Elsie.

"Yes."

"I didn't know that," remarked Danah, pleasantly surprised. "What were you?"

"A gravedigger."

"A gravedigger?"

"It was only pretend, Danah. Don't make it seem ghoulish. It wasn't a second job or anything."

"I would never even want to pretend to be a gravedigger." Danah joined Bob at the table after topping up her own drink. "Once, a Sunday school teacher wanted me to be the Virgin Mary in a Christmas pageant and I refused. I got into quite a bit of trouble for that."

"Why?" asked Elsie, wiping her mouth on a plain white paper napkin.

"I think I was afraid of getting possessed or something." Danah felt the power of alcohol hitting her system and reached for her second slice of pizza. "I hope you're seeing someone, mom, 'cos you're pretty weird!"

"What do you mean *seeing* someone?"

"You know, a head shrinker."

"Elsie, don't be rude to your mother."

"No, Bob. It's OK. I mean, that's what these kids say now. It's better that she talks to us. Some kids stop talking, you know." Elsie shrugged. "So, tell me what happened at the audition, Elsie."

"We ran out of time. She did Ophelia first. I know Janet will get it. She should get it. She did a good audition."

"Do many kids want to be Hamlet?" Danah was hedging. What she really wanted to know was if any other girls wanted to be Hamlet and how stiff the competition appeared.

"Of course they do."

"Why?"

"Because the play's called *Hamlet*." They all laughed. "Is it OK if I go to Erika's for a sleepover? It is Friday."

"Sure, honey," said Danah.

"Are her parents going to be home?" asked Bob.

"I guess so."

"Well, if you find they aren't home, you call us and we'll pick you up," said Bob.

"That's not going to happen again, Dad. That was Erika's brother's fault anyway. He doesn't even live there now."

"As long as we're clear on the rules, Elsie," cautioned Bob. Elsie ran upstairs to prepare an overnight bag.

Danah cleaned up the kitchen and made a pot of coffee while Bob drove Elsie to Erika's. By the time Bob arrived back, Danah was sitting on the couch, staring into powdery, pale ashes in the cold fireplace. Bob brought over the paper and offered her the Home Section.

"No thanks," she said, faintly.

"Oh, I thought you'd be interested. There's an article on home offices." Bob read the Metro Section. Danah stared at ashes and listened to the wind in the trees. She noticed the occasional ping of the coffeepot retaining its heat. The house creaked as it weathered the winter cold and Danah appreciated being sheltered.

"Did you have the workmen here today?" asked Bob.

"Just Norm as usual. Oh and Electric Ed came by briefly."

"That's what you call him? Electric Ed!"

"Only in my head."

"Are there a lot a lot of Eds working on the house?"

"Yeah, there are. When I ask for a referral now I *expect* the guy to be called Ed. Bob put the paper down on the glass coffee table. He smiled at her, and she took this as her cue to elaborate. "Electric Ed's face twitches like a rabbit. He barely speaks. I've wanted to ask him if he was ever cast in *The Wind in the Willows* as a child. He'd be perfect as Mole. I'm used to the twitching now. The way he does it, you can almost see animal whiskers moving. But today, I swear he burrowed into the house. One minute he was outside tacking loose wires to the siding. The next second he appeared beside me, behind the counter in the kitchen. And he stood there blinking, as if adjusting to the light."

"Sounds like the makings for a children's story! By the way, do you want to come into school and read to the kids this year? Literacy Week is next week." Danah picked up the Home Section. "You liked reading to the kids last year, didn't you?"

"I did, but I don't know, Bob. I never know when the

workmen are going to show up, if they're going to need to get into the house to shut off power or something, or when there are going to be questions I have to answer. I have to be here all the time." This answer sounded so persuasive that she believed it.

"OK, but don't you get sick of being in the house all the time?"

"I am a happy shut-in! Why are you so bothered about me being in the house all of a sudden, anyway?"

"I'm not bothered. Are *you* bothered by it? Are you really happy being in the house so much?"

"Well, I'm sure we're getting a better deal out of the workmen because they know I know what's going on all the time. I know what they're supposed to be doing."

"You're doing a great job. I don't mean to sound like I don't appreciate what you're doing." Bob looked like he might read the paper again.

"But, well, since you brought it up, I do sort of wish I were doing something that was more, well, *mine*."

"What do you mean? You're the general contractor, you drew up the plans, you came up with this whole idea here."

"Yes and no."

"Yes and no?"

"Don't snap at me or I won't feel like getting into this."
Danah felt like an inarticulate parent wasting the principal's time.

"I'm not snapping."

"Well, you sounded angry just then. Maybe not now, but just then you did."

"What are you trying to say?"

"I don't know. There's something, something that's sort of wrong and sort of getting in my way and I honestly don't know what it is so I can't . . ."

"What I don't get is why you don't feel like you have your own work."

"I know."

"You are a social media consultant. You have clients. You are also a general contractor."

"I know. I guess it's that my work always seems to be invisible. Things felt stale, flat to me today. I sort of have a fake way of being around the workmen. I try to be one of them, I suppose, and of course I am not. Oh, I don't know, Bob. I'm just in a funny mood. That's all. I feel nervous, edgy. I feel the way you feel before you do something important. Thing is, I don't have anything important coming up."

"It might be stress. You're doing more than you think. When I told Mrs. Myette about what you're doing, she was very impressed."

"No offense, Bob, but your secretary and I are not exactly peas in a proverbial pod. I mean, I'm pretty staggered by the thought of what she does, to be honest. Hasn't she been a secretary for about thirty years? How does someone stick at one thing for so long? I guess she likes what she does."

"My point here is that you underestimate all that you're doing, and you probably need a break."

Danah walked over to the steps leading down to the front door and looked at the boarded up doorway that used to be a coat closet. She walked back towards Bob. "You know, I get the feeling that filling in that breezeway is important in a symbolic way, if that doesn't sound insane. I feel like two parts of me are about to be connected somehow."

"It'll be nice to get to the garage without going outside."

"Yes, but it's more than that. This breezeway was a cold place running through the middle of our house and we never saw it as a problem until very recently. The house came that way and we accepted it -- but filling that space up with a window seat, a big couch, a wall-mounted screen, making it a room leading to a pool, making something comfortable and warm out of nothing . . . it's going to change the feel of the whole house. Can you picture it yet?"

"More than before. The little concrete foundation walls help. But no, no, I can't really see it yet."

"It's funny seeing something that's not there."

"What? Do you think you have psychic powers?"

Danah made a funny, teasing face at him, while absorbing a stab of guilt about Litany. "No, but it's as if I'm learning to trust my imagination, I guess."

Bob stood up and arched his back. "How could I have forgotten to tell you?" he said.

"What?"

"Wait till you see this." He walked downstairs to the front door where he had left his briefcase. "Do you remember me telling you I hired a new first grade teacher? Well, she's a film nerd. She's got a thing about old British movies. For some odd reason I started telling her about your father—something I never do." He came back upstairs holding a DVD out towards Danah, who could not move. "It's your father!"

Bob might as well have been presenting an iPhone to a cave man. The concept of a disc containing moving images of her father and a record of his voice was unimaginable.

"Here! Aren't you going to take it? Are you OK, Danah? You look like you've seen a ghost."

"Well, yes. Watching my father now, for the first time, at the age of forty-six would be like seeing a ghost, wouldn't it?" Bob patiently placed the video on the glass coffee table. "What's the movie called?" she said, as if she were illiterate.

"*The Dark Stranger*," said Bob. "Let's watch it!"

"Now?"

"Don't you want to see it?"

"I didn't expect this today."

"We don't have to watch it now. I thought you'd be curious. I have to admit, *I* am."

Danah stared at the cold, gray fireplace ashes, and without lifting her eyes, she said: "I don't know if you're ever prepared to find a parent." Then she reached for the video. She saw the romantic leads locked in a faded, romantic pose. "It was made in 1946. I'm forty-six. I wonder how old my dad was when he made this."

"You don't know when he was born?" said Bob, gently.

"No."

"I probably shouldn't have sprung this on you the way I did."

"It's OK. I'm glad you did. I can't quite picture you talking about my dad to one of the teachers."

"I know, I agree. It took me by surprise, too. Maybe this was bad judgment on my part. I can give it back to her on Monday."

"I think I'll go to bed and watch some junk TV."

"You don't want to see it?"

"Maybe tomorrow. It's going to take me some time to get used to the idea of him sort of coming alive again. Don't watch it without me, will you? I think I want to watch it by myself, maybe tomorrow. I want to see him before you do, or even Elsie does. I mean, isn't that normal? A girl usually meets her father before her husband meets him, right?"

"It's very emotional for you, Danah. I can see that now. I hadn't realized. I got caught up in the glamour of saying my father-in-law was a movie star."

"It's not glamorous to me."

"No."

"Bob, can you imagine how weird it is to have a famous father who probably had a fan club, and was seen on stage, in movies, on television, and who even had his own BBC radio show, and yet you never met him? Not once."

"Did Vera ever say why she divorced him?"

"Money. He was irresponsible with money. I think he even did jail time. And then she said he was a womanizing alcoholic."

"I can see how that would put a person off."

"Yes, a wife; but he was still my dad. I'd like to think there was some good in him. I never thought to question what Vera said, or to find him. He lived in England, we were in America. I never felt a pull towards him . . . until now."

"Are you glad I got hold of his movie?"

"I am, Bob, thank you. I'd like Elsie to see him and know that she shares her passion for acting with her grandfather as well as her grandmother. But don't tell her about it until I've watched it by myself, OK?"

"You got it."

That night Danah fell asleep quickly. She dreamed she was signing autograph after autograph. There was a never-ending line of people who knew who she was, although she herself did not know. She woke feeling very unsure of herself.

"Where did you put that DVD?" she asked Bob, as they nestled together.

"With my socks."

"Perfect!" said Danah. "No one would think of looking there."

"There's no rush to get that back, by the way," added Bob, giving her a kiss on the cheek on his way out of bed.

The weekend passed uneventfully. It was cold and wet. Danah picked up stray nails in the construction areas and vacuumed. And meanwhile, she grew accustomed to knowing the DVD of her father rested in peace and it seemed to her that the socks had a normalizing effect on the DVD so that by the time Monday arrived she peeked at the DVD and sent a prayer to her father, thanking him for finding her as best he could. Norm arrived a little later than she expected.

"Rented a drill for the day just to keep things interesting!" said Norm, cheerfully, when he arrived around 10:30. Danah could not tolerate the noise of the drill. I must leave the house today. Quite apart from breaking the feeling of being under house arrest, I should go out because we need groceries. She walked over to the sliders that ought to open onto a deck and stared at the uneven ground she raked yesterday, after Norm left. She had scraped together plastic cutlery, broken glass, endless cigarette ends, take-out lids, and a child's compass.

Norm had arrived with an assistant today. She saw them holding Dunkin' Donut coffee cups. They stood where the deck footings would be, laughing about something. She scuttled back into the kitchen. I don't want them thinking I have nothing better to do than to watch them joke around. She emptied the dishwasher. Norm waved at her from the backyard. His assistant had disappeared. Usually, Norm knocked on the front door first thing and they talked over the day's work. Not today. Just that brief exchange about the drill. Danah took out the wild bird feed from under the sink and headed for the red, metal birdfeeder outside the front door. She opened the double set of doors and came face-to-face with Norm's helper. He froze. She stood there anticipating an introduction. After a moment, he lifted his head and almost met her eyes.

"I'm working-with-him," he said. Could his name really be "I'm-working-with-him?" She strained to see traces of a Native American bone structure in his cheeks. She wanted to say, "Hello, well, I'm Paying-the-both-of-you!"

"Norm's a good guy," she said, and the kid rushed around the corner back to Norm.

I must go out. Yet she walked back across the living room and dining room to the sliders. Clutching the rusted handle on the slider in both hands, she pulled hard. Norm came towards her. He pointed at the wooden plank nailed across the doorframe to prevent people from opening the door. She nodded and smiled. He picked up a stray piece of wood and pried the nailed plank off the doorframe. She tugged at the door again. Nothing gave. Norm made a hand motion, indicating she needed to twist something. She flipped a metal dial at the base of the handle. With one more tug the door opened begrudgingly. Norm looked at her. She had forgotten what she wanted to say. Norm grinned.

"Progress!" said Norm.

"Yes." She stepped out to join them, dropping down about two feet. I-work-with-him stopped drilling and wiped his face on his green T-shirt sleeve—a limber shoulder roll.

"If it was easy, we'd all stay home," said Norm.

She had no earthly idea what he meant since she did stay home a whole lot and nothing seemed that easy. "You got that right!" she said, still trying to think of what it was she meant to say in the first place. The two men knelt on their strapped-on kneepads, either side of the first hole. They took turns stretching an arm into the hole and pulling out soil and rocks. "I'm going out for a while," she said, just to hear herself say it really. Telling them I'm going to leave the house makes it more likely to happen. "I won't be long."

With her keys and teeth clenched, she walked through the front door and the screen door and shut them gently without locking them. She considered going to the bathroom again. She closed herself into her black Toyota, reversed around Norm's red truck and took shallow breaths all the way to the grocery store. Milk, bread, food, toothpaste, she repeated like a mantra. She took a left into the strip mall housing Stop & Shop and TJ Maxx. Instead of going to the Stop & Shop, though, she sauntered into TJ's and went straight to a rack holding a cobalt blue mohair cardigan. She looked for the size and saw a label with a black and white checkered border announcing *medium*. She read the word over and over again. She kept hold of the cardigan and walked over to Active Wear. She stroked a soft, white skirt with a lacy overlay. She picked up the matching top, again seeing the word *medium*, and quickly replaced it on the metal rack. "Why does it say *medium* everywhere?" she muttered, on the way to the shoe section. There was a little bench free and she sat on it, contemplating the cardigan and its provocative label. Her eyes drifted further afield and fixated on a shoebox marked *medium*. I may be losing my mind, but I feel a huge pull to take this seriously. The spirits are telling me to see Litany again.

She went to the pillows section and called Litany. She had just had a cancelation and could see Danah next Monday afternoon. Danah felt 10lbs lighter after making this arrangement.

Norm took Tuesday off and the following Monday, also. He wanted to help a friend install kitchen cabinets. Danah had the house to herself. She opened Bob's sock drawer after Elsie left for school. She stroked the DVD case the way you stroke a dog you don't trust, removed the disk from its case, and fed it to the bedroom DVD player. She immediately needed a pause to collect her defenses, so she went downstairs and made herself a big blue glass bowl full of buttery popcorn. Back on the bed in the master bedroom, she pressed *play* on the remote, and shadowy figures began to move around the screen to the sound of tally-ho British voices. She couldn't bring herself to make any adjustments in contrast or brightness. After all these decades, she felt she must take it as it came. A young Irish girl eavesdropped on a man telling a story about fighting the English and keeping dear old Ireland proud. As Danah watched the brave girl travel alone to Dublin, it occurred to her she might not recognize her father if she saw him. She made an effort to follow the story and get caught up in the action. And then she saw him. She couldn't make out the story clearly. Her father was a bogus British officer handing over a fake prisoner. She couldn't make out whether her father was a good guy or a bad guy. A flashlight lit his face momentarily. He said good night and was gone. Then there was a car chase. Was that it, she wondered? She ran the tape back and freeze-framed her father who stood quivering in shadows. She could not imagine how this minor character might recur. It was all about the Irish girl and an Englishman, and whether the Irish girl would wake up to the

Englishman's belabored efforts to charm her. She tried to be a good sport and watched more. She noticed the locations and told herself she was looking at the same things her father had seen. And then he came back. He did a funny walk in a hotel with the police watching him. He tried to look innocent and overdid it in a Chaplinesque way. There was a slapstick chase and fight. He was funny. She was so pleased that he made her laugh. When the movie ended, she called Bob.

"I just saw my dad."

"Was he good?"

"Brilliant! He was funny. He did a funny walk. He did funny faces. He wasn't afraid of the stars. He had scenes with them, but he did his own thing. We must make a copy. I'd like to thank that teacher who loaned us the DVD."

"She'd like to meet you," said Bob.

"Does she have any more of his movies?"

"I'll ask her."

"OK. I know you have to go."

"Wouldn't it have been a bummer if he sucked!" said Bob.

"Bob! You can't say that at school!"

"Yes I can. I'm the principal!"

"Thanks for finding the movie for me. I love you."

The rest of the week and the weekend could not go quick enough for Danah. Eventually, Monday arrived, the house emptied and Danah scooted out of town to see Litany without telling a soul. She had been tempted to tell Holly at one point, but she knew herself well enough to know that telling Holly meant putting complex feelings into words and she no longer wanted to protect herself by being skeptical. It was time to suspend disbelief and that was best done alone.

Danah's appointment was at 10:30. Recently, she had become phobic about the highway. It was something about the wide, straight, direct access of it. There were no obstacles, nothing to delay a person from going where he or she intended. Merging cars seemed horribly aggressive. Not wanting to arrive emotionally drained she took country back roads to Litany's house.

The same old rusty cars were parked in Litany's driveway. The house appeared a little smaller than she had remembered it. She knocked and heard Litany call out to come in. There was an airless quality to the house. Danah fought back the urge to leave. She guessed Litany was in the back room finishing up a reading. She sat on the dark green loveseat again. She pushed her fingers through holes in the multi-colored, crocheted blanket draped over the back of the couch, obsessively threading her fingers back through another hole so they could touch a thumb and form a circle.

"I'm ready for you now, dear. I'm sorry to keep you waiting. I was on the phone. I'm doing a lot of teaching and, well, let's get started, shall we?" Litany led the way down the dark, narrow hallway to the room of readings. Danah wondered what Litany called the room where she gave the readings. The wood-burning stove smelled relaxing. Danah knew the drill: phone on the table, tap record, and be calm. They sat facing each other at the wooden picnic table as Litany sent up a cleansing prayer.

"As I come into your vibration, I have someone. I hear the word, *gratitude*. I see a gentleman from the other side. He resembles you at the eyes and chin. He's dressed like an old-fashioned gentleman. I hear 'gratitude' again but I'm not getting any verification. I'm, it's unclear. Do you have a question, dear? Let the spirits hear your voice."

"What is my father doing?"

"I can't say for sure. He's lying down. He's in a fog. He's not able to think clearly. He is sorry. He is sorry for a lot of things in his life. He cannot believe his life ended the way it did, so suddenly. There were so many more things he wanted to do. He is offering you a tiny, silver spoon, a baby's spoon. He wishes he had fed you as a baby. He is very, very sad." Litany broke into an unintelligible babble for a few moments. Adrenaline surged through Danah, and she considered making a run for her car. Litany's head was tilted so far backwards that Danah couldn't see her face. Then, Litany coughed and rearranged herself on the bench as if she had only just sat down. "I see you as a baby. You had a head of curls. You and your mother are on a large, ocean-going vessel. You might be two years old. You are asleep in a stroller. A man is watching over you, a man in uniform, a young American soldier. You have been left to fend for yourself many, many times. You know how to take care of yourself. Do not doubt that. I see you didn't know whether or not to like yourself for a long time. You are beginning to like yourself now. Do you have another question?"

"Does my father have a message for me?"

"You are already on your way, he says. He is proud of your

determination and glad to see you accepting things you cannot change. Don't be surprised if someone named Anthony or Tony becomes important to you. Your father likes to see you smile. He wants you to give yourself permission." Litany nods. "Yes. Permission not to not hold yourself back, permission to feel things, to let your feelings show or not show. He is glad you gave yourself permission to come here today." Litany was silent. "Is there a child around you? A young girl? She has a touch of your father. More than a touch. Look at her. This one who looks at you, who tilts her head, she is an old soul with deep roots in your family. Your father communicates with you through her. He has done this many times and you will notice this now. He is in a fog. That's all I'm going to get today."

Litany closed with a prayer invoking protection and guidance which left Danah feeling vulnerable and shaky. She had come so close to hearing something specific from her father, but he stopped short again. Why does he have to bring Elsie into it? Litany handed Danah her phone, and Danah dutifully followed as Litany led the way back to the front door.

"Can I ask you a question?" said Danah, hesitantly.

"Yes," said Litany, matter-of-factly.

"Do you remember anything you said during my reading?"

"No dear, I thought I explained the first time you came. That's why you have the tape. You can listen again." Danah overcame the urge to explain that the reading was stored in the cloud and not on a tape.

"Yes, I understand that. I wanted to ask something different."

"Yes?"

"What would it mean if every time a spirit appeared it was in a fog?"

"It usually means murder, dear." Danah lost a heartbeat. Litany's landline rang, but she saw the shock on Danah's face. "I'm sorry dear. Perhaps I shouldn't have answered." The phone continued to ring. "I will pray for you," said Litany, reaching for the wall-mounted phone. "Ask the spirits to help you. You know your way home, right?" she said, before disappearing. Danah let herself out.

"Murdered? My father was murdered?" she said aloud in the car. I should never have got involved with the occult. I'm so stupid! I opened myself up so wide that now I believe this trash, that's the problem. What should I do? By the time Danah saw familiar landmarks, she had named her prime suspect: Bernard. He had always been jealous of Stewart. I've got to find out the circumstances of Stewart's death. I think he died in a home for old actors— something Hall. Did Bernard take any trips to England around that time? Fifteen years ago . . . what was I doing fifteen years ago? I was pregnant with Elsie. *Murder* is not an easy word to forget, she thought, trying to put it out of her mind and focus on the road. Then she remembered Vera telling her to remember that everyone dies. How much does Vera know about my father's death?

Upon re-entering her house, Danah checked e-mail on her desktop computer: one from her mother talking about the weather and the flowers in her garden; one from Holly asking if she could come over after school. "Things are not going well with Paul. I'm freaking out!" wrote Holly. *She's* freaking out, thought Danah. She called Holly back and was hugely grateful to leave a message. She declined the invitation, giving no reason. Next, she microwaved a mug of purified water from the fridge door and dropped in a Ginger Twist tea bag. Ginger because it was my grandmother's favorite flavor, and Twist because that's what my knickers are in right now, she thought, pushing hard to regain perspective and a sense of humor. She took the mug and walked towards the front door to inspect the framing for the breezeway room. She stopped dead. A metallic switch plate had been mounted on the wall. A magnetic strip with the word *gratitude* had been stuck on it. She put her right hand over her heart. It must have been Elsie. But wasn't Elsie still at school?

"Elsie!" she called out.

"What?" Her voice came from upstairs.

"Did you do this?" She was pointing at the word.

After a brief moment, Elsie flew downstairs and landed beside her mother.

"It's the magnetic poetry grandmother gave me. I just found it again."

"So you put it there this morning?"

"My god, mom, I know you're strange and everything, but is it really necessary to carry on like this?"

"No, really, Elsie, be serious. Tell me when you got the idea to do this." Elsie scrunched up her eyes and placed her index finger on her brain.

"About 10:45 this morning. It was quiet. It seemed like a normal day. I was in study hall."

"And why are you home at this time of day?"

"Early dismissal for conferences, remember?" Elsie slapped one hand over her eyes and the other stretched towards her mother. "Wait! I know what you're going to say next . . . How did you get in, Elsie? Am I right? See, see! Well, the all-seeing Elsie hears a word beginning with N . . . nothing! No! Norm! Norm let me in!" Elsie bounded back to her room and Danah was grateful not to be interrogated about her own whereabouts and activities.

Danah approached the magnetic *gratitude* strip with extreme caution and tickled the upper right corner of the rectangle until it curled towards her, and once confident she had it she tore it off like a Band-Aid, anticipating pain that never came. She closed her fingers around the word. I could continue to ask for signs, for proof, but I know I'm holding it right here in my hand. She took the word to the couch.

Gratitude was not a word Danah used actively, except at Thanksgiving. Vera had very rarely expressed gratitude. She remembered her mother saying she felt grateful for not having to go anywhere on Sundays. She herself had been relieved about getting various examination results, getting through college, that sort of thing, but not really grateful. As an adult, she felt grateful for Bob, for her daughter. Danah actually felt guilty about not being more grateful.

"Are you OK, mom?" asked Elsie.

"I'm fine, honey. It's just this word, it's caught me by surprise. What made you choose this word?"

"It was the first one out of the box. It spilled out onto the kitchen counter all by itself. Gosh, mom, I don't know anyone who takes words as seriously as you." Danah smiled at the compliment. "Does it connect with your work or something? Is that why you're looking at it like that?"

"Yes," said Danah, lying. "I'm reading a ghost story written by a client, and it was just uncanny that you would have picked this word out because the heroine in the story finds *gratitude* highlighted in a book she's reading, and it's a message from the ghost of someone she had loved a long, long time ago. What do you think it would mean if a ghost did that—if a ghost brought the word *gratitude* to you?"

"Assuming I believe in ghosts, which I probably do, I'd say that the ghost was saying he was grateful to the woman for what she was doing."

"*He* was grateful to *her?*"

"Yes."

"Wow!"

"What's the big deal? Anyway, you don't get to change the story do you, mom?"

"No. I can't change other people's stories. I haven't finished reading the one I'm talking about. I couldn't guess how the word *gratitude* was supposed to be taken. *He* is grateful to *her*. That's great. I really hope it's true, that it turns out that way. That's a wonderful thought. I didn't expect that. Thanks."

"You make it sound like these characters that someone else invented are yours. You really get inside stories don't you!" Danah felt a pinch of guilt. If only Elsie knew how I hide behind words, how words keep me from doing things I should do. What if I told her that her grandfather might have been murdered and how I suspect Bernard? Contemplating the word *gratitude* wouldn't seem like the thing to do then, I don't suppose.

"Workmen!" sang Elsie.

"Now?" asked Danah, jumping up.

"Earth to mother! It's Monday afternoon. People are still at work."

A black man in a one-piece coverall stood at the door. She read his yellow truck: "Bugs Be Gone! We out-bug bugs!"

"Good morning, madam. BBG," announced the man, putting out a hand to shake hers.

"BBG meaning Bugs Be Gone?" she asked, shaking his hand.

"Exactly right, Mrs. Reynolds!"

"Well," she said, leading him around the back of the house where Norm had built the stage for the deck and office. "We're doing some renovation here, as you can see, and I'm thinking we might be stirring up some old nests."

"I'll soon find out if something is bugging you!" he said, with a charming smile. "No structure is immune from infestations. Did you know termites benefit the environment?"

"Wait a minute! Whose side are you on?"

"There are no sides in this, Mrs. Reynolds, just tunnels. Have you seen any bugs?" His patter sounded rehearsed, but Danah thought he performed it well.

"No."

"Can you tell the Termite Swarmer from the Termite Soldier?" Danah pantomimed ignorance. "Wings. Swarmer's got wings," he informed her.

"Is that like having game?" she said.

"It's a lot like having game . . . for him, not for you. You seen any wings 'round here?" She opened her eyes wide and shook her head. By this time, they had arrived at the place where the new office would adjoin the house. Danah expected him to scrape wood or dig holes in the ground, but he stood talking: "We have a baiting program. It's a non-invasive way to kill."

"Brilliant," said Danah, suddenly picturing Bernard on his back, waving legs and arms in the air in a futile attempt to get on with his life. "So it leaves no traces?"

The guy nodded. "We can install the program with minimal disturbance to you."

"And then the killing will begin, without us hardly noticing?"

"You got it, Mrs. Reynolds. The termites are already destroying your house. It's time to fight back."

"How do you know?"

"They're invisible."

"That's how you know?"

"They go very deep, madam. How old is your house now?"

"Twenty years."

"Right, well, chances are . . ." He started poking around, but it looked like it was for show. Danah wondered why they called this an inspection when his bottom line thus far and been the words 'chances are.' "A Termite King is an inch long," he said, looking at the ground. Danah scratched her upper arms. "Slab house is it?"

"A concrete foundation, yes."

"The Subterranean Termites can travel along cracks in concrete, you know."

"You sort of have to admire them."

He smiled and his brown eyes looked right into hers. "I do," he said.

"Do you, really?"

"Like you say, these little critters take action, they're also ambitious, they work nicely in teams, and they know their place in the organization."

"Perfect employees, really!"

"You could say that, ma'am, yes."

"So how do you feel about killing them every day?"

"It's a living."

"But how do you feel about your job, having respect for the critters like you do?"

"Pays the bills. Can't complain. Good benefits." He was leading her back to his truck.

"So the killing part doesn't bother you, then? You don't get nightmares about it?"

"No." He was checking off little boxes on a form on his clipboard.

"Do you keep all the poisons and traps in the van?"

"Yes. Ready for anything!" he said, handing her the clipboard and a pen. She signed, confirming he had completed a free inspection.

"What would happen if a person swallowed some of the chemicals you use on termites?"

"They aren't supposed to do that, ma'am. A person would have to dig deep into the ground and pull apart the baiting system.

It's very unlikely, ma'am."

"Oh. OK. Good. I mean, I have a child. I'd want everything to be safe. That's all."

"So, I'm leaving you with our booklet, Mrs. Reynolds. There are pictures of the common bugs found in a household such as yours. I'll send you my report in a week or so. Thank you for your time, Mrs. Reynolds."

"Thank you."

5 ONLY CRAZY SOMETIMES

"Thanks for coming over." Danah avoided Holly's eyes.

"Harry, do you still like chocolate chip cookies?"

Holly's son nodded emphatically three times and then let his chin rest on his chest – a statue, a tribute of sorts to melodrama. Danah smiled and reached her hand out to him.

"Come with me!" They walked hand-in-hand to the kitchen. She pulled open a bi-fold door to reveal a pantry. Cereal boxes stood in height-order, the bread bin was empty and clean, labeled containers of nuts were stacked, and replacement cans stood in line behind their leaders.

"Can I have those?" asked Harry, dropping Danah's hand to point.

"You bet!" said Danah, giving him an unopened, double-barreled packet of Oreos.

"Not too many, Harry," cautioned his mother. Harry climbed the weaver's chair at the island and then broke open the packaging while Danah fetched a square, white side plate for him.

"Decaf or herbal?" asked Danah.

"Whatever you're having."

"I was going to have what you were having." Danah paused between the coffee maker and the shelf of tea.

"Who likes making decisions?" Danah hesitated: "C comes before T for tea. Let's have coffee."

Danah went about the business of grinding beans, positioning a filter, and filling mugs with microwaved water to absorb the ceramic chill.

"Want some milk, Harry?"

Harry nodded. His smile revealed a mouth of Oreo teeth.

"That's enough cookies, Harry. He'll never eat lunch now," Holly said to Danah.

"What *are* friends for?" asked Danah, wistfully.

"Can I watch TV now, Auntie Danah?"

"You are such a sweetheart for asking, Harry. You know where it is. I'll bring you some milk in a minute, OK?"

"Key dokie!" said Harry, tumbling off the stool and racing upstairs to the master bedroom—the only room in the house with a television.

"So, what's going on?" asked Holly, brushing crumbs off

Harry's bar stool onto her hand.

"What do you mean? Is something going on?" Holly backed up her question with silence and raised eyebrows. "Well, to be honest, I've been avoiding everyone, if that makes you feel any better." Danah glanced at Holly's eyes for the first time that day.

"You've been busy."

"Not really. Well, yes, I have been working hard with the house. But, when I'm not working, I don't know, I haven't been able to make myself do much of anything. Elsie and I had two bowls of cereal for supper the other night because I couldn't face going to the supermarket and Bob was working late."

"Oh, that is sad. You've got to snap out of it."

"I'm stuck." Danah carried the coffees over to the coffee table. "Oh! I forgot Harry's milk. I must take that to him. Prince Harry! He's so cute, Holly."

"Thanks. He keeps me sane."

"It's funny that," Danah looked over her shoulder at Holly, "funny how kids drive us crazy and keep us sane. I'll be right back." Danah delivered the milk and found Harry talking back to a cartoon. As Danah came back downstairs, her innards lurched at the sight of

Holly reading the magnetic poetry strips on the switch plate by the front door.

"Did you do this?" asked Holly.

"No. Elsie did. My mother gave her a box of magnetic poetry years ago . . ."

"She's so creative. Just like you. I love this one: 'Whisper beneath bitterness.'"

"What?" Danah felt panicky and quickly joined Holly by the door. She had to see these words for herself. She pressed each word with her index finger as if it were an elevator button designed to take her to another level.

"I'm sensing a ghost around me," said Danah, staring through the black-and-white rectangular words to a dusty, gray notion of her father. "There's something going on. I'm not sure what is happening."

Holly was lost for what to say to her old friend. They let the moment pass in silence as they walked back to the couch and settled in with the familiar warmth of coffees. "How's your mother, Danah?"

"I have no idea what she's thinking. I know what is blooming in her garden. That's all she's telling me. That's it."

"Are you angry with me for some reason?"

"Do I seem angry?"

"Angry or bored. Maybe bored by me. When you didn't return my calls I thought maybe you were tired of hearing about the affair."

"Why are women are so quick to blame themselves for things they have absolutely no power over?"

"So, I can talk about Paul?"

"Sure."

Holly changed her position on the couch to sit cross-legged. "I've always felt secure about Paul, you know that. He's tall. He's sexy . . ."

"Paul is a very cute guy. So cute in fact, that if he weren't your husband I'd never dare talk to him! He's a fitness trainer for God's sake! He could host a reality show called, Extreme Good Looks. Good looking men have always frightened me."

"I think Bob is *very* attractive. I don't think I've ever told you that, have I? I like the way he looks so conservative and then he says outrageous stuff! He's sort of the male version of the school librarian fantasy -- an elementary-school principal who lets his hair down."

"You don't have to sell me the guy. I already married him! And I still love him, although I don't hear myself saying that very often."

"What do you love about him?"

"Oh my God! Really, Holly? What do I love about my own husband?" Holly held her ground silently. "OK, it's actually a good question: These days, I love him for being a very present father. I love hearing Elsie say daddy and I call him daddy on her behalf. Is that bad?"

"I heard on a chat show that women pick fatherly types all the time."

"Oh god, it *is* bad. What happens to women like that?"

"I don't know. I had to pick Harry up from school. I only got to watch the first half."

"Oh well, what were you going to say about Paul?"

"Paul? I don't remember. What was I saying?"

"That you've always been secure about him."

"Right! But I'm not anymore."

"What's changed?"

"Nothing. Nothing's changed. He's always worked long hours. He was self-employed when I met him. He was a trainer then, we own a gym now. That was our goal. He's always worked around young, beautiful women. But I feel like recently I just can't touch him, I don't mean physically, I mean I can't get to him the way I used to. I can't decide if he doesn't care what I think anymore or if he's suddenly more content and sort of serene. Maybe he has out-matured me."

"Are you working out at your gym each week?"

"No, I haven't for a while. You think I should go over there more?"

"I do. You'll pick up a vibe when he sees you there. Ask him if you can help out at the gym. See what his reaction is. Tell him you want to become a nutritionist, or something, and you want an office there."

"That's good!"

"People literally poison themselves with the stuff they put into their mouths, Holly. They can die without ever knowing what they did wrong. I had an expert here the other day. He respected termites, but he said there are creatures destroying my house and it's time for me to fight back and he said they won't even know if I bait and set a trap."

"That sounds a bit dramatic, even for you, Danah. I hate to run but it's noon! I've got to go. Harry! We're leaving, honey. I've got him in an afternoon program for a while."

Danah repeatedly banged the small Chinese gong on her kitchen island until she heard Harry approach.

"What's that noise?" asked Harry.

"It's the sound of you leaving!" said Danah. Holly laughed.

"What?" said Harry.

"We've got to go, Harry. It's time for school. Get your coat on," instructed his mother. "I think I'll drop in on Paul this afternoon and maybe work out. Thanks, Danah. That was good advice. Get your coat on, Harry."

"Oh! Did I tell you that Elsie might be getting the role of Hamlet in the school play?"

"No. Hamlet's a man, isn't he? I don't know that play very well."

"They don't seem to care if a boy or girl plays Hamlet. It's the same play either way."

"I hope she gets what she wants. Let me know."

"Bye, bye, Auntie Danah," Danah bent down to hug the bundled boy. She put on her own white ski jacket and walked with them to their car. When they drove away, Danah realized she was not alone, because Norm's truck was still there, although she couldn't see or hear him.

Norm had brought the office and the breezeway room to similar stages of completion: they were both ready for a framing inspection. After that, Danah understood from Norm, it would be quick going to get the electrical work roughed in—assuming Electric Ed could fit them into his schedule. Danah so appreciated the concept of living in a construction site, and she thought how satisfying it must be to know, as workmen do, what needs to be done before what, and what can legitimately wait.

Norm must be here somewhere. She turned sideways to squeeze through the wooden studs of the breezeway room. Once inside, with wooden bars ahead and behind her, she muttered — "My prison house!" knowing it came from *Hamlet* and feeling it to be true for anyone carrying a terrible secret. Then she stepped out the other side, to the back of the house, and saw Norm taking a cigarette break.

He had finished building the railings on the deck and was leaning his elbows on the one-by-six that now ran around the top of the uprights. His head turned and smiled at her, and she admired the fact that he held his position, feeling perfectly entitled to his break.

"Another day in paradise?" she said. They both stared into the marshland.

"You bet!" he said, with his gaze still fixed in the distance. The index finger on Norm's right hand, hanging over the edge of the railing, was bloody.

"You hurt your finger!" exclaimed Danah, feeling immediately to blame.

"I did, didn't I!" Norm smiled and blew smoke through the gap in his front teeth.

Danah fought off multiple impulses to mother him. She could not come up with a nurturing line that wouldn't insult his intelligence. "That's gotta hurt!" she said, finally. He laughed out loud, and she figured that was as good a dose of medicine as she could give him.

A pale gray bird with a wide wing span circled above the marsh very slowly, focused on prey.

"That's a marsh hawk," said Norm, pointing at it with his cigarette.

"And that's a handsaw!" pronounced Danah, pointing at a handsaw propped up against the railing.

"And your point?" said Norm, turning to lean on his elbow and relaxing into a friendly smile.

"Oh! Point? No point really. Just reminded me of something Elsie said this morning. Some lines from a play. There's one that goes: 'When the wind is southerly, I know a hawk from a handsaw.' It means I only seem crazy sometimes."

"Now that I understand!"

Norm put the cigarette in his mouth, bent down, and picked up the saw by its black, shiny handle. It was shaped like a capital "P." He demonstrated how the thin metal handle, attached to either end of the blade, could rotate the cutting edge. "I used this to add some curves to the main uprights on the decking. Everyone just calls it a saw, but, technically, it's a coping saw. It can come at a piece of wood from any angle." He leaned the saw up against the railings of her new deck.

"That's what coping is, I guess. Learning to come at

something from more and more angles," she said. A comfortable silence elapsed until Norm stubbed out his cigarette on the soul of his boot.

"Have you been thinking about beams?" He was now leaning with his back to the railing.

"Beams?"

Norm signaled to Danah to join him on the far side of the deck. They stood on a scrap of plywood balanced across the floor joists between the studs in the office framework. He unhooked his metal tape measure and shot it up to touch the rafters.

"This horizontal one here is a collar beam" He tapped the beam and then retracted the metal wand by pressing his thumb on the central, red button. Danah inwardly smiled at the thought of how many workmen had unhooked their lengthy, metallic wands and extended them in front of her when there really was no need.

She looked up at the cold, blue sky beyond the rafters. Norm briefly removed his green baseball cap and scratched his head. He extended the metal wand again and walked the length of the almost-an-office, tapping the three collar beams.

"These guys. Do you want them exposed?" He hooked the

tape back onto his worn, leather belt.

"Yes. Definitely. Let's expose them. Yes, that's exactly what I want. I will expose them." Norm didn't appear to be listening. He was engrossed in measuring something.

"Might as well phone in an order for wallboard today," he said, with his back to her. "I'll give you the numbers later."

"Thanks," said Danah, sensing her cue to exit. "By the way, have you got an electric sander I can borrow?"

"What you going to do now?"

"Refinish some of the wood trim. The banisters are pretty knocked about."

"That's it?"

"I thought I'd re-do some of the trim on the kitchen cabinets and the island, too."

"I think I happen to have two sanders with me in the truck today."

Danah followed him over to his truck. The sides of his pick-up were lined with two long, silver boxes that looked like coffins for thin people, in Danah's eyes.

"I've got this one," said Norm. "It's a belt sander, smoothes large surfaces." He handed it down to her and then rummaged for the other one. "Here it is. This one finishes surfaces. You'll want to get two grades of sandpaper. One rough, to start, then two hundred to get it ready for stain. Do you know what kind of stain you need?"

"Someone told me it looked like Colonial Maple."

"My guess, too."

"This one's too heavy for me, Norm. My arms can't do it," said Danah, handing back the belt sander.

"Try this. Here's some sandpaper to start with. We'll have to cut it down to size. Got some kitchen scissors?" Norm jumped down from the back of the truck. "This is a fifty. You'll need to go over it with a one-twenty before staining." They walked back into the house. Danah hung her jacket on a coat rack. Norm cut the paper into a small rectangle, secured the ends with the use of a lever and demonstrated the circular motion and pressure required.

"Thanks, Norm." He went back outside and she started working without even thinking to eat lunch. She worked for an hour. Seeing the dents and scratches disappear satisfied her. The only problem was the residual layer of orange dust on everything in creation. She figured she would vacuum later.

At two-thirty, Norm appeared and asked her how it was going.

"I've got that order for you," he said.

"What order?"

"Wallboard for the office and rec. room."

"Sure. OK. I'll get some paper and write it down." Danah had an account at the local lumberyard in her name. They gave her ten percent off if she spent a certain amount each month. If Norm bought anything himself, he showed her the receipts and added no mark-up. After Norm gave her the specifications, he hovered. Danah slid the sander button to the "on" position, signaling that it was time to get back to the job.

"Thing is, I don't know if you should place that order just yet."

"What?" said Danah. She turned off the sander.

"You probably want to wait to place the wallboard order."

"For what? What are you talking about? Why wait?"

"I'm taking a month off."

"What did you say?" she asked, fighting for presence of mind. Norm flashed one of his toothy grins at her.

"I'm not taking a vacation. I have another job. You're not my only customer, you know." This stung Danah. She felt abandoned.

"Obviously," she said, straining to introduce some impersonal professionalism. "But this is a job too, isn't it?"

"My other customer's been waiting a long time. I promised I'd squeeze them in."

"Well, that's just fine, Norm, but you're currently employed here. You can't leave me with this mess for a month. Besides, it's not good for the framing to be exposed to winter weather for a month."

"It'll be fine. I've told them I'm starting Monday."

"This is so unfair of you to walk out like this with no warning." Danah knew her face was flushed and her neck mottled with a rash of anger. He grinned. "It's not funny, Norm. I'm really surprised at you trying this on. It isn't like you at all." She rambled and slid back onto the typical lecture she gave Elsie when she disappointed her.

"It's not about being fair. It's about earning a living. Sometimes I have to juggle a couple of jobs."

"Fine. I understand that. It's obvious that you would. I'm a freelancer too, you know. I do know something about juggling jobs.

But what I don't do is lead an employer to believe he or she can count on me to finish a job on time and then jump ship in midstream."

"Well, I don't know about your kind of work. I'm telling you that I'll be here tomorrow for my paycheck and I'll call you when I'm ready to come back." Danah stomped past him and went up to her bedroom, slamming the door behind her. She regretted how childish this appeared.

"Fuck, fuck, fuck, fuck him," she said, pacing up and down.

Not long after this the door opened and in came Elsie.

"Hi, mom! What's wrong?"

"That shit, Norman, is taking off for a month!" Danah experienced mild guilt at using the word *shit*.

"When?"

"Well, exactly! That's the point. You get that and you're fourteen years old. Well, he doesn't get it. He thinks it's OK to take off any damn time it occurs to him to be some place else."

"So, he's leaving now? I saw him putting stuff in his truck."

"Damn him. What a bastard he turned out to be! It would serve him right if I hired someone else to finish the job. That's what I should do. I'd like to see his stupid face then."

"Well, if you need to talk to him, mom, you should go now. I think he's packing up."

"I bet he's taking his damn sander with him, too. To hell with him. To hell with his sander."

By the time Bob arrived home, Danah was on her third glass of wine. She had dropped Elsie at her soccer game in between glasses one and two. She worked herself up into quite a state rehashing her skirmish with Norm.

"I thought you two got on well. I thought you liked him," said Bob, pouring himself a glass of wine.

"*I* thought I liked him, but how can you like a man who leaves you in the lurch like this with no warning, and who basically accuses you of creating and perpetrating the entire capitalist infrastructure just to keep good men like him down in the ditches."

"Danah, my love, you are over-reacting."

"Oh! Lovely! Now you're taking his side against me. What is it? Do I walk around with a 'Betray me now!' sign pinned to my back, or what?" Bob laughed, and sipped his drink.

"You're right. It's annoying to wait a month while he goes off and does god-knows-what, and then have to pray that he comes back. And you've worked so hard keeping everyone on schedule. I know this is hard for you."

"You're damn right it's annoying. I want this over. I'm sick of workmen in my house. I turned down a project because I knew I couldn't get it done fast enough with all the interruptions I get. It would serve him right if I hired someone else. In fact, I'm going to make some calls."

"You can't fire him."

"Why not?"

"Because it's his name as general contractor on our construction loan. Look, we're getting a really good deal with this guy. If he really were acting as the general contractor he'd be hiring guys, charging us double their rate, and pocketing the difference. And that way we couldn't afford to get it done. Just write off the next few weeks."

"No. I won't. It's a matter of principle. I guaranteed him months of work. That's worth something these days. I've let him hire his friends. I'm tired of people giving me half a story and walking all over me so that everything's hunky dory comfortable for them. No more. I'm standing up for myself this time. I bet Norm wouldn't behave this way if I were a man. I bet his other customer is a man. I bet that's it. I'm not having it, Bob." She drained her third glass.

"OK. I understand that, but can you convince Norm?"

"I'm not thinking of *convincing* him. I'm thinking of just making it clear that *he* is a jerk, that I'm *not* a jerk, and *he* works for *me*." They both laughed because it came across like an English lesson. "I should check my e-mail. I'm expecting some notes from a children's publisher. I haven't checked in since this morning. Norm threw me for a loop."

"Have you eaten?" asked Bob.

"No. I didn't even eat lunch now I come to think of it."

"I'll make something. What time do we pick up Elsie?"

"Erika's dad's going to bring her back." Bob made a fire and then started making dinner.

Danah clicked and double-clicked her way through the icons and boxes until she saw the nice yellow envelope poking out of her virtual mailbox. Nothing from work. One from Valleygirl38, alias Holly. When will Holly admit she's forty-two and not thirty-eight? She clicked open the letter and read the following:

Thanks again for the really good suggestions this morning. I went to the gym and Paul seemed really pleased to see me. He likes the idea of having a nutritionist available to members, so I'm going to look into that. I'm so glad I took some action on this.

Hope all's well with you. Love, Holly

Danah envied Holly. One simple action, one simple visit to Paul's workplace, and her mind had been put at rest. Why, oh, why can't I think of what to do about the possible murder of my own father? She sat staring at article headlines: lose 20 pounds in a hurry; the 100 most popular baby names; and celebrities' reconciliations. And *this* is news, she said to herself, sarcastically. What if they knew what I know? Wouldn't they break out a dozen new headlines within the hour? *Psychic Uncovers Murder; Old British Actor Murdered by Car Salesman; Daughter Allows Murder of Father to go Unmentioned for Fear of Upsetting Mother.* That's it. God forbid that I should ever upset my mother. Her first husband cheated on her. That's all I need to know about it, right? He did her wrong. It begins and ends with her. It doesn't matter that he didn't cheat on me, his daughter. It doesn't matter that a girl needs to know her father. It doesn't matter that a creative father and daughter are forbidden to know each other even a

129

decade after the divorce.

Danah clicked "Reply," and wrote the following to Vallleygirl38:

Dear Holly:

I'm really glad you went and checked out the gym situation for yourself. Quite honestly, I feel jealous of how easily you have resolved your problems.

I, on the other hand, am sitting here furiously doing nothing. Norm betrayed me this afternoon, Holly. He announced he was taking next month off and to hell with me and my petty, selfish desire to see my house finished. He basically said he would come back when he felt like it.

I'm not handling this well. I know that. I'm getting so angry, I'm scaring myself. Holly, I haven't told anyone this, but I'm pretty sure my stepfather, Bernard, murdered my father. I've figured this out from a few things Litany told me. I went to see her again. It kills me that I'm not doing anything about it for fear of upsetting my mother.

Bernard always hated any mention of my father's name. Before they moved in together, he made my mother destroy or throw out every photo of my father, every newspaper clipping, every scrapbook with him in it, every theater program, and every film review. My mom had an enormous poster from a movie they were in together and when I asked her if I could have it, she said, "Oh, you

wouldn't want that old thing, darling, I threw it out years ago." Can you imagine
how Elsie would have loved to have had that old thing on her wall?

Anyway, the thing is, I believe Bernard murdered Stewart somehow. I
know it sounds far-fetched. It happened fifteen years ago and I have no real
evidence except what I feel in my gut. The dreadful thing is I'm just carrying on as
normal, like nothing happened. But I cannot imagine what to do. What can I do?
It's making me crazy. I don't feel like going anywhere or doing anything.

"Supper's ready!" called Bob.

"I'll be right there!" Danah deleted all but the first two
paragraphs and then added this:

Don't worry. I'm not really as crazed as I might sound or seem. I'll talk
to Norm tomorrow and work something out. I love you like chocolate, dear friend,
D

After dinner, Bob sat on the couch with his laptop,
surrounded by various professional journals, and wrote notes for an
up-coming speech he would be giving at the National Association of
Elementary School Principals Convention.

Danah sat staring into the fire. Suddenly, the doorbell sang
out half its normal ring. She heard a single "ding," and stood up
expecting to see Elsie at the door. No one was there. Bob kept on

working as if he hadn't heard anything abnormal. It happened again. Danah was filled with the thought that her father was trying to get in, to remind her to take action. She had read on a website about how ghosts communicate through gadgets to get our attention. Specifically, there had been many cases of the telephone ringing for no reason and lights going on and off. A person experiencing this was often filled with thoughts of a particular dead friend or relative.

Ten minutes later, the doorbell rang as it should: ding-dong. Elsie came floating through the door restoring normal. It was nine o'clock: Elsie's official weekday bedtime. Danah left Bob in his professional oasis and followed Elsie upstairs. She sat on Elsie's bed and watched her unpack her soccer bag, conscientiously conveying dirty clothes to the washing machine on the landing.

"Have you heard who's Hamlet yet?"

"Mom, you've asked me that every day for a week. I think you want me to be Hamlet even more than I do!"

"So, you haven't heard?"

"No. We're working on getting ready for the mastery tests next week. I'm sure Mrs. V. will tell us after we get those out of the way. Except that I don't want to jinx it, I'm sure I'm going to be

Hamlet."

"*Play* Hamlet, darling. You're not going to *be* Hamlet. No one can *be* Hamlet. That's the problem, really." Danah straightened up the row of pandas sitting on the windowsill.

"What do you mean?" Elsie unwrapped a piece of chewing gum.

"Well, he talks about the important difference between seeming and being. You'll see, but don't get your hopes up too high. Maybe Mrs. V feels she's got to give it to some kid who needs a boost of confidence, or something. There are often completely unpredictable and invisible reasons why things happen, or don't happen, especially in the theater world. You know that."

"I know, but I also know I'm getting that role for sure." Elsie pulled a notebook from her backpack.

"Do you know, Elsie, something very weird happened tonight while I was waiting for you to come home."

"What?"

"The doorbell dinged twice without donging, and each time it dinged, it made me think of Stewart, of my dad."

"You never think of him." Elsie stopped turning pages in her textbook.

"Well, I do now. I've been thinking of him more and more."

"Do you even remember seeing him?"

"No, I don't. I left England when I was about two years old, and I never went back to look for him. Vera convinced me he wasn't an important part of my life."

"But he was your father."

"I'm only just beginning to realize that now." Danah kissed Elsie goodnight and went to bed while Elsie finished some homework. Danah and Bob lay in bed and watched a local TV news story about a brave woman saving a little girl from drowning in a lake.

The next morning, after a solid night's sleep, Danah discovered that Norm had left his sander for her on the front doorstep. She felt grateful and prepared to start sanding the kitchen, thinking that, just maybe, he hadn't bailed out on her totally. When she heard his truck pull up, her stomach got queasy. He knocked at the front door: two heavy knocks. Usually, she left it unlocked for him, but not today.

"Just a minute," she yelled. She breathed some good, deep

breaths privately. Then, she opened the glass door and strictly forbid herself to speak.

"Working on the trim?"

"Yes," she answered, without welcoming him into the house.

"I was thinking," he said, slowly.

"Yes?"

"You might want to try another abrasive on that wood. There's lots of abrasives. Call the hardware stores. I think there's one that's a liquid. You can rub it on. The old finish sort of bubbles off."

"So I wouldn't get all this orange dust all over the place, you mean?"

"Right."

"Sounds good." Danah took a step backwards.

"You know, I don't think I said things the way I meant to yesterday," said Norm. Danah's heart raced. "What I meant to say to you is that I don't mean anything personal, it's just about money."

"Well, that's fair enough, Norm, because I feel the same way. It *is* all about money, *my* money. Bob and I are borrowing a huge amount of money to do this. We don't have this money just sitting around someplace. We're borrowing it from a bank at an interest rate.

We'll be paying this off for the next thirty years, Norm. It's nerve-wracking. But this is the thing: The sooner we can finish this work, the quicker we can convert the construction loan into a normal mortgage and get the borrowing rate down. Added to this is the fact that *you* are not my only contractor, Norm. I have a bunch of other contractors lined up and scheduled on the basis of when you led me to expect your part of the job would be complete. If you bail on me for a month, you're bailing on all those other people too. They are counting on your work getting done first, and I don't know how it's going to work out if I have to reschedule everyone. Do you see what I mean? You gave me zero notice." Danah held her shaky breath.

"OK. I can see what you're saying. I can see it. I'll call my other client tonight and tell him I can fit him in on Fridays and weekends. How's that?" The toothy grin was back. Danah's normal breathing pattern returned, too.

"That's great, Norm. I really appreciate that. I just didn't know what I was going to do. That's a relief. I'm going to the hardware store. Thank you, Norm. I'm really grateful."

"So, we can go ahead and get the inspector back," said Norm.

"The specter?" said Danah.

"Dead-dog Bob!" said Norm, grinning.

"You like that name, huh?" said Danah, greatly relieved that the whole world was not privy to her private madness. She entered her minivan and surfed the driveway on a wave of euphoria.

The hardware store was next door to a pharmacy, and a huge parking lot sat out front. A woman working at the hardware store, wearing an orange apron, convinced Danah that a liquid abrasive would be more mess than it was worth. So she bought more sandpaper and returned to her car. She wasn't ready to go home. She turned the engine on and ran the heater. She watched the pattern of people arriving and departing, hoping there would be meaning in it. She sat there until she wasn't compelled to note anything. She sat until she was simply sitting.

I'm asking for help. I need a sign from the spirit world that I am in fact communicating with my dad. Then I will take action. Please give me a sign that you are listening. She immediately felt moved to turn the engine off and enter the pharmacy. She cruised the aisle of cards, hoping to feel a pull towards one greeting or another, but she couldn't honestly say she felt the pull. It's not a good idea to muddy this up with words. Words are too demanding, too misleading. She considered moisturizers and skin care products. She stopped in front of the beautiful blue liquids that promised deep cleansing. For a brief moment, she felt perhaps she was doing just what she should be doing.

On her way out, she held the heavy door open for an elderly man who walked using a stick. She wrapped her fingers around the set of keys in her jacket pocket. She stopped beside the driver's door. Something shone up at her from the ground -- an elegant watch. She bent down, taking it with her right hand. It was a ladies' watch with a narrow, black leather strap. The hours were engraved in the circle of silver around the glass face: Gucci. She climbed into her car and slammed the door shut. She stretched the watch out on her lap. If I were to believe, if I were to actually believe finding this watch was a sign, what exactly would this watch be telling me? She laughed a sharp, hard laugh. What does a watch do? It tells time. It's time, isn't it? It's time for a whole lot of things I've been putting off.

Arriving home, Danah took the watch off and laid it out in front of her grandmother's photo on her bedside table. She spent the afternoon sanding, vacuuming, and Windexing orange residue off kitchen surfaces. It wasn't until she lay in bed with Bob that night that she talked about what had happened.

"A funny thing happened on the way to the pharmacy today," she began. The lights were off, and she couldn't make out Bob's facial expression. She didn't tell him the prayer part, the asking for a sign. Instead, she tried to make it sound obvious that there was something mystical about finding a watch at that moment, in that place. Bob did not make the appreciative noises she wanted to hear. "Isn't that amazing, Bob? I found a Gucci!"

"You didn't think you should turn it in at the pharmacy?"

"Normally I would."

"You seem a bit wacky, but I can tell that finding this watch means a lot to you. Why does it mean so much?" Bob cuddled up to her, and she felt aroused by him and his boxers.

6 BETRAYAL?

"What are you going to do today?" asked Bob, briefcase in hand.

"I don't know. Why?" asked Danah, from the top of the stairs.

"No reason." He descended the half-flight of stairs to the coat stand by the door. She came down the half flight from the second floor to the first, and stood where he had spoken a moment ago.

Bob wrapped a gray scarf around his neck and crossed the ends over his white shirt and red tie before reaching an arm into his navy blue, woolen coat. Danah balanced on one leg for as long as she could.

"Why are you standing on one leg?"

"Feels good," said Danah. "I get tired of always standing on two legs." Bob looked at her as if she had a problem.

"Are you going out today, honey?"

"Prolly not," she said. "If you really, really want to know what I have planned for the day, I'll tell you." Bob waited. "Stains."

"Stains?"

"Most women avoid stains and spend time shopping for stuff to remove stains, don't they! I like staining. Are you OK with me liking it, Bob?" Bob put down his briefcase. He took a moment to study the rough floor designated for tiling. When he lifted his head, he revealed his podium face, assumed a speech-giver's stance, and drew a deep breath.

"Relax, Bob! I'm staining the wood trim I sanded last week."

Bob smiled and put his hand on the door handle. "Going now. Full day. Later," he said.

"Kiss?" asked Danah, eager to delay his absence.

"Naturally," said Bob, climbing four steps and leaning in to kiss.

"Kinda makes you wonder how, quote, *natural*, kissing is. I mean, we so often have to remind each other, don't we? My hunch is that it probably isn't all that natural an instinct after a certain amount of time with someone. I like to kiss when I think of it, but I don't think of it very often. Maybe not much of it was done at all before cameras were invented. Kissing makes for good close-up shots. I like watching movie stars kiss. Has anyone ever written a history of the kiss? Have you ever heard of something like that, Bob?"

"No. I never have. Got to go now. Happy staining!"

"Yes."

Danah spent the morning staining the kitchen, living room, and master bathroom. She enjoyed the directions on the can of wiping stain—*WARNING Respect the fact that you are working with a toxic substance.* That's so great. I can work with something toxic if I know it's toxic from the beginning. What's hard is *creeping* toxicity. Bernard is the prime example of a toxic substance that ought to carry a written warning. How much simpler it would have been if I'd known he intended to be a veneer of a father, a polyurethane coating of a man who made things look immediately shiny. I assumed fathers and stepfathers added something good to a family, a shine that would make the family resilient and complete.

As Danah worked on the thirsty wood surrounding the hand basin in the master bedroom, she silently puzzled through the details of the murder as she knew them. If Bernard did kill my dad, does Vera know? She couldn't not know -- they are always together. Why would they care about Stewart, who was four thousand miles away? It makes no sense. I don't have all the facts. She dipped a finger of an old T-shirt into the reddish liquid and drew as many circles as she could until the stain ran out.

"Ha!" Maybe that's why Bernard always wants to be there when mom calls me. He needs to know that she isn't letting any clues drop. He's there to remind her whose side she's on—his, not mine. Forget all that stuff they tell you about the thickness of blood. She looked at the reddish brown stains on her own hands. Danah felt the grenade of venom forming in her stomach the way it always did if she allowed herself to focus on her stepfather. Damn it, I've had enough of hiding out and avoiding. She capped the tin of stain and lay the T-shirt down on newspaper. She pushed her hair away from her face with the back of her hand and looked at herself in the entryway mirror. "I'm taking you out to lunch," she said. "I insist. It's my treat. You deserve to be seen and heard."

She washed her hands and then dressed in newly laundered jeans, a black polo neck, black boots, Elsie's big woolen hat and blue ski jacket. There were no good-byes. Since it was Friday, Norm was working on his other job. The speed at which she left the house shocked her.

Driving through the downtown area, she noticed the local

firemen hosing down a fire truck, and she remembered something Bob had said about the next town over building a new fire station. An ex-teacher of his had converted the old fire station into a restaurant. She and Bob had been meaning to go there for a while. Danah continued along Route 1 for a while and then took a left turn for the green. The restaurant, called The Fire Place, commanded frontage on the south side of the green. It was a brick building and arched, wooden doors, painted turquoise, had replaced the two enormous arches that had acted as garage doors for the fire trucks. People were streaming in, and Danah followed the crowd. She hung Elsie's jacket on a pegboard by the door but forgot to remove her woolen hat.

It was spacious inside. The most noticeable feature was the central brick fireplace that spiraled up through the ceiling, presumably where the fireman's pole had once been. Metal columns supported the ceiling, and velvet swags of fabric hung between them, forming a partial maze. Many intimate dining spaces had been created with high-backed, pew-type seating arranged in clusters and corners. Danah was quickly shown to an ornate wooden chair in a nook designed for a person to eat alone, privately. The waitress wore tight, red pants. Danah's high-backed chair had a big, red cushion on it, and she sank onto the chair with pleasure. Behind her, hanging above the dividing line between Danah's chair and the people behind her, hung three pots of trailing English ivy at different heights on invisible wires, which added additional privacy to her cozy spot.

Danah ordered a chicken quesadilla and a glass of house wine. The room was noisy; nevertheless, she could make out exactly what the couple on the bench behind her was saying.

"What do you mean, 'wacky?' I mean I can be wacky too!" said a woman. A man laughed.

"You've always been wacky, Holly." There was a pause in which Danah stared at a framed poster of an antique fire truck. She sat upright and strained to hear what her husband was saying to her best friend at the table behind her. "Danah can be very funny, of course, but she's mostly serious. Now she seems distant, odd." Another pause. "And she used to care what she looked like. Now she grabs any old thing. She wears Elsie's clothes!"

Danah took off Elsie's woolen hat and sat on it.

"And she's become obsessive about magnetic poetry. She creeps up to it like it's an Ouija Board or something, like it has powers. I don't know, Holly, I just hoped maybe you could help me know what to do." The waitress gave Danah a glass of house white and she sucked it up like soda.

"Do? Why have you got to *do* anything?" asked Holly.

"Well, I feel bad for her. She doesn't want to go out or do anything."

"Yeah. She told me she felt stuck. She used that word: *stuck*. I don't know, Bob. I think she's stressed out. It's a big responsibility being a general contractor. Norm nearly bailed on her last week. She's making so many decisions, and she's not that sure what she's doing."

"Every time I think I'm getting somewhere, that she's going to open up, she starts babbling at me about something totally unrelated."

"She did sort of babble to me on the phone the other night. She'd been watching the Animal Channel. She said she'd watched a family of chimps, and that her whole life she'd gone along loving chimps, even wanting one of her own, and then, while she was watching this show, she said she suddenly recognized they are not what you think. She said there is a scary darkness in them," said

Holly.

"Exactly! What the hell does that mean? Last night, I reminded her of her dad's movie, because that had seemed to make her happy, and she gave me a monologue on coping saws and how you have to learn to come at a problem from many different angles."

"What movie? A movie with her dad *in* it, you mean?"

"Yes."

"Oh, my god, Bob! When did she see that?"

"A couple of weeks ago."

"She never told me that. That *is* strange. Why would she keep that from me? Isn't that the first time she ever saw her dad, as an adult, I mean?"

"Yes. You see what I mean? She isn't her normal self."

The quesadilla arrived for Danah. She held up her half-full wineglass and silently pleaded for more.

"More?" said the waitress, as if she were talking to a foreigner. Danah nodded enthusiastically, holding the glass out to the waitress who obediently took it and then tactfully placed it back on the table so that Danah could drain it dry.

"I'll be right back."

"One day she talked to me about not being what she seemed to be. I had no idea what to tell her. Sometimes, I feel like she's talking with a person I can't see," said Holly. A pause.

"Do you think she's dabbling in the occult?"

"Why?"

"Because she seems to be in another world half the time."

"I know she doesn't believe in psychics because she said that to me once," said Holly. Danah received a second glass of wine, and the waitress removed the first glass, which was now empty. Danah tried hard to swallow a mouthful of quesadilla and succeeded.

"Danah is a good person, Bob. I don't need to tell you that."

"What do you mean, 'good?'"

"I mean she doesn't compromise. She's different from me that way. I try to make everyone happy never mind what. She's not like that. She won't pretend to like someone she despises, and she despises her stepfather. She doesn't think he deserves respect for marrying her mother. And Bernard does sound like a pig. I've never met him, of course, but I think even I would have trouble making nice with him."

"I wish she'd bitch about him behind his back and get over it like that. That's what everyone else would do. But she broods. She can't accept and move on," said Bob.

"That's what I mean. She's not like everyone else. She's got high standards on hypocrisy and gossiping. She really tries hard not to do either one. That's what I mean about her being good. If you're her friend, you really know she's your friend. She won't betray you. Does that make her crazy?" asked Holly.

"Probably," said Bob and Danah felt a stab of betrayal.

"Well, then, we should all be crazy," said Holly, but Danah didn't hear this. She could still hear Bob saying he thought she was insane.

"So you think it's Bernard who's making her crazy?" asked Bob. Not anymore, now it's both you *and* Bernard who are making me crazy.

"I think that's a big part of it. She doesn't trust him near Elsie, and it makes her sad. This is not the grandfather she wished for Elsie. She's not sure she's ever seen him sober. And she can't plan anything with her mother without him getting involved."

"Why can't she just give Bernard a break?"

"Are you forgetting what happened?" said Holly.

"What?"

"When she went down to Florida soon after Elsie was born, Bernard refused to come to Connecticut because he was in a bowling tournament, and you couldn't get any more time off, so she took the baby down to meet her grandparents. She wanted it to be so special. Do you remember?"

"Vaguely." Danah felt crushed hearing Bob say that it was only a vague memory. She slumped in her chair.

"You remember," prodded Holly. "She took the almost newborn Elsie down there. The plane was delayed. She had to sit on it with no air conditioning. And it was blazing hot when she arrived in Tampa. Elsie got a fever. You remember this, right?"

"Oh right. Didn't Bernard rush back to the condo to watch some game on TV and refuse to take them to a doctor until the game was over?"

"Yes, and he wouldn't allow her to drive his precious Lexus. Her mother went along with Bernard. She didn't want to upset him. Danah ended up calling a cab and took Elsie by herself. She didn't even know where the nearest hospital was. It makes my blood boil just telling the story. He's the most selfish man."

"I know. I know. And it must be disappointing after seeing the movie and knowing how interesting her real father was," said Bob.

"Seeing him in the movie probably brought that home to her the other night."

"Bernard always manages to cause a bad atmosphere whenever he comes up here. I hate introducing him to people if we're out somewhere. He is an embarrassment. You never know when he's going to have one of his attitude problems."

"And I remember her saying that Bernard gave her a lecture in the commercials of the football game, telling her how fussy mothers are these days and how everyone would be better off if they just popped a few pills and relaxed. That's when Danah let him have it, and they've barely spoken since. I don't blame her. What rotten luck getting stuck with him for a stepfather and never knowing her real father! That's a double whammy," said Holly.

"You OK?" the waitress asked Danah. She nodded and pointed to a pecan pie on the A-frame menu sitting on the table. "Eat that? You?" asked the waitress. Danah nodded eagerly, thrilled to meet someone who understood her needs. "Coffee?" continued the waitress, pantomiming the act of drinking from a cup. Danah smiled and blinked once, signifying 'yes.' The waitress promised to return.

"Danah has more integrity than anyone I know. She won't play the dutiful stepdaughter, I know that much," Bob said. "Bernard doesn't get under my skin, but then I never felt he owed me anything. So you really think this is about how Bernard and Vera have let her down?"

"I don't know. But she was upset looking at a photograph of her mother, father, and herself a couple of weeks ago. Buried stuff hits you in middle age."

"Did she show you her Gucci watch?"

"Yes."

"What did you think?"

"It's very nice. I wish I'd found it."

"No, I mean the way she reacted to finding it, like it was some kind of a divine intervention. I thought her reaction was weird. I tried to be happy for her because she seemed relieved or something, but, well . . ."

"I don't know, Bob. I honestly don't know what to tell you. Maybe you should just be direct with her and ask her what's going on."

"I tried that. She just says that's a good question and wanders off repeating the question. Once, she talked about how we should all spend more time asking questions, and less time answering them. She said questions tell you more than answers."

"Well, that's kinda interesting. She can be quite the philosopher, can't she! Listen, maybe it's nothing. Maybe it's nothing more than winter doldrums," suggested Holly.

"Maybe I should just arrange to take her out dancing? I have been pretty tied up with work recently."

"Maybe we should all go out to dinner?"

"That's an excellent idea, Holly. Yes. But I must get back. No, no! This was my treat. Leave this to me."

"Thanks, Bob. We must do this more often!" There was a silence.

"Let's not tell Danah about our lunch. She might get the wrong idea entirely, if you know what I mean," said Bob. Holly laughed.

Danah assumed they exchanged a look and she hated them for it. She bent over double, with her face inches from the plate, as they got up to leave. After a few minutes, she stood up, looking over the top of her chair and saw them talking as they put on their coats by the door. She scanned the other diners for familiar faces. Recognizing no one, she sat down. She put two elbows on the table, covered her face with her hands, and began a deep, silent sobbing. It felt good to let something out, but she soon put a stop to it and wiped her face on the fire red napkin. All she could think was how deadly tired she felt.

The waitress plonked down a coffee and pecan pie with whipped cream. Danah looked up and she meant to smile, but instead, out came the words:

"I don't trust anyone."

The waitress looked alarmed. "Have you changed your mind about desert?"

"No, no. This is lovely. I'm sorry. I'm learning a part. I'm memorizing lines. That was one of my lines. One of my character's lines I should say. I'm sorry. This is great. Thank you. I'm so sorry." The waitress backed away.

Danah felt as fragile as meringue on water. She finished dessert, paid the check, and walked to the door. She looked for her white ski jacket, but it wasn't there. After examining every coat twice, she remembered she'd worn Elsie's jacket, which brought Bob's comment to mind about her not caring about her appearance, and she felt stabs of red-blooded anger about him betraying her like that and then she felt angry about Holly seeing Bob without telling her first.

Danah arrived home to see Norm's truck there and her front doors off their hinges.

"Oh! This is horrible! Horrible!" she said, with her hands to her head.

"You left the front door unlocked. I just took it one little step further!" quipped Norm, coming up behind her.

"This is too weird seeing this. I'm so unhinged today already, you have no idea, and now I have to actually look at this! I really can't bear it, Norm. I think I'll lose my mind if you don't get those doors back on pretty quickly. I need my front doors, Norm. I need to close them. Actually, I need to lock them. When can I do that?"

"Don't worry. I'll have them back in no time. I have to shave three eighths. I got a call from your tile guy. He's coming by next week. I need to raise the doors to allow for the thickness of the tile."

"OK, Norm. I see. I'm just so worn out today. I wasn't expecting anything to happen. I wasn't expecting to see you. That's all. I know you have to unhinge things, doors. I know you must do that sometimes. It's the only way to get things done, right?"

"Right," said Norm, looking concerned at how upset Danah was acting.

"I'll do something. I really will. It's OK," muttered Danah as she walked through the gaping hole in her house.

She wanted to disappear into sleep, but she was too nervous to lie down. In any case, the bed she shared with Bob was not her idea of an ideal destination at this moment. She opened up the loyal pantry doors and was rewarded with the sight of a full bag of pistachios. Pouring them into a black, ceramic fondue pot reminded her how she had introduced Bob to the concept of fondue and made her realize how much she'd like to stick him with a fondue fork. How could he go behind her back like that? And how could he coax Holly into betraying her, too? How could Holly meet with Bob secretly and deliberately keep her out of the loop? A husband telling another woman that he does not understand his wife does not fill that wife with warm feelings.

Danah cracked open one little pistachio skull after another: plick, plick, plick! Then she popped a Pepsi. I could have married another man, an exciting, intuitive man who rode horses and took me on adventures. What was I thinking marrying a man named Bob Blanko? I have to give my mother credit here. She did point out his name to me. And I began having real doubts about our marriage after staying home for a year with Elsie. She swigged Pepsi, feverishly snapping multiple pistachios. I should have had the guts to move on, to go discover more than safe choices. I could have moved to New York, got a full-time job, and supported myself. Divorce is awful, but people continue, the kids cope, a new life emerges. What would Elsie's second birthday party have been like if I had divorced him, I wonder? It could have been great . . .

There I am, driving over to Bob's house for Elsie's party in my sports car. He still lives in Connecticut in this house, except it's falling down. His latest young girlfriend, let's call her Young Jilly, has insisted on throwing the party. Not having yet had the pleasure of celebrating a biological reproduction of her own, she has gone overboard with Bob's money. There are balloons tied to trees a mile away from the house. I walk in like any other parent, except that I appear childless, and I have to fight the urge to explain that I am the mother of today's birthday girl. We are directed to the living room. White, helium-filled balloons hang everywhere, dangling silver strings. The dining table is covered in a white satin table cloth. White vases holding white, satin roses are everywhere. Was there perhaps another occasion on Young Jilly's mind when she picked out these decorations? Why hadn't Blanko told her about primary colors and how two year-olds like them? The white balloons look as festive as IV bags. Oxygen seeps out steadily.

"Mommy, mommy!" cries dearest Elsie upon seeing me, and I run to hug my precious. She is not wearing the denim overalls I sent. No, she is dressed in an overly frilly pink thing. Is that make-up on her twenty-four month old face? Children I don't even recognize are opening gifts meant for Elsie. Bob is nowhere.

Some boy I've never seen before, who looks suspiciously large for a preschooler, comes in carrying a large stick. He is moments away from ruining Elsie's party. I hold back. I hope like hell a responsible blood-relative is following him and will do what is required. He holds the stick aloft and circles for a victim. I feel a powerful urge to run away and check e-mail for passionate notes from my boyfriend, who is a gypsy king performing on Broadway for a limited time only. The boy closes in on Elsie.

"Put the stick down!" I say to the overwrought guest. He won't. Not to be outdone, I open his sticky fingers for him, and take the weapon for myself. This improves my mood considerably. The feel of a solid stick in my hand is an unexpected pleasure. I take a step backwards and hope no one will insist on taking the stick away from me.

Bob appears with a piñata. He leads game after age-appropriate game with these kids, who transform themselves into models of good behavior under his supervision. He remembers to take photos. He plays just the right mix of CDs. He dances with Elsie. He leads the merry band to the dining table fit for a princess and brings out quite the prettiest cake I have ever seen: a chocolate dome covered with daisies and rosebuds iced onto the surface as if tossed by magic. He has thought of everything. My precious Elsie is ready for her close-up.

With the cake over, Jill has a bright idea. She sends them out onto the driveway to play. It's April, the sun is out and the children can run the sugar off outdoors. What possesses a woman of thirty-something to wear ankle-socks with a lace frill around the top? The frills slip out from under her jeans like false teeth losing their grip.

I decide to use Bob's phone to make an urgent international call; and as I barrel around a corner to his office, I go flat bang into Bob. This is more spontaneous bodily contact than we had in the last two years of our marriage.

"Oh, *there* you are!" he says. "Did you bring the goodie bags?"

"Follow me," I say, knowing better than to give a man directions to something sitting on his own kitchen counter. We arrive to find Frilly Jilly already handing them out to wide-eyed children and observant parents who might mistakenly think she's a dear for finding panda-shaped bags, panda key rings, panda pencils, and black-and-white non-toxic modeling clay.

"Would you like to stay for coffee? We're having some," says Jill. Bob and I smile at each other. "Coffee" used to be our code word for sex.

Danah got back into working clothes and carried on with the staining. She wiped circles of stain onto the needy wood. The ironic thing is that here I am, busily leaving marks, stains, and all I can think about are people who sneak around me trying to leave no traces.

"Your doors are back on their hinges!" called Norm. Sweet, sweet words.

Danah picked up her checkbook and walked through the hinged doors to join Norm. "That's a load off my mind to see them hinged again," said Danah. Norm came out from the cab of his pickup and handed her his bill for the week's work with the receipts for materials he'd bought. Danah checked the math in privacy after she'd given him a check. He'd never made a mistake yet.

"Gracias," he said, with check in hand. "See you Monday."

"Yes."

"You take care now." These words brought tears to her eyes.

When Bob arrived home, Danah was staining the towel racks in the master bathroom. They were custom-made to match the frame around the swing doors between the bathroom and bedroom.

"I'm home!" shouted Bob. She did not reply. "I'm home!" he repeated, from the bedroom.

"And why is that then?"

"What kind of question is that?"

"What kind of answer was that?" He ignored her. He changed into jeans and a dark green sweatshirt.

"Would you like to go out for dinner for a change?"

"Would it be a change for *you* to eat out?"

"We haven't been out together to eat for a while. Elsie's doing homework. She can make a sandwich. I thought it would be a nice change of pace."

Danah let out the kind of sigh people make when leaving this earth. She walked through the double swing doors to confront her opponent.

"I very much want to eat in."

"Are you feeling all right?"

"No. Many, many things are wrong at this time. Can I leave it like that for now, Bob?"

Bob went downstairs and microwaved a frozen lasagna. As Danah dropped her stained clothes in a pile ready for tomorrow's shift, she heard him call her. She put on white pajamas and her yellow dressing gown before joining him.

Two tall, white candles glowed on the dining table that was covered with a black tablecloth. Normally she liked the severe cloth. Tonight, she saw a coffin, a wake of sorts. Bob held out a glass of wine to her.

"Here's to the great job you're doing on the house!" He raised his glass, and she watched him drink. "I didn't poison yours."

"Very interesting," she said, quietly.

"Danah, I've had enough. Snap out of it! Sarcasm is boring!"

"Oh! Principal Blanko is displeased. What to do?" She helped herself to lasagna from the kitchen counter, sat herself down at the table, and began to chew.

"What the hell is wrong with you? Spit it out!"

"I don't know what *it* is."

"Issue!" sneezed Bob. Bob's sneezes often took the form of a word. Damn right, there's an issue. Bob possessed a considerable lexicon of sneezes which included: outcome; I chew; I sue; octave; and I seize. He had an uncanny knack of making choices appropriate to the moment. He once sneezed "I Ching" in a Chinese restaurant. Another time, when they had dinner guests and Danah had not cleaned the house, he sneezed, "Vacuum!"

"We can't go on like this."

"How shall we go on, then? Should we carry on behind each other's backs, perhaps? Would that be preferable?" Bob looked cowed. "Was that the *it* you wanted me to spit out? Probably not, but here goes, anyway. You took Holly to lunch today and talked about me." Bob looked shocked and stared at her from across the table. Danah made a Twilight Zone noise.

"Well, what options do you give me? How am I supposed to figure out what's going on with you?"

"So you cheat on me, thinking that'll fix everything?"

"I did not cheat on you, Danah! I resent that."

"I'm so sorry. What is the correct verb for taking out my attractive best friend to lunch secretly and giving her the 'I don't understand my crazy little wife' routine?"

"I have no romantic interest in Holly, and you know it. Cut out the bullshit. I was asking her what was upsetting you. That was it."

"I know exactly what you said."

"How?"

"I sat at the table next to you."

"You did not."

"Ah yes! You would know more about what I do than I know myself, wouldn't you?"

"We would have seen you."

"So how do I know that you complained about me being wacky and wearing Elsie's clothes? How do I know you told Holly not to tell me about your little lunch?"

"Holly called you."

"Oh now you're betraying your trust in her already! Should anyone have faith in anyone anymore?" She pushed her plate away and the wedge of lasagna toppled over.

"OK, I admit, it was a dumb thing to do. But in my defense, I have to say this is what women do all the time. If you have a problem with me, I bet you go running to Holly with it, and you don't even have to answer that. It's OK. I'm OK with you talking your thoughts over with a friend. I guess men are just not allowed to do that. I get it."

"Find your own damn best friend and leave mine alone."

"If you would just relax a minute and open up, just maybe I could help you!"

"I'll tell you what really, really got to me. What really hurt me was the way you only *vaguely*—and that was your choice of word— you only vaguely remembered how badly Bernard treated Elsie and me in Florida. Which means you didn't remember how excited I was to take my baby down to meet her grandparents, how I got over the fact they couldn't be bothered to come here, how I rose to the occasion and had high expectations for a visit that I'd cherish my whole life. And then I was treated like, well, so many unwashed dishes. And I called you from the emergency room, me crying, and baby Elsie crying in my arms. I had never felt more abandoned or angrier in my life, and you remember this "vaguely?"

"Of course I remember it. Bernard's a selfish bastard, and I got pretty upset myself up here in Connecticut that day, totally unable to help you. I know all that, but what I don't know is how long you've got to hang onto this for, getting angry over and over again. It's not doing anyone any good. I want you to stop punishing yourself for something you had no control over. Let's agree, one more time, that he's a no-good bastard who doesn't deserve a granddaughter, and then let it go."

"It sounds great, it really does. I would love to let Bernard go. But how do you fire someone who is married to your mother?"

"It stinks. You're right. He comes in a package with your mother. You shouldn't have to put up with him. I wish Vera had married anyone else, or no one. But she married Bernard."

"Well, it helps to hear you say that. You weren't saying that in the restaurant. You were making it sound like I'm insane."

"I love you, Danah!"

"OK, I'm going to let it go!"

"Dad!" yelled Elsie from upstairs. Danah had forgotten she was home. "I need help with math."

"Coming!" he called back. Danah cleaned up what mess there was and soon followed him upstairs. She lingered in the doorway to Elsie's room. Elsie was looking into Bob's eyes as she recited some rule or other. "You can do it!" he said to her. Danah went on her way down the hallway. She recognized self-pity rising. Maybe if I'd had a father who said that to me, I wouldn't be so full of doubt about myself. She went back downstairs, not yet able to embrace the intimacy of her own bedroom. She looked in the pantry for advice. Her hand gravitated towards a can. The label said: 'Cured Pork.'

"But *how*? *How* was the pork cured?"

7 FIFTEEN YEARS AGO

Danah decided to walk along the stretch of beach facing her house. Bob and Elsie had left for school. Norm wasn't due for an hour or so. She crossed Beach Road without bothering to look for traffic and descended a flight of weather-worn wooden steps that led to a narrow walkway across marshland and then to a sandy beach with dunes. She rested her back against a mound of sand and breathed air mingled with seaweed. The tide was out, and she saw many little kingdoms of sand, each one created by trapped water. She picked herself up, kicked off her clogs, and dipped her toes in the cold pools so carelessly abandoned by the sea.

After ten minutes or so, she climbed back up to Beach Road and joined the growing ranks of neighbors getting early morning exercise. A graceful man with silver hair came gliding by on roller blades. A woman in her forties walked behind her for a while, scolding her dog and pulling him up short on his leash because he would not heel. The woman and her dog finally passed Danah. The doggie tirade faded into the distance. Danah wondered how the woman spoke to her husband, if she had a husband. There was a woman coming towards her wearing a long, pink skirt. She had long, gray braids and real walking boots. Am I supposed to meet this woman? The woman walked quickly past her, giving her a nod.

Danah imagined, for a moment, that nothing was accidental or irrelevant and everything happened for a reason. What if I were supposed to find Bob and Holly together that day? What could I possibly learn from that? Danah studied two women approaching her. She suddenly turned around to be ahead of them, to shut them out of her line of vision. A cold wind picked up, and large spots of rain splattered the sidewalk. Danah rushed home. In her absence, Norm had arrived and opened the garage. She saw him from the other side of the road. He was busy carrying in his tools and sawhorses out of the rain. She waved at him, hoping he wouldn't talk to her, but he immediately walked down the driveway towards her.

"You've got to order the doors and windows today," he said, with a cigarette dancing on his lips.

"Okay," she said, dragging out the second syllable. She recognized the tone of voice she normally reserved for dentists whenever they suggest a series of costly, painful visits. And in the same way Danah always hoped the dental receptionist would not get specific about dates on her way out of the office, she now walked away from Norm and entered her house. A few minutes later, Norm was beside her in the kitchen, holding out some brochures.

"Can't do this without you!" he said, handing her an Anderson catalog and a Marvin one.

"Anderson? Marvin? she said, accepting the catalogs. They sound like those characters from that movie, *Dumb and Dumber*, don't they?" Danah put both catalogs face down on the kitchen counter and walked away from them towards the stairs, trying to show Norm she had other things to do.

"You've already got Anderson in this house, so you probably want to go with that," said Norm, holding his ground. As Norm continued to talk about the various merits of different styles of windows, Danah searched for a way to tell Norm that she already had these catalogs and did not like the idea of anything being 'double hung.' She wanted to say that the whole notion of cutting a hole in a wall and inserting a window freaked her out. She preferred to live with the illusion of windows and walls coexisting from the beginning. The idea of marking out an exact spot for a window was like having to pick out a live fish to eat. It was not something she was comfortable doing. She did not wish to contemplate the conception, birth, or life of a fish. She liked the illusion of fish coming into this world coated in lemon butter. She hesitated now because she knew this might seem outlandish to Norm. However, thus far in life, she had managed to escape designating spots in walls for holes and condemning specific fish to death.

"Well, take another look at the plans we gave the town," Norm continued. "You'll need two pictures, a slider, and a glider for the rec. room."

"Sounds like a photography assignment at a baseball game."

"Might take a while to get them. You better call today," said Norm, exiting through the front door.

Is there an emergency I can attend to instead, wondered Danah, trying hard to come up with something critical but not life-threatening. She put a mug of purified water into the microwave. When it was done, it seemed to scream louder and longer than usual. She dropped a lemon tea bag in the grey mug and remembered a monstrous pile of laundry awaiting her that could qualify as a moderate emergency. Then Norm's electric saw started up and reminded her of the dentist.

She found the building specs in a box in the corner of her bedroom. She took them downstairs and placed them beside the window catalogs. She flipped through the first few pages of the Anderson catalog. They always start out non-threatening. She admired the cathedral-proportioned windows showing royal blue light outside. Turning back to the contents page she noted the page numbers for 'sliders.' After a sip of tea and some eyeballing of sliders she turned to the back for the fine print, the ordering information. There were line drawings of doors and black holes where the locks and handles should be. She flipped back to the comfort of color photographs. She circled simple, white windows and sliders while mentally shuddering at the memory of free-floating windows and doors. Norm can place the order and quote the exact sizes over the phone, she decided. She was running the catalogs back to Norm when she thought she heard a truck pull up. She looked through a front window and was not at all pleased to see Holly arriving uninvited.

Danah found Norm on the back deck, looking at the office framework. She ignored the doorbell. She explained her choices to Norm and handed him the catalogs.

"OK. I'll call in the order. No problem," he said, rolling them up and inserting them into his back pocket. "By the way," he said, quietly, "I've got deck envy!"

Danah laughed a hearty laugh. "That's a good line. Deck envy! I'll use that."

"That was the doorbell."

"Right." Danah walked off with a smile on her face until she remembered it was Holly at the door. She greeted her with raised eyebrows, wondering if she were here to confess cavorting with Bob the other day.

"I just dropped Harry off at pre-school and I thought I'd see if you were in."

"Well, it depends on what you mean by 'in,'" replied Danah, coldly. Holly came into the house and took off her coat.

"How are you?" asked Holly, hanging her woolen coat on the rack.

"Let me see. I'm definitely not over the moon, which is probably a good thing, because then you know you're in for trouble."

"I don't know how you know what to do all the time, with the house and the workers, I mean."

"I don't."

"Well, you still keep going, that's the amazing thing. And it's looking great, it really is. I bet you're adding so much value. I can see it working now. I couldn't see it before, you know, I couldn't really imagine it. You're so good at imagining things, Danah." Holly followed Danah up the stairs into the kitchen.

"Am I? I'm good at imagining things?"

"I've wanted to see you." Holly settled onto the cobalt blue barstool at the kitchen counter.

"Really?"

"You're hard to get hold of."

"Here I am."

"What's wrong with you? What do you want me to say?"

"I want you to say what's on your mind."

"I'm your friend, Danah. You're acting like I've done something terrible."

"Have you?"

"No!"

"Sure? It's just that when my trusty, old girlfriend drops by unexpectedly, which is totally out-of-character by the way, I have to wonder if someone put her up to it." Holly walked over to the sliders and looked at Norm on the unfinished deck. Danah remained at the kitchen sink. She started clattering some breakfast dishes.

"OK. Big deal. Bob and I had lunch." Holly approached the kitchen island. "Why? Because he's worried sick about you, and I'm not happy about the way you are right now, either. Is that what you wanted to hear me say?" Danah wrestled with her response. There were so many answers she could have given. "Bob's worried about you."

"Let me guess why: I've changed. I am no longer myself. I am no longer very funny. I am quiet. I am angry, or maybe depressed. I've stopped exercising and started wearing Elsie's clothes. I don't go out enough. I only talk to workmen. Is that what he said?"

"Yes."

"Oh! Mr. Blanko, what a piece of work! So reasonable, so considerate, a pillar of society, and so solicitous of his wife's well being. But can the man *talk* to that wife of his? Can he? Hell no, he runs off and talks to her best friend instead."

"He doesn't want to risk upsetting you more."

"Well, now you can run back to him and tell him I'm mad as

hell and very upset, thanks to the both of you."

"Is that what this is all about? Bob and I having lunch?"

"I never said what this is all about."

"But you are upset with me for having lunch with Bob, among other things, right?"

"Well, let me think. First you drag me to a psychic because your marriage is rotten, then you are spotted out with my husband. I guess, when I put it that way, it does trouble me." A brief silence elapsed in which Danah found herself wanting to ask Holly if she would always be her friend. "You should have told me you were going before you went. Then I would have known where your loyalty was."

"Danah! He's worried about you. I hate to say this, but sometimes you are difficult to talk to. I had to agree with him about that. He thought maybe I knew what was bothering you. And here I am to tell you what we said."

"So, did you tell him we saw a psychic?"

"Absolutely not! You're acting paranoid. I made a promise. I keep my promises." Danah set two glasses of orange juice down on the island. "I thought about telling you, I wanted to. But Bob was so definite about keeping it a secret." Danah looked skeptical. Holly answered Danah's look: "You're right; I should have tipped you off."

"Well, I shouldn't have doubted you. I'll tell you what really pissed me off. It was Bob making it sound like Bernard did nothing to me down there in Florida, that it was me who was out of line."

"You should tell Bob that."

"I did. We talked. We sorted some things out. It's so frustrating that there has to be a crisis before Bob and I talk to each other."

"He was worried about you. He said every time he gets close to talking to you, you change the subject and act nervous. He's sensing you're afraid of something. Are you?"

"Of course I am. Isn't everyone afraid of something?" Danah rinsed her glass in the sink.

"What are you afraid of?" asked Holly.

Danah turned to face her and thought for a moment. "Putting on weight, running out of things to say, dementia, death. The usual, really."

Holly smiled. "Why didn't you tell me about seeing your dad in a movie?"

"Oh that. Bob got all excited about that too. It's painful. I have a lot of mixed feelings. I told Bob it meant looking at the dad who never wrote to me, never called me, never found out where I lived, or what I was doing with my life. He's not just any movie star to me."

"You should give yourself more credit, Danah. You're taking on a lot of stuff right now and handling it."

"I don't know how well I'm handling anything. There's a lot of stuff I haven't handled that I should have handled." She looked out at the sky.

"You're too hard on yourself."

Danah smiled. "I'm sorry I went off on you, Holly."

"It's OK. By the way, when did Bob tell you we had lunch?"

"He didn't tell me. I was there. I heard it all for myself."

"What?"

"I was there. I sat at the table behind yours. I heard every word."

"I can't believe you did that."

"Did what? What did I do?"

"You eavesdropped! I can't believe you just sat there listening to our private conversation."

"Oh, so now I'm going to hear about it from you?"

"I don't like that. I wouldn't have done that. I wouldn't have just sat there and listened in. That's not right."

"So now I owe *you* an apology?"

"I think you do."

"Well, it was like finding your kid's diary open on a page with your name on it. What are you going to do?" Danah flicked crumbs off the kitchen counter. They looked at each other without pretense. "I guess neither one of us is perfect. That's disappointing."

"Well, I'm glad we got all this out in the open, anyway," said Holly, putting her own empty glass in the sink. "No more secrets from each other from now on."

"I was raised on secrets. Secrets are a way of life for me."

"That could change," said Holly, walking toward the front door.

"If it does, I won't tell you," said Danah. They laughed.

"I'd better be going. I've got a load of groceries to get. Paul's parents are coming over for dinner tonight." Holly put her coat on.

"Say hi to them from me."

"I will," she said, doing up her buttons.

"Harry's lucky to have grandparents so near."

"I'm glad I got the nerve to come over and we talked." They hugged goodbye.

Danah uncharacteristically felt an urge to do laundry and actually ran towards it. She turned on the dryer to fluff up the clothes that had sat there for a day. Then she began folding clothes and this gave her time to play back what had just happened with Holly. Her friend had been direct and quick to forgive. Danah realized she herself would have held a grudge for a while if positions had been reversed. However, she could not picture herself in a restaurant with Paul. Despite all the years she'd known Holly and Paul, she couldn't recall a single instance of talking with Paul when Holly wasn't around.

Inspired by Holly's example of directness, Danah pulled out her smart phone and tapped Vera's number.

"Claude," said Bernard. His last name was Claude and he insisted on answering his home phone as if he were still at his secondhand car dealership.

"This is Danah."

"What do you want?"

"I want to speak with my mother." He clunked the phone down on a hard surface and yelled for Vera. If there were a kill-him-now option right now, what would I do? If there were a button to press that would release a poisonous gas in his ear, I'd do it.

"Darling! Are you OK?" Danah was about to reassure her mother when Vera added, "Just a minute, darling, hold on!" Danah heard her mother saying goodbye to Bernard and Bernard telling her what time he wanted supper waiting for him. "I'm back. Sorry about that, Bernard had to go out."

"Is he going to the car dealership?" asked Danah.

"No."

"Where is he going then?"

"He's spending the afternoon at the gun club, dear. He's in a competition or something. He was in a hurry."

"Bernard has a gun?"

"Oh yes. I thought you knew that. He's held a permit ever since, well, since before we were married, I suppose."

"He doesn't *hold a permit!* He *holds a gun.* How can you allow a gun in your house? That's very un-British of you, mother."

"Do you know, I don't even think about it anymore. Bernard says there are a lot of nuts around, and it's safer this way."

"So it's safer for an old man who can barely walk, and who already has one hand on a walking stick, to go stumbling around *with* a gun than without one?"

"Danah! Don't call him an old man, and he doesn't go stumbling around. You make him sound awful. You're not being nice."

"Yeah, well, guns aren't very nice, either. They don't tend to bring out the best in people. Are you honestly OK with him having a gun around, mom?"

"It's difficult, Danah."

"What's difficult?"

"It's difficult explaining this to you. I know you don't like him, but I love him. I do. He's very good to me. We are very happy together. I see how other couples are. I think I'm lucky."

"So you probably carry a gun too?"

"No I don't!".

"Why not?"

"Oh my god, Danah, you should have been a lawyer."

"Why don't you have your own gun?"

"Because I don't like guns."

"That's what I'm trying to get at. Are you forgetting to ask yourself if you're OK with things? Do you automatically give in to everything he wants at this point? You've got to speak up, mother, if you don't like something. That's what you've always told me." The dryer buzzed, signaling dry clothes.

"I'll think about what you've said, OK? Meanwhile, please be civil to him. He is my husband, and I do love him, darling. Try to accept that." Danah jumped up to sit on the warm dryer.

"It's very hard to be civil with him. He never has a kind word to say to me. Never has. He never asks about Elsie."

"It's nothing personal, Danah. He's the same way with his own kids."

"Oh well, if he's nasty to everyone, that's OK then. I guess I'll stand around with them one day talking about how consistent he is. Thing is, he's never introduced me to any of my step-siblings, has he?"

"Hold on there. I'm going to tell you something, Danah. Don't try to poison me against Bernard. It won't work. And that's all

I'm going to say on that. Now, did you call to talk about Bernard, or was there something else?"

"Can I ask one more question?"

"What?"

"When did he start carrying a gun?"

"Oh! I don't know, about fifteen years ago, when we got married, I suppose."

"Wow!" Danah hopped off the dryer and pumped her fist as if she had just won the U.S. Open.

"What? What did I say?"

"You told me when you got married. You got married fifteen years ago, didn't you?" Vera made a series of flustered noises.

"What does it really matter now?"

"I don't know. I never did understand why it was so important to you to keep it secret in the first place. So where did you get married to Bernard?"

"London."

"London, England? Why would you go all that way?"

"Please don't tell Bernard I told you any of this, Danah."

"No problem. We don't talk to each other, remember?"

"Well, no one really approved of our marriage, as you well know. His kids didn't like me any more than you liked him. We thought we'd get married on a vacation and avoid the, well, you know. "

"Interesting," said Danah, feeling lightheaded from the flood of new information.

"Now, you really must promise not to breathe a word of this to Bernard. He'd kill me if he knew what I'd said."

"Would he?"

"What?"

"Would he really kill you?"

"He'd be very angry. Danah, just promise me not to repeat any of this."

"I won't talk about it."

"You know, darling, Bernard is really very good to me. He's taking me on vacation soon. Some stocks just went sky high. A lot of men would keep that from their wives, not Bernard. He said we could go on a trip and I could choose where. Isn't that sweet of him? There's someone at the door. Danah, can you hold on?"

"OK." Danah heard a muffled exchange between Vera and a

woman.

"Can you hold on a minute? I have to find my purse," Vera said to Danah.

"No. I'm sorry. I really can't hold on any longer. I have to do something. Bye, mom."

After they hung up, Danah convinced herself there was more to this story. Vera was so agitated, and there was a tone in her voice that was entirely new.

8 ELSIE IS HAMLET

I don't *think* I would kill him, but I could surprise myself. Danah had woken up early with an urge to literally get her house in order, and so she was picking up Elsie's room, having already Cloroxed the bathrooms. It was a long-standing habit to clean while trying to make a decision. If I found out he really did kill my father, and it was easy to do away with Bernard . . . well, you never know, Big Panda, you never know. Danah chose a small panda to nestle with Big Panda. This man has made me angrier than I ever thought it possible to be.

The sight of Elsie's organized room satisfied her. She wished everything could be so deliberately arranged. If only my life were this tidy. Returning to her own bedroom and the makeshift office, she summoned her favorite browser, went incognito, and entered the words: "fat man" and "gun" in a Google search. The top three entries amused her wicked self. She couldn't believe there was a Fat Man website devoted to selling accessories with a cartoon fat man on everything. She clicked on Guns 'n' Stuff. The stuff with the guns turned out to be golf clubs, jewelry, books on African game hunting, gym bags, teddy bears, engraved knives, and sauces. All these items were emblazoned with a blue and yellow gun logo and the company's name: Guns 'n' Stuff.

Clicking on "sauces" brought up bottles of steak and barbecue sauces with names like "44 Magnum" and "Saturday Night Special." Danah read all the text, hoping to find the words *killer sauces*. I could add a little something poisonous to the sauce and then give it to Bernard. After he died, Vera could sue the company and win a settlement claiming she believed the description, "killer sauces," had been intended as a joke. But Danah did not find those words. They must have run this copy by their legal department.

She clicked on the wide-necked bottle of "Saturday Night Special" to get the details, only to be greeted with the following message: *an error occurred*. She was offended, as if she had been morally judged. Briskly, she returned to the previous screen and selected "44 Magnum" instead. She laughed out loud at the idea of bumping off Bernard for a mere $3.95, plus the cost of the shipping and poison. Another error message occurred. It read, *Supply address of the remote client*, and it dawned on her that Bernard was indeed remote, for which she was extremely grateful. Clinging to the site despite several more error messages allowed her to discover that some Guns 'n' Stuff products could be purchased in bricks-and-mortar retail stores. The list of real-world stores did not include Connecticut. The nearest one was in Maine.

Truck noise from the driveway reminded her it was the hour for workmen to arrive. She logged out and ran from the computer as if from a crime scene. Grabbing a blue corduroy jacket, she went out to greet today's guys.

"Here comes the boss lady!" said Norm. A quick glance at the trucks choking her driveway told her she had the roofers, the tile guys, and Norm on hand.

"Morning, Dan. Do you want the trucks moved back from the house?" she asked the roofer. He had a broad, sunburnt face with no wrinkles, as if nothing had ever bothered him.

"Could move them back," he said, gazing at the sunbaked shingles that had curled in a valiant attempt to escape their fate. "Yep," he added, and this one 'yep' set off a furor of engines and hand signals. The tile and roof people backed their vehicles onto the street. Norm reversed his truck onto the grass on the right, halfway down the driveway.

"Guess we're gonna need valet parking before long," said Norm, walking towards her. It pinched Danah's nerves to see that the roofers stayed in their trucks and broke out coffee and food. "It's lunchtime for them," said Norm and she smiled at him for reading her thoughts. "Dan said he was up patching a roof at five this morning. Probably don't want to work on a roof in the heat of the day is my guess." Norm pushed the brim of his cap up and walked off.

Trying to re-enter her house involved navigating around Rich who was crouching in the foyer. He was a sizeable Italian. Danah assumed that the younger kid outside was Rich's son. Rich scooted closer to the stairs to allow Danah access. Then, she heard what could have been a classroom of children dragging their fingernails down a chalkboard in unison.

"What was that?"

"Tile cutter," said Rich, snapping a chalk line. Roughly ten minutes later, when Danah next glanced over at the foyer, there was a grid of orange chalk lines. Something is taking shape, at last, she thought, with such relief. These amazing men know what to do and they do it without hesitation. How can I be more like that?

A loud, mechanical whirring ripped the air. This time, she ran outside for an explanation. Another truck had arrived. This one was red. Its open-caged back held a riding lawn mower and various tools for yard work. Danah spotted a man wielding a chainsaw on the far left of her property. As she stood, watching him slash his way through the brush, something struck her as odd, and she also became more and more certain that she had not hired a man to cut brush for her.

"Have you been up close to this guy?" asked Norm.

"No. What do you mean?"

"I'm surprised the birds are still singing. Let me put it that way."

"Breath?"

"Drunk as a skunk."

"I've never understood that expression," she said quietly. Danah and Norm stood there, watching the chainsaw man swerve left and right, carving a chaotic pathway through the underbrush.

"I'm pretty sure I didn't hire that guy. I've never seen him or his truck before," said Danah.

"You're kidding me!"

"Unfortunately, no." They witnessed a spindly birch tree fall.

"I liked that tree. What the hell does he think he's doing? Norm, will you tell him to leave?"

"Not me."

"Please," she added.

"That's why you get paid the big bucks, boss lady," he said, cheerfully, before striding back to the safety of his own power tools.

Summoning her boss-lady powers, she marched towards him, expecting the sight of her would prompt him to shut off the motor, but he continued.

"Hello!" said Danah, waving wildly.

"Yes, ma'am," he said, after shutting off the chainsaw. He kept the blade upright and ready to slash at a moment's notice.

"I think there's a mistake."

"What? You like the brush?" His breath polluted the great outdoors, and his eyes slid from one thing to another, never finding focus. He and the chainsaw lurched towards her.

"I didn't hire you. I think you pulled into the wrong driveway," said Danah, taking a small step backwards, and hoping Norm was monitoring the body language.

"Yeah?" he said, staggering sideways.

"Uh huh," nodded Danah, trying to give him the impression they were in complete agreement. The slasher held the blade like a baby and looked rejected. Danah wondered if she should hire him to trim a few trees as a safe way out.

"I know," he said, and jogged toward his truck. He slung the chainsaw in the back, murdered the gearbox, and backed out of the driveway.

Meanwhile, a FedEx truck had silently parked in the street and a uniformed man had delivered a shallow box to her doorstep. She decided to open it later. By two o'clock, she couldn't stand to hear one more staple shot into the roof. She'd managed a few calls to editors and public relations people. She knew what she was supposed to do, but she couldn't settle. She had promised to pick up Elsie after school today because it was Elsie's birthday. Elsie couldn't stand fuss in the morning, so she had asked her mother not to acknowledge her birthday until after school.

Danah joined the convoy of minivans and more impressive cars she couldn't name all waiting to make a right turn into the middle school. Having made the turn and parked near the reddish-brown school building, she felt mesmerized by students forming groups and then separating as if they were the stuff of lava lamps. Three girls with linked arms danced an off-to-see-the-wizard routine. It wasn't until they had collapsed into laughter that Danah realized Elsie was one of those girls. Danah beeped her car horn and waved. Elsie returned the wave, said something to her friends, and then ran towards her mother.

"The best news! The best ever! Oh my god, mom! Shall I tell you?" said Elsie, through the driver's window. Danah paused for a moment, trying to think what on earth it would be.

"Oh, it can't be true!"

"Yes!"

"You didn't!"

"I did. I really did!"

"Go on then, say it!"

"I'm Hamlet! I got the part! Can you believe it?"

"Oh Elsie! I'm so happy for you. It's so exciting. Get in the car, honey." Elsie double-skipped Oz-style to the passenger's side. She swung her backpack ahead of her, and Danah's spirit soared to see Elsie's face so clear with happiness. She started the engine.

"Can you believe it, mom? And Janet is Ophelia. I knew she would be. She's good. She's got the hair, but she's good, too. Rebecca is Gertrude. And a kid who's new this year is my father. It's the best." They drove the access road to the main road in silence.

"That's the best birthday present ever!" said Danah, pulling out onto the main road again and making a left. "Have you got much homework?"

"No, I got most of it done in study hall. Oh my god, mom, I nearly died waiting for the cast list. Mrs. V. said she'd put it up by the end of the day, and she only put it up last period. I was so psyched when I saw my name on that board. I almost want to go back and look at it again now." Danah threw Elsie a smile glowing with pride.

"Well, I want to treat you to something. Can you think of something you'd like to do right now?"

"I have to call dad. And then, I don't know, maybe we could go to CVS and get a bunch of magazines."

"Let's take the magazines to the coffee shop. Maybe I'll go berserk and buy myself a magazine." Elsie gave her mother a look as if to say, you are so weird. "I honestly don't remember the last time I bought a magazine."

"It's definitely time then," said Elsie.

"Yes. It is time," said Danah, staring at the face of her Gucci watch. They parked in the CVS parking lot and entered the heavy, double set of glass doors.

"What kind of magazines do you want?" Elsie's eyes traveled the rows of glossy covers.

"I want pictures that'll get me thinking like Hamlet. Mrs. V. said we should make a montage of things that'll get us into the role. Eventually, we're going to bring in pictures and things and talk about how they relate to our character." Elsie dialed her father's number with her back to the feminine products.

"That's a good idea. You can put them on your bulletin board. Is it a big production? Are you going to do evening performances for parents?"

"In about six weeks. Wait! I got dad. Dad! Guess what? No. I got the part of Hamlet in the school play. I know! That's what I said! Thanks. OK. Here's mom." Elsie handed her phone to her mother and browsed the wall of magazines.

"Yes, I'm proud of her too. Great timing, yes. What time are you coming home? Oh. OK. We'll meet you at the restaurant then.

Yes. Bye." Danah poked the phone to end the call. "What did he say, Elsie?"

"He said 'What a great birthday present!'"

Elsie picked up three fashion magazines full of androgynous, brooding models, many of whom wore black. She also took *Extravagant Homes*, saying this would give her a sense of modern palaces. Danah bought *Simple Times* and three kinds of chocolate.

Driving home from the coffee shop, Danah said, "Do you think I'm shrinking?" They stopped at a red light.

"Shrinking? What do you mean—*shrinking*?" Elsie looked at her mother.

"I mean, do I seem smaller?"

"Of course not. Why?"

"I don't know, I just thought the women in the coffee shop seemed bigger than me, that's all."

"You should be happy, then." Elsie returned her eyes to her magazine.

"No. I don't mean they were fat. I just have the sense of being less than, although I know I'm not, it just felt that way, of course. It's the way I've been feeling recently."

"Why are you telling me this? Shouldn't you be telling a shrink?"

"I don't want to talk to a shrink about shrinking." The light turned green. "I figure you already know I'm a bit crazy, so I can tell you how I really feel."

They arrived home to an empty driveway. The landline rang as they entered the house. Elsie ran to get it.

"Gran! Guess what! I'm Hamlet."

Danah poured herself a glass of wine and listened to Elsie grill Vera about playing Shakespeare. Elsie discovered that Vera had once played Rosalind in a theater in Chichester, Sussex. Danah put her hand on Elsie's shoulder and told her she wanted to talk to Vera when she was done. She went upstairs to lie down, watch the local news, and sample chocolate.

"Mom! It's Vera on line one!" yelled Elsie from downstairs. Danah smiled. She picked up the phone on Bob's bedside table.

"Thank you." Danah sprawled across the bed. "Hi mom. Good news about Elsie, isn't it?"

"Marvelous, darling. She'll make a wonderful Hamlet. It's a very interesting idea to cast a girl in that role. It normally is women who hesitate and have trouble making decisions, isn't it!" This comment startled Danah and she saw, in a flash, that she herself had been playing out the role of Hamlet for the past few months. *How could I have missed this? I even have Bernard starring as the evil stepfather.* "Are you there, dear? Danah?"

"Yes." *I am more* here *than I've been in a long time, mother.*

"Yes, you're right. Hamlet does seem female in many ways."

"Elsie invited us to see her in the play." Danah wanted her mother to come up to Connecticut without Bernard.

"Have you said anything to Bernard about guns yet, mother?"

"As a matter of fact, I did, yes."

"And?"

"And it didn't do a blind bit of good."

"What did you say?" Danah rolled onto her back and studied settling cracks in the walls.

"I asked him if he could keep his gun at the gun club."

"What did he say?"

"He said, 'No.'"

"That was it?"

"No. I told him I didn't really like having a gun in the house.

And he said he knows what he's doing. He was rather unpleasant for a day or two afterwards. He didn't talk much."

"I'd say that was a clear victory."

"Now then, Danah, be nice."

"So that was it, then?"

"Unfortunately, no. I think he's been going to the gun club more frequently than before. He placed fourth in that shoot-out the other day. He was quite pleased with himself for that." He's always pleased with himself. "I don't think it's worth making a big fuss about it, darling."

"Well, I'm glad you questioned him anyway. Questions are important. Really, at the end of every day, we should sit down with a journal and try to remember all the questions we asked. It would tell us a lot about ourselves." A long pause.

"What are you doing for fun these days, dear?" asked Vera.

"Fun?" said Danah, in the tone she'd use if she'd seen pork chops on a vegetarian menu.

"Yes, dear, fun. Are you having any? What are you doing for Elsie's birthday?"

"We're going to a sushi restaurant tonight, and we're giving her some money to go on a shopping spree."

"Well, if you ask me, I'd tell you to stop working so hard."

"I can't. That's how I earn a living." Danah sat up, cross-legged and aggravated.

"So, what's the last thing you did for fun?"

"I took myself out to lunch at a new place in the next town over," said Danah, hoping Vera would not dig for details.

"Well, I'm very glad to hear it, dear. You know that if we lived closer, I'd insist on taking you to the theater with me once a month."

"What a lovely idea!"

"Well, we'll come up and see Elsie in *Hamlet*. Send me a postcard with the dates of the performances. We'll come for the weekend. Maybe we can see the show twice? I sent Elsie a check for her birthday, but she said it hadn't arrived. Did you check the mail yet today?"

"Yup. Not there. It'll come tomorrow."

"Let me know. Goodbye, darling."

The next morning, Danah came downstairs at 6 am to find Elsie already on the couch with a notepad, laptop, and her paperback copy of *Hamlet*.

"Good morning, Hamlet."

"Good morning, mumma. Mrs. V. wants us to write a synopsis of Act One, up until Hamlet shows up. And I have to learn some lines. I hope I can pull this off."

"You don't usually say that," said Danah, arranging a filter in the coffee maker.

"What?"

"I've never heard you talk about 'pulling something off.'"

Elsie laughed, "That's true. I never say that. Except I have now." Danah shivered. "I really want to do well, mom. It's not easy being Hamlet. Can you help me?"

"After I make coffee, OK?" Danah stared at the maze of rain sliding down the windows until the coffee maker burbled, signaling that a full pot of coffee was now available.

The two of them sat cross-legged on the black, leather couch. Danah took the copy of the play and flipped through the first twenty pages.

"I think of all the Shakespeare plays, this one takes the longest to get Hamlet onstage," said Danah, trying to find where

Hamlet first appears.

"Mom, it's the *only* Shakespeare play where Hamlet comes onstage. Hamlet does not appear in any of the other plays."

"You know what I mean, Clever Clogs!"

"You mean this one takes the longest to get the *main character* onstage."

"Right. See, he walks onstage in Act 1, Scene 2, but he doesn't speak until line 68, and that's an aside," said Danah, showing Elsie line 68.

"What's an aside?" asked Elsie, taking the script.

"It's when you say something onstage, but not to the other actors. It's as if you're thinking out loud. So what do you think Shakespeare is trying to tell us about Hamlet by introducing him like this?"

"That he's not good at being direct? That Hamlet is comfortable on the sidelines, commenting."

"Yes, I think so. You should be writing these observations down, Elsie, while this story is still fresh to you. Are you keeping an actor's notebook? These observations will be good to look at later. Why do you think Shakespeare makes us wait so long to see Hamlet when his name is the title of the play?"

"Because it's about waiting, or something?"

"This is coming to you very easily, isn't it?"

Elsie shrugged and studied the first few pages of the script while Danah sipped particularly good Sumatra. "Have you ever seen a ghost, mom?"

"No, I can't say I've really seen a ghost, but I may have felt one. I've been aware of things whisking away from me to the right or left, and getting the feeling that something beyond my understanding just happened right in front of me."

"So, basically, you believe in ghosts?"

"I suppose I do."

"If someone told you they had seen the ghost of your father and they had a message from him, would you believe it?" Danah briefly entertained the idea of confiding in Elsie about the psychic. By the time she had collected her thoughts into a reply, Elsie added: "Mrs. V. says the ghost tells Hamlet to kill Claudius. What were the words? Oh yes! 'Revenge his foul and most unnatural murder.' So the ghost tells Hamlet that his stepfather poisoned Hamlet's dad and stole his dad's wife, right?"

"Right, but you're getting ahead of yourself. You've got to write a synopsis of the opening. I'll tell you what happens, basically. There's a changing of the guard at night in the castle where Hamlet lives with his mother and stepfather. Hamlet's best friend, Horatio, joins two guards who've seen a ghost appear on the two previous nights. It's the ghost of Hamlet's father. Horatio watches for the ghost and sees it briefly . . ."

"We read that part. Horatio says, 'This bodes some strange eruption to our state!' Here, I'll show you." Danah sat stunned. Could this really be my father making her point out these words to me? First, the psychic asks me to place the words *strange eruption*, then Dead-dog talks about heaving and avoiding strange eruptions, and now Elsie? "See, here, line 81."

"Yes," said Danah, without looking at the script, "I know. I've heard that line before, 'some strange eruption.' Yes, I know that."

"OK, so, this is my question: Can you trust a ghost?"

"I wish I knew." Danah said, remembering Vera saying that Stewart was untrustworthy.

"Can a dishonest person become an honest ghost?" asked

Elsie. Danah was dumbfounded. "And, most importantly, do we have to believe someone just because they are dead?" Danah laughed. "What's funny?" asked Elsie.

"You are. You are, honey. You are really amazing. I've never heard anyone talk like that about Hamlet. You're going to do a fabulous job in that play, you know."

"But really, couldn't a ghost lie? He could play tricks on people. Hamlet's father is jealous of Claudius, right, so he might lie about having being murdered . . ."

"Thing is, Elsie, you have to take it all in context. Most people in Shakespeare's day were superstitious and they believed in truthful ghosts. So you really have to believe the ghost is telling the truth, or the play doesn't work. And also, don't forget, Claudius confesses to killing Hamlet's father."

"Oh yeah, I forgot that part. Well, I think Hamlet should speak up whether he believes in ghosts or not. I think people should speak up. And the harder something is to say, the more it's worth saying. Why does he wait so long to say something?" Elsie leaned her head to the right. Danah had goose bumps and the distinct impression that Stewart was present. These words didn't sound like

Elsie's. *This young girl who looks at you, who tilts her head, she is an old soul with deep roots in your family. Your father communicates with you through her. He has done this many times and you will notice this now.* "What do you think?" asked Elsie.

"I think you're asking some really good questions," said Danah.

"Thanks, well, here's another one. Mrs. V. asked us this the other day: 'What makes *Hamlet* tragic?' What would you say?"

"Off the top of my head I'd say the lack of communication is what is tragic. It leads to so many deaths."

"What I said in class was, the really tragic thing about Hamlet is that he never feels comfortable being honest. He can't tell people what he's really thinking. That's sad."

Danah's eyes stung with tears and she wished she could let it all out. She got up, ostensibly to refill her coffee mug, and turned her back to Elsie.

"It's a tough part to play, Elsie, even for a grown-up." Elsie continued to browse the opening pages. Danah stared through rain on glass. "Has Mrs. V. talked about remembering emotions you've experienced that parallel your characters'? It can help you play a scene truthfully.”

“I don’t know what you mean.”

Danah approached her daughter again. “Well, for instance, let me think . . .” Danah sipped her coffee and sat down. “Well, the Ophelia thing, OK? In order to get under Hamlet’s skin when he rejects Ophelia and tells her to go away and become a nun, you need to think of a time when you’ve pushed someone away. It needs to be someone you once liked.”

“Does it have to be the boyfriend/girlfriend thing?” asked Elsie, biting the skin beside her thumbnail.

“No, just someone you once liked and then told to get lost, basically.”

“Jennifer Chapman!”

“So, tell me how it happened.”

“Remember her? Remember her? She was my best friend in second grade. Then, I didn’t see her in third grade. Then we were put in the same fourth grade class, and she thought we were still best friends, but I was best friends with Erika by then. She got really clingy and annoying. Once, I literally shoved her away from me in the playground. She started crying and I said, ‘Get used to it’ and walked off. It sounds really cruel now, but at the time I thought it was the only way to get through to her."

"Perfect. So, think of that when you play that scene with Ophelia. If you keep an actor's notebook, you can write down parallel, real-life moments for all your major scenes."

"That's good, mom. I really didn't know what he was doing in that scene. Now I get it."

"Doing that helps you play scenes from the heart instead of the head. It helps you *feel* what's happening."

"You should come in and talk to the class about acting. You're really good at it."

"No, no. That's all I know, really."

"Did you ever act?"

"Some days, that's all I do." Danah grinned.

"You know what I mean."

"When I was about ten, I got cast as Alice in *Alice in Wonderland*. I loved it. I remember that teacher better than all the others: John Davies. I had quite a crush on him. He was a student teacher."

"Did Vera help you?"

"No. No, I don't remember her being there. And there never was a performance because we ran out of time. In my yearbook, that year, John Davies wrote: 'Would have made a perfect Alice. Pity we didn't finish.'"

"That's sad."

"Nice that he was so sure I'd be good, though. Come on, Hamlet, you'll be late for school."

"It's a big deal playing Hamlet, isn't it."

"It's really something, yes. Finding out on your birthday that you're going to play Hamlet is really something. Something happened yesterday, Elsie. We can say that."

During that conversation, something happened: Danah decided to tell more truth.

9 GIRLFRIEND TALK

A bottle of Chardonnay, named No One Will Know, beckoned Danah from the pantry floor and then she spotted a bag of unopened Hershey's Kisses on a shelf at eye-level. She was reaching for the wine when her phone rang. Guilt made her quickly grab Kisses instead. A methodical obliteration of Kisses began the moment she saw Holly's face on her phone.

"Am I interrupting?"

"No, it's more like you are staging an intervention. I was seriously about to start on a bottle of wine and throw a pity party for myself. Now, I'm going to eat an entire bag of chocolate Kisses instead. Good timing, Holly."

"I wanted to ask you when *Hamlet* is on. Paul and I want to come and support Elsie."

"It's not for another month. I'll get you tickets. Don't worry about it. I'm already dreading seeing Bernard, though." The phone was on speaker and lying on the kitchen island as she maniacally unwrapped one Hershey's Kiss after another. "One of the awful things about him, apart from his cold fish eyes, is that he manipulates

211

situations to the point where it looks like *I'm* the controlling one. I always come off looking bad." She pushed a white kitchen cabinet closed.

"He sounds very hard to be around. I feel sure I will dislike him."

"Thanks. That would be very helpful. Not enough people are on my side against that man. I'm warning you, though, he'll suck up to your face, but then, behind your back, he'll say something like, 'Well, she sure missed the boat, didn't she,' or, 'I can't see what that husband of hers sees in her.' He's a total creep. He lacks for nothing, in terms of creepiness."

"Let's talk about Elsie. Are they doing the original *Hamlet*? I'd have thought that was way too difficult."

"It's a modern adaptation, but they are studying some speeches from the original in class. She's got such a good teacher, Mrs. V. I hope Harry gets her one day. I wish I could get Bernard out of my mind, Holly, but I can't." They paused. Danah reduced the last Kiss to chocolate rubble, scrunched a fist full of silver wrappers, and walked them over to the garbage, under the sink. Then she opened a tin of cashew nuts and studied them.

Holly said, "I've started going through Paul's wallet and pockets for receipts, clues really, to see if he's keeping things from me."

"You *still* think he's cheating on you?"

"I do."

"But you didn't find anything, did you?"

"I don't know. I found a receipt for two coffees and three pastries at a place in West Hartford I've never been to. But I can't accuse him of having coffee with someone, can I? I mean, it sounds really ridiculous now that I'm saying it out loud. Although, I have to say, he never eats pastries."

"Why don't you come right out and ask him? Ask him, say, 'Did you kill my father?'"

"What? '*Did you kill my father?*' What are you talking about?"

"What am I saying? Sorry! I must be thinking of . . . Elsie in *Hamlet*, or something. Sorry about that!"

"So, I should confront him? Is that what you're saying?"

"No. Men hate that. What's he doing that's different?" Danah focused on this conversation the way someone afraid of heights might stare at a tree on the far side of a ravine. She hoped helping

Holly with her worries would bring balance into her own world.

"I don't know. I just have this horrible sinking feeling. I think I'm losing him."

"How would you describe his mood?"

"He's usually pumped up, bubbly. He used to start conversations with me. But recently, he's been quiet. It's me who has to start every conversation. I'm lucky if he chimes in with *yes* or *no*."

"Maybe he's morphing into a normal guy. Normal guys don't spontaneously talk to their wives after the first decade. You knew that, right?" Danah pulled out a blue bar stool from under the island, sat down, and made inroads into the cashew nuts.

"Are you telling me Bob doesn't talk to you?"

"Yes. That's what I'm telling you."

"But I've *seen* him talk to you."

"No, you've seen him *talking*, but he's not really talking to *me*. I think that's part of what makes him a good principal. He loves talking in meetings when it's not very personal. But when it's just the two of us, well, it doesn't feel personalized."

"I don't know what to do, Danah."

"What if the four of us go out to dinner, and *I'll* try to make

Paul talk? I'll start describing the plot of a book I'm reading -- a love story where the wife suspects the husband of having an affair. The wife has an affair to try and get even, but she finds out he never had an affair and they end up getting divorced -- sort of a middle-aged, messed-up Romeo-and-Juliet thing."

"That's depressing."

"It's not your story, Holly. It's not even a real book. I'm just making this up as I go along. We could watch Paul's face and see if he looks guilty."

"That's even more depressing."

Danah laughed. "You could always come onto him at an unscheduled time and see how he reacts."

"Unscheduled?"

"Well, isn't your sex schedule fairly fixed at this point?"

"No. I have to say we're unpredictable. It used to be that if he came home unexpectedly during the day, and he was wearing his gym clothes, he looks so good in workout stuff, I'd just take him down!"

"Oh my god, Holly! If you weren't my best girlfriend, I'd hate you! You've got to go easy on me here. Some of us aren't married to Atlas, mine's more like Encyclopedia Man."

"Relax. It hasn't happened for a long time. For one thing, he never drops in unexpectedly now. That's why I'm worried. Yes, let's go out to dinner after *Hamlet*, the four of us. He might let something slip when we're all together."

"You know, if you question Paul in front of us, you're likely to get a direct response."

"What's the question?"

"That's for you to say. 'Are you cheating on me?' seems a bit harsh. Say something more like, oh, I don't know. You'll think of something. The timing has to feel right. If we don't manage this at the Hamlet dinner, we'll do it another time."

"Thanks Danah. Just having a plan makes me feel less stuck."

"Well, I have to get back to my glamorous life. I had a septic man here this morning."

"A septic man!"

"Jealous?"

"You mean he cleaned the septic, not that he himself was actually septic?"

"How do people do that?"

"They don't think about it."

"Wouldn't it be nice not to think so much?"

They ended the call. Danah continued staring at her phone. She had made it to the other side of the conversation without further incident. *How could I have blurted out* Did you kill my father? *I am losing my grip. Will I lose it with Bernard? He could shoot me dead if I accuse him and I'm right. I wonder if he was armed when I visited them in Florida?* She opened the bi-fold pantry door and looked longingly at the wine rack. *I will not start drinking at two o'clock in the afternoon, mid-week, alone in my kitchen,* she told herself, several times before pouring her first glass.

She went upstairs to the office-in-the-bedroom and tried to work. She read over her social media plan for a book launch. She played around with the wording of a press release. *Why do I spring into action with a plan to solve Holly's problems and not even mention that I have quite possibly stumbled onto a murder? Not just any murder, mind you, the murder of my own father by my own stepfather.* Over the years, Danah had tried to make peace with Vera's choice of second husband by reasoning that Vera didn't want to grow old alone, that she was tired of taking care of herself, and that domineering Bernard did at least pay bills and have money in the bank. What if it were more sinister? Danah's stomach lurched as if on

a theme park ride. If Vera had somehow conspired with Bernard,

well, Danah couldn't think about it.

10 DECIDING TO ACT

By the time Elsie popped her head around the bedroom door, Danah had been on the computer for quite some time without accomplishing anything.

"Hey, mom!"

"Hey, sweetheart! Good day?" Danah stood up. Her lower back cramped up and ached. She resolved, for the twentieth time, to find a better office chair and followed Elsie downstairs into the kitchen. She made herself a Lemon Twist tea. Elsie poured a tall glass of orange soda and put a bag of popcorn into the microwave. Danah wiped down the island counter.

"Can you help me, mom?"

"I imagine I can. I usually do, don't I?"

"Did something happen? You're all hyped up."

"I don't know if something happened. That's the problem."

"What?"

"Oh, it's just this project, this project I'm working on. Some people aren't good at communicating directly. I'm not sure what's going on. I'm sorry. What do you need?"

"I need help learning a speech. Can you help me?"

"Yes, I'd like that. We've also got to start thinking about your costume. Has Mrs. V. talked about that yet?"

"No, mom. No. I've got to do this speech now." The microwave let out a high note of insistence as if on Elsie's behalf. Danah watched Elsie slam the microwave door and empty out the hot paper bag of popcorn into a large, blue glass bowl, spilling some onto the floor. "I don't know if I can do it!" said Elsie, through a mouthful of buttery explosions.

"You can do it. Mrs. V. knows you can do it, and so do I." Danah gave Elsie a quick tickle. "And so do *you* know you can do it, Missy Miss!"

"I know I think I can do it . . . but I could be wrong."

"The speech already! Give me the speech." Elsie birthed a yellow binder from her bulging backpack.

"Is everyone's binder yellow?"

"No, just mine. I chose yellow because Hamlet's a coward."

"Are you nuts? He's not a coward!"

"Well, we had a class discussion, and we said he was." Elsie carried the bowl of popcorn over to the couch. Danah relaxed, and remembered she was talking to a child, a precocious child, but a fifteen year old child nevertheless. She sat down next to Elsie and closed her fist on popcorn.

"Think about it, Elsie. Think about why he's hesitating. He's been told his father was murdered by his stepfather. Imagine calling daddy a murderer, and accusing me of aiding and abetting him. Those are fighting words. You think long and hard before you turn in a couple of family members for murder, especially if your only material witness happens to be a ghost."

"You take it so seriously, mom. It's like I almost believe it's happening for real, in our family, when you talk about it."

"I'm just trying to make it sound real for you."

"So you don't think he was a coward?" asked Elsie, more settled now that she had consumed almost an entire bag of popcorn. She pushed the first joint of her index finger around the bottom of the bowl like a broom and sucked off the salt. Danah leaned back in her chair-and-a-half. She brushed off remnants of popcorn buds as she spoke.

"It's very rare that anyone decides to act. What I mean is that it's very rare when someone takes an action they were not conditioned, raised, encouraged, or trained to take. Very rare. Hamlet is contemplating stepping away from all the roles he knows and all the ways of behaving that his family and friends expect from him. He will not act without thinking. He will not act impulsively out of anger. It's not easy to deliberately choose an action. The vast majority of so-called actions people take are not actions at all. They are *re*actions. They are reacting, not acting. Hamlet is attempting a pure act, if you like, taking an action that no one is asking him to take. He's thinking about doing something that has no definite results or benefit that he can see. He won't even get a clear conscience. And the world will go on if he does nothing."

Elsie frowned, sighed, and made another sweep across the bottom of the bowl for salt.

"It's sort of like being an author," Danah continued. "No one comes begging a first-time author to complete something. But there he is, or she, determined to struggle through it, strangely compelled by invisible forces. And the day the book is finished is a day the writer feels he, or she, did something important. And to my way of thinking, that kind of sustained, conscious action is heroic and rare. You can't toss out the word *coward* at someone who hesitates about something so courageous."

"So Hamlet is like a writer with writer's block?"

"Not a bad analogy."

"But he calls *himself* a coward."

"Isolated people under stress call themselves a lot of things. Writers are hard on themselves. And no one can really help them do what they have to do." Elsie flipped through the script to find her speech. "Elsie, try to think of an action that would be totally out-of-character for someone, and then you've got a true piece of action. Think how hard it would be for that person to take that action."

"Like me dropping out of school?"

"Well, yes, but dropping out of school isn't courageous."

"No, I know!"

"OK, take this for an example: if you loved every English teacher you ever had, you majored in English at college, and then you taught English and wrote for a living . . . where was the decision to act? I don't think I've ever acted, for example, and most people don't. They do what's expected. Given my track record, I can't think why I would ever expect myself to take real action."

Elsie's phone burst into song. "It might be the ghost of my

father! We were going to go over lines together." Elsie gave herself a brushing down and fluffed up her bangs before answering. It was Erika. She slumped. "Can I study at Erika's tonight?"

"OK, but I want to hear this speech first. Can you eat dinner there?"

"Can I eat at your house?" Turning to her mother, she said, "No problem."

"What is it, 3:30 now? I'll get you there by 4."

Elsie flapped through the yellow binder in search of the lines she needed to learn.

"I don't want this binder to be yellow now," said Elsie.

"What do you want it to be?"

"Black. No, grey. Grey would be good because it isn't black or white."

"I'll try to find a grey one. You don't usually see grey binders, though. Actually, I wouldn't mind having one myself."

"Here it is. It's the part after the actors show up at the palace."

"OK. Just give it a plain old read-through."

"Here goes: 'What a rogue and pleasant slave am I!'"

"Peasant! Peasant slave, not *pleasant* slave!" They both laughed.

"'What a rogue and *peasant* slave am I! It's monstrous that this actor can get so worked up over a fiction, while I can't bring myself to do anything about my father's murder! If that actor had my reason for grief, he'd drown the stage with tears and cry more loudly than human ears could hear. I must be a coward. I unburden my heart by talking, and I'm still talking, not doing anything! I've heard that guilty people watching a fiction similar to their crime will sometimes confess. I will have these actors perform something like the murder of my father, and watch my uncle Claudius very carefully. Maybe that ghost was a devil, trying to tempt me into murdering an innocent man. But if my uncle shows any sign of guilt tonight, I'll know he's guilty. The play's the thing with which I'll catch the conscience of the king!'" Danah applauded.

"You read that really well"

"But it's so much to memorize."

"It is. It's quite a good adaptation Mrs. V. found."

"I should start with one line, then two, and keep going, right?"

"You got it! I don't think you need me. I'll give you half an hour and then take you to Erika's, OK?"

"I'll do the other homework I've got now."

"By the way, what's Erika? In the play?"

"Rosencrantz."

"That's a great role, too. Tom Stoppard wrote a whole other play about Rosencrantz and Guildenstern." Elsie waved her mother away, and Danah put in a load of laundry. She smiled, thinking of herself as a 'rogue and pleasant slave.'

11 UNDERSTANDING THE VILLAIN

After dropping Elsie at Erika's, Danah went to the local coffee shop, The Daily Grind, for a decaf cappuccino. While standing in line, she again had the sensation of shrinking, or as if others were growing and she had stopped growing. Sitting in the window-seat-for-two was a blonde woman in her mid-forties who was positively glowing. She was talking to a man who could be her father. Danah was stabbed by thoughts of never having met her own father. Meanwhile, she stared at the man holding up the line with his endless requests. Apparently, he needed to order an infinite variety of half-pound bags of ground beans, enough to satisfy a large corporation hosting a convention of coffee connoisseurs. Danah turned to the glass front door for relief and witnessed the entrance of a small, bald man with a wet T-shirt sticking to his rubber belly. Then it got worse. She recognized him, and he recognized her.

"How's that house of yours coming?" said the Pool Guy. Danah wished she could remember his name. Greg? Gary?

"We're getting there!"

"Been servicing an indoor," he said, rolling his eyes to heaven and tapping his wet T-shirt. "Some of the customers are screaming and shouting today!" Danah watched how sweetly the father-figure cleared the table and held the door for the blonde woman. "You're not the screaming type," continued the Pool Guy, "but believe me, some of them . . . not you. You are tolerable." I am not tolerable, she wanted to scream. I am tolerant, tolerant! Instead, she smiled meekly. "Some of them just wasn't born to wait!" he added.

The line finally moved up one. That man had literally left instructions for the coffee to be sent to other states. There were now two people ahead of her.

"You put the chlorine sticks in and shock the pool and then you tell them, 'Wait four hours before you swim.' Next thing, they're calling Maggie asking if it's OK to swim yet. We'll be out servicing your water before you know it!" he said, all smiles.

Danah no longer wanted a coffee, but she felt it would look too stupid to leave after waiting the best part of a week on line. When she finally slumped into the privacy of her own car, she was not happy. Then she found Bob's car parked on her side of the garage. He's probably parked on the left for ten straight years, and today is different?"

"You look nice!" Bob said, from the kitchen.

"I am nice," she snapped back, because she hadn't forgiven him for having lunch with Holly.

"Wine?"

"I have coffee," she said, holding up the waxed cup. "But actually, wine is a far better idea." She poured out the coffee and gave Bob's cheek a kiss.

"Where's Elsie?" He handed her a Chardonnay.

"Erika's. Thanks. I'm just going to check e-mail." She took her wine glass upstairs to the bedroom, to her desktop computer. She had an e-mail asking her where the stuff was that she knew she had sent out earlier. Drinking her wine like water, she attached some files and clicked resend.

The sound of jazz piano from downstairs relaxed her a little. She rejoined Bob, who had now put supper on the table. He is not the villain.

"Stupid files I sent this morning never arrived. I had to resend them," she said, by way of trying to excuse her bad mood. Fully realizing how self-involved she was being, she tried hard to flip that switch and instantly become a better wife. "You were home early!" She sat down, facing Bob at the other end of a six-person dinner table.

"I can sneak out once in a while. It was quiet after classes today. No crazy teachers. No crazy parents. How was the septic?" He cheerfully reached for a baked potato.

"How was the septic?"

"Didn't the septic man come today?" Serving herself three meatballs and not liking the look of any of them, made her irritable again.

"Issue!" sneezed Bob.

"When they removed the small, stone lid from the hole in the ground, I felt like we were exhuming a body. It felt creepy." She cut open a potato and assessed the white mush inside the dry skin.

"What's the capacity?" he said, before cramming an entire meatball into his mouth.

"Twelve hundred and fifty," she said, proud of being able to talk like a man.

"That's the size for a four-bedroom."

"Good for resale," she said, realizing how easy it would be to hop and skip and jump through life with Bob having conversations like this and meals like this because they appeared to make Bob content. He has meatballs. He has a wife. He has an impersonal conversation. But she knew they both wanted more than that.

"Don't you like them?" he asked. She was frowning at her plate.

"The meatballs? To be honest, they are grossing me out. Maybe it's talking about our septic system while eating?" Feeling horrible about blaming Bob for this conversation, Danah realized she must accept responsibility for not talking about what was preoccupying her.

"So, what did they say about that smell?"

"Marsh gas."

"OK. Good."

"Well, good that nothing's broken, but not good that there's nothing we can do about the stink."

"It's gone now."

"Yes." Danah poured herself a robust glass of wine. "Do you think murder is always wrong, Bob?"

"Murder?"

"Yes, murder." She took a mouthful of potato without butter

and felt a little giddy from saying murder out loud, twice.

"Without getting into the particulars of a specific murder, yes, I'd say it's always wrong. Are you thinking of murdering someone, dear?"

"Well, actually I was, yes." She forked butter onto her potato.

"Anyone I know?"

"Bernard."

"Oh! We're back to him again?"

"I'm actually trying to move ahead now and murder him." Danah stared at the food on her plate. "I don't know why I took these meatballs. I'm a vegetarian."

"Yes, I know, but sometimes you eat meat."

"I'm not really a vegetarian, then, am I?"

"Not a strict one, no."

"If meat is on the table, I eat it. I have a tendency to just go along – that's why murdering Bernard has been all uphill so far, I suppose."

"Unless someone else starts murdering him first, and then you can just go along with them." Bob laughed at his own joke and she loved him for letting her talk crazy.

"Absolutely right." The possibility of someone else murdering Bernard comforted Danah and gave her strength enough to reject the meatballs. She finished her wine with crackers and cheese. Bob poured himself a little more wine and had a few crackers too. "I'm so, so extraordinarily happy I didn't give in to those meatballs. You expected me to eat them, didn't you?"

"I never know what you are going to do," said Bob.

"I can go food shopping tomorrow," said Danah as the house phone rang. "It's Vera."

"How do you know?" asked Bob, as Danah walked towards the landline.

"I don't know. Hello?" The wine made Danah want to sit.

"I think we're going to drive up, dear," announced Vera. "Bernard's got a new Continental he wants to take for a ride."

Bob started unloading the dishwasher.

"Uh, huh. By the way, Elsie wants to know if Bernard knows *Hamlet*."

"I shouldn't think so. Not his cup of tea really, is it?"

"Well, I guess Elsie is wondering would it be his cup of tea, figuratively speaking, if he knew the story. She wonders if Bernard would be sympathetic to Claudius."

"How could anyone be sympathetic to Claudius? He is the villain, dear."

"But Claudius doesn't think of himself as evil for the most part. Elsie has to explore Claudius' character for homework. I told Elsie that if anyone could side with Claudius, it would be Bernard." Danah wondered if she herself were being the villain at this moment.

"That's not very kind, dear." A pang of guilt at being bad did not deter Danah for once.

"I'm not trying to be kind, mother. I'm trying to help Elsie with her homework. And another thing that came up when she was studying her scene with Gertrude was the fact that she couldn't tell if Gertrude was really loyal to Hamlet. She asked me why Gertrude, who notices every little detail about Hamlet's behavior, is so oblivious to Claudius' cruelty?" Danah held her breath, amazed that she had said this.

"She's in love with Claudius."

"Oh."

"Yes. I'm sure that's it."

"Oh."

"I can't wait to see Elsie. It's not long now. Shall I bring a meat loaf up with me?"

"No! Please don't."

"My meat loaf isn't that bad, is it? You've always eaten it in the past."

"It's just that Bob put meatballs on the table tonight, and I almost ate them. Why doesn't anyone, including me, remember that I'm vegetarian? Anyway, I managed not to eat the meatballs, and I'm going to make more of an effort to be what I am from now on."

"I'll think of something else to bring, then."

"You don't have to bring anything, mother. We'll eat out after the play, and then we'll figure it out as we go along. We could go grocery shopping together."

"I have to go. I can hear Bernard's car pulling up."

"OK, then. Bye."

Danah had hung up and was trying to understand why her mother hung up when her own front door slammed. Elsie was home. She looked upset. She slid her backpack across the floor and pulled open the fridge doors.

"OK. What really pisses me off," began Elsie, "is that *Hamlet* didn't have to be a tragedy."

"No?"

"No! Claudius would have been smart to be nicer to Hamlet. He should have made more of an effort to talk to him, to do things with him, you know. Then Hamlet might have accepted the way things were."

"Do you honestly think a prince could be happy in a blended family, Elsie?" asked Danah, grateful to have passion expressed openly.

"Yes. Yes, I do. If they had remembered to treat him like a prince."

"You may be right. So, you're going to play an angry Hamlet? She's going to be a fascinating Hamlet, don't you think, Bob?"

"Outstanding."

12 ALMOST THERE

The next morning, after Elsie and Bob left, Danah toured the unfinished office and the unfinished recreation room. I *can* make things happen. I can act. The new windows and doors give the space credibility. Sections of bare wallboard joined one another with taupe-colored mud stripes. Multi-colored wires dangled from rough-cut holes. Danah picked up a box of assorted brushed aluminum switchplates. No more cold, damp breezeway running through the heart of my house. The garage door now opened by pressing the button Norm had relocated to the garage wall, on the left, when exiting the rec room. She had made a chalk cross on the garage wall where she wanted the button to be, and now it was there. Pressing the button seemed to release a thought: if I get clear about what I want, it happens. As the garage door lifted, it revealed more and more of the newly paved driveway. Norm's truck pulled up. Danah walked towards Norm, smiling.

"Just couldn't wait for me to arrive, huh?" he said, cigarette in hand.

"Good morning! I've just been walking through the rooms.

It's all looking great, like real rooms now!"

"Well, yes, that was the basic goal."

"I can't believe you're almost finished."

"You're going to miss all that banging and dust now, aren't you?"

"It will be strange not having work going on around me." Danah picked up a stray nail.

"Ed'll be here today. We passed the electrical inspection."

"Dead-dog was here yesterday?

"Son of Dead-dog!"

"I'm slightly sorry I missed that. So what have you got left to do?" Norm strolled into the recreation room through the garage. He studied the walls and ran his hand over the joins in the wallboard.

"Trim, mostly. Got to sand the mud in places. Do you want me to prime these walls?"

"Can I paint the trim that's going around the windows and doors before you mount it? It would be so much easier to paint them if they were lying across the sawhorses."

"Normally, I don't allow that—customers making things easier for themselves. But I'll make an exception for you."

"You're good to me!"

"You'll have to work fast, mind. I'll measure and cut first. I'll put them on the sawhorses for you. Do you have the paint?" She led the way back into the garage and kicked a couple of cans of paint. "Start stirring, lady!"

"What, *now*?"

"Now would be a good time."

"I have to finish my coffee first, then I'll be back."

"Spoken like a pro. You might have a whole new career in house painting!"

"Very funny!" Re-entering the house from the recreation room through a door where there used to be a wall felt empowering. Compulsion drove her to check e-mail and she had one from work that told her about a new marketing campaign for a children's book she would be working on. The large, thin print and yellow background were hypnotic. She stared at the screen until the words receded and a ghostly image of Stewart emerged. As soon as she realized what she had seen, the ghost dissipated.

Maybe I need to take that stuff that makes you think straight. If only I could remember what it's called: Gink-something, Ginko-something. She typed 'Ginko' into Google search and saw thousands of links to Ginkoba. She clicked on a few of them and scrolled through a few pages on each site. Ginkoba supposedly helped a person focus, but had not been approved by the Food and Drug Administration. Naturally, she felt more confused than ever. What I really need, she thought, is a pre-Ginkoba product. A product that will clear my thoughts enough to focus on making the decision about which Ginkoba product to buy.

"Danah!" yelled a man. It was a second before Danah remembered that Norm had been waiting for her.

"Almost there!" she called.

13 THE KISS

"Well, I reckon that'll about do it," said Norm, taking one power tool after another from the garage into the back of his pickup. Danah stood halfway between the garage and the truck, following his actions as if watching a tennis match in very slow motion.

"You've done a great job, Norm. Thanks for all your hard work. I'll be recommending you to everyone."

"Don't go recommending me too soon. Got enough backed up as it is! I've got to help my brother-in-law install kitchen cabinets this weekend."

"Here, this is yours." She handed him his final paycheck. He stuffed it in his back pocket. "The bank inspector should be here this afternoon."

"OK. Well, I'm out of here. Call me if you need me." He jumped into the driver's seat, backed up, waved, and drove off. Danah felt as if she were stranded in a departure lounge with no ticket or destination. She sat down on the bench where Elsie waited for the bus and wished a bus would arrive for her. People had led her to expect that she would hate the invasion of workmen, but she already missed them.

Then, a red Ford Explorer shot onto her driveway and stopped in front of the garage. A tall man with tan-colored boots, who filled his pale blue jeans beautifully, and had a head full of thick blonde hair, strode towards her.

"Excuse me, ma'am!" She noted a soft, southern accent, "You Miss Reynolds by chance?"

"Who wants to know?" She smiled; knowing her line was a bit corny, but at least she had resisted the temptation to slip into a southern accent. The man extended a strong hand towards her.

"Rick David. I'm an inspector with the bank." She got up from the bench and gladly shook his hand. "My card."

"Yes, I was expecting you next week, Rick. What happened to the other guy? Alex, I think his name was." Danah held open the front door for him.

"Guess they put him on another site, ma'am. They like to keep us on our toes."

"Well, what do you need to see?" Danah led him through the front door and then to the kitchen.

"Just about everything new around here, this being the final inspection."

"Are you Danish?" she asked.

"Now, how would you know a thing like that?"

"Blonde hair. Just a wild guess, really."

"Well, yes I am. My grandparents on my mother's side were from Copenhagen."

"My father was Scottish," said Danah. "His name was Stewart."

"That a fact? Thought I heard an accent."

"No, not me. My mother sounds English, although she gets mistaken for Australian half the time, but I sound like I'm from the northeast at this point."

By this time, David had spread paperwork all over the kitchen counter. He selected a particular checklist and secured it on a transparent clipboard. They wandered from room to room discussing the house. He complimented her on many choices and asked if she'd consulted a professional decorator.

"Thanks. No. No, I've pretty much made all the choices myself." She tugged hard at the old slider opening onto the elevated deck.

"May I?" asked David.

"Please!" Another smile passed between them. He pulled the slider open with one hand and followed her onto the considerable deck.

"Oh, Lord! I'm jealous now! This is real nice. I'm living on a boat, for the summer months. It's been a dream of mine. I bought the boat the day my divorce came through. I like it, but it's a little cramped inside and kind of exposed on deck. It's mighty private back here." Danah kept walking.

"Yes. That's why my husband and I have stayed here so long. It's a convenient location, but it's also private, as you say. Hard to find both." Danah led David through the office and recreation room.

"Well, Mrs. Reynolds, I congratulate you on a job well done. You have a lovely home."

"Thanks, yes, we like it. And what happens next then, exactly?"

"I'll phone in my report today and the final draw on the loan will arrive in your account by 11 am tomorrow. Sometimes, the bank sends out a second inspector on the final payment, you know, but I wouldn't expect that." David had one hand on the front door knob.

"OK. Great. Thanks so much. Enjoy your boat!"

"Sure thing!" They shook hands.

Danah heard his vehicle start up and pull away. She poured a glass of orange juice and did what she often did when she didn't know what to do: She checked e-mail. She clicked on some news headlines and was startled to see the date. Bernard and Vera would be arriving in just over a week. Her stomach turned. Damn that man! I'd be thoroughly looking forward to this play if it weren't for him. I don't even know why he's coming. He hates theater.

Danah knew she must get on with her work, but she sat there silently wishing Bernard ill. Feeling guilty and ashamed, she did an incognito Google search for "Easy Death," not thinking she'd get much of a response, when up popped over a million results. Her eyes drifted down the first page of links and she felt sobered to think of the hundreds or thousands of people with terminal illnesses who must search these sites daily, looking for relief. She felt as if she were trespassing, however, when she found a site touting a video called, *An Extremely Easy and Civilized Finale*, her morbid curiosity drove her on, and she double-clicked. She found it hard to gauge the tone of this site. It sold pens, postcards, and tote bags with the words

Civilized Finale emblazoned on them. A yellow heading caught her attention. It read: "Die Now, If You Want To . . . but first take our quiz." "Are they serious?" she said aloud. Her face showed total disbelief, but this site inspired her. She quickly took a legal pad over to the bed and wrote a quiz for Bernard:

1. Do you have an irreversible character problem?

2. Do you make others suffer?

3. Have you explored alternatives to being a jerk?

4. Have you ever expressed remorse for being a total asshole?

5. Do you have anything scheduled that you really can't miss?

She read the list back to herself and let out one nasty, hollow laugh then tore up her list. She longed to be free of her hatred for Bernard. She reached over to her bedside table for the photograph of her father and put it under her pillow. Soon she fell asleep, wrapped in a soft, blue comforter.

A car appeared in Danah's dream. A man kept beeping the horn. She was supposed to go for a ride and, although she was terrified about disobeying him, she refused to move. The car grew larger. No, it was getting closer. The horn insisted on immediate and total surrender. Danah longed to comply. She woke to the sound of a real car horn. She ran to the bathroom window and peeked down onto an exotic, black-and-red sports car. Paul, Holly's husband, was beeping the horn. As if she had a crush on him, she ran a comb through her hair and moisturized her lips, before scampering down to greet him.

"Oh good, you are here!" Paul performed an impossible, sideways maneuver and leapt neatly over the low-slung curved-top of his car door. The warmth of the sunshine surprised her.

"Is this car yours? It's like something from a James Bond movie, or something! I don't even like cars, but this one is a wow!" She walked towards the car slowly and carefully, as if she were still in the dream.

"Hey! What about me? Do I get a hug?" Paul looked like the stuff of a summer romance in an Italian fishing village. He wore long, baggy black shorts and a black workout shirt that was all openings. He had a deep tan despite the fact that summer hadn't even begun and a smile that kept you thinking.

"How've you been?" asked Danah, giving him a restrained hug and hoping she wouldn't be rendered mute by his good looks and flashy car. "Tell me about this car, Paul."

"Wanna go for a ride?"

"Now?"

"Once around the block?"

"Shouldn't we both be working? Oh hell! Let's go!" After locking the house, Danah opened the little red car door and felt the pleasure of changing her mind.

"I bought it last week. It's a Morgan," said Paul, backing up with one arm along the top of her seat.

"I love the look of it -- that cute, red body with a black belt over the bonnet. I've never seen a car like it."

"It's made by a family-owned company in Malvern, England—the oldest family-owned and continuously producing manufacturer in the world. The company started in 1909. They made 3-wheeled sports cars at first. They're coach built, which means there's a hardwood frame, and the metal body panels get nailed to that. The framework rides on a steel chassis with a pillar independent front suspension that's been unique to Morgan from the beginning. There aren't that many of them. Very few leave the U.K. There's usually a 5-year waiting list for a current model in Britain. This one is a '78."

"It's fun to see people looking at this car!" They drove in silence to the end of the seafront promenade, then turned around.

"It's a fun car. I'll have to store it in the winter." Danah squinted at a tiny rocky outcropping a few hundred yards from shore. She thought she saw someone waving from it.

"Why did you come to see me, Paul?" asked Danah, as they pulled into her driveway and came to a halt. She wanted him to take that sideways leap out of the car and he did. The trick was to have massive upper-body strength. They walked towards the front door, and she began her customary fumble for keys in her bag.

"I'm thinking of expanding the health club, and Holly's been telling me what a fantastic job you've been doing with your house. I figured talking to you might inspire me into action."

"Me inspire someone into action? That's funny!" She had the key in the lock and struggled with it until it suddenly gave in and she stumbled over her own threshold.

"Wow! This tile is just what I want. Very practical. Doesn't show dirt, does it? And to use the tile in between the steps like that . . ."

"Risers. The vertical bits between the steps are called risers.

I've gained a whole new vocabulary, which for me was a lot of fun. Writers don't often suddenly increase their vocabularies at this point in life. There were times I felt like I was speaking a secret language. One day I said to Ed, the electrician, 'Want a center feed on that?' and he said, 'Yeah.' I felt so proud." Paul stopped at the wall of windows, smiled at her, and gazed at the new, elevated deck.

"They must have thought you were pretty cool to pitch in."

"What do you want to build?"

Paul returned to the island and leaned his forearms on the counter. "I need a bigger daycare room. I hadn't counted on so many young mothers working out."

"I wish I'd joined a gym with daycare after I had Elsie. It took me ages to get back into my clothes." Paul raised an eyebrow.

"You know what I mean, get back into the pre-pregnancy clothes." She felt deliciously self-conscious as she put muffins on black plates and poured orange juice into glasses. He was studying her, and she liked being on the test.

"And then we need some specialty rooms. There's always one new craze or another. And I'd like Holly to have her own office. She's getting more and more interested in becoming a nutritional consultant. She has good ideas." He stood the other side of the island and ate the cranberry-orange muffin in hungry bites.

"Thanks for the ride, Paul. It really blew the cobwebs out of me!"

"You don't talk like anyone else, you know that?"

"That's about the nicest thing you can say to a creative person." She slipped onto a barstool and sipped juice.

"Do you write your own books? I mean, original stuff?" Danah smiled a shy smile, while stroking the granite countertop.

"I have been toying with an idea. I think maybe I could write a play."

"What's stopping you?"

"I don't know, maybe the fact that it's hard."

"Don't let that stop you. Renovating this house was hard. You did that. Putting an office out there, along the far end of the deck, was a terrific idea. Must get great light there."

"And it's quiet. I think I got most of my renovation ideas working alongside the workmen. I got in the swing of it and watched them make things happen. Are you handy?"

"What do you have in mind, pretty lady?" They laughed.

Danah led him out onto the large deck.

"I once built a tongue-in-groove floor." She raised her eyebrows at him. "Straight up. No kidding. Built it with my dad. The tongue went smack into the groove every time! I guess he did most of the work. I was about ten or twelve at the time."

"It's tongue *and* groove, Paul. Not, tongue *in* groove!"

"You think you're pretty funny, word-girl, don't you?"

"Yes, I do. So, what I'm getting is that you are not at all handy. Am I right?"

"Least handy man I know." They leaned on the railing and looked out to the marshes.

"Well, I have an excellent carpenter to recommend. He doesn't do fancy, finely measured stuff, but he's honest, reliable, and hard working. I wouldn't recommend my electrician. You'll have to submit a detailed plan to the town's building department. You'll meet Dead-dog!"

"Dead-dog?"

"I know. You'll be amazed at the cast of characters who show up. Dead-dog Bob is the building inspector. They say he shot a homeowner's dog during an inspection. Blam! Dead! They say he carries a 9 mm, but I never saw it. And then there's Son of Dead-dog, of course."

"I might have to hire you just to protect me!"

"Come and look at the rec. room." She held open the black, wooden gate for him and walked down a flight of unfinished, wooden steps that led to the Pennsylvania Bluestone around the pool. They entered the recreation room through the Anderson slider.

"I'd put a pool table in here. What a great space!" His dark shadow on the stark, white wall towered over her.

"You took part of the garage to make this room, right? Amazing! This'll be great in the summer—walking straight out to the pool from here."

"I took ten feet from the garage that had become a dumping ground. We can use this as a guest room, too. That couch pulls out into a king-size bed. My mother and stepfather will be in it next week."

"You don't sound too thrilled."

"You've heard of the wicked stepmother, right? Well, he is an equal-opportunity wicked stepparent." Paul laughed.

"I know. It's not politically correct to hate family. But this man is less connected to me than the Man in the Moon. I'm forty-six years old, and I don't feel like pretending . . . We avoid each other fairly successfully."

"But he still pisses you off?"

"Every chance he gets."

"Well, my advice . . . do you want advice?"

"Sure, go on."

"Shoot for no regrets. Ask yourself if you'll regret doing or not doing something, and then make a decision. In the end, you've got to live with yourself!"

"True."

Paul opened the slider and walked back onto the Pennsylvania Bluestone around the pool. The height of the elevated deck to the right, and the old trees all around, made this the most secluded part of the property. "When are you going to open the pool?" Paul made soccer moves with his feet, while gathering scattered debris into a pile.

"When it's been warm for a while." She stared at his mouth. He looked at her. They both took a small step towards each other, and kissed the kiss usually only read about. It lasted a good, long while. Danah's hands went from either side of his face, to his hair, to his considerable shoulders. All this time, her eyes were tightly shut. When she needed air, she opened her eyes. "We kissed!" she said, in an expression of shock, horror, and delight. "You kissed me!"

"What are we going to do?" she said, feeling the sickening swirl of panic. She crossed her arms and watched him kick the ground.

"Do? We don't have to do anything," he said, facing her.

"I think you are wrong about that."

"Love is not a bad thing, Danah. Why are you afraid of it?"

"Love? You're talking about love! Are you nuts? We kissed, Paul. It was a midlife moment, or something. God, don't talk about love! For God's sake, don't talk about love!"

"You don't have to be afraid of me now. You're still you, Danah. I know it's not the convention to exchange that kind of kiss, but we're not conventional people."

Danah uncrossed her arms.

"Have you gone completely insane? Paul, you just kissed me."

"And you kissed me back. Two consenting adults kissed. It's not the end of the world." His eyes were the color of clear honey in sunlight, and they captured hers, which were darting around looking for anything but him.

"Slight simplification! Two married, not-to-each-other, consenting adults kissed. Granted, it might not be the end of the world, but it's surely the end of our little lives as we knew them."

"Nothing terrible happened."

"So, this is the new plan? You're going to take women for a ride in your Morgan, kiss them, and return home to Holly a happier man because nothing terrible happened?"

"That was uncalled for."

"What? Mentioning the wife or the car?" He looked away and smiled in spite of himself.

"You can be a lot of fun!"

"So, you're refusing to answer my question?"

"There was a question?"

"Is this morning a typical morning for you?"

"No."

"How so?"

"Oh stop it! I'm not on trial."

"So, you do have something to hide? Miniscule indiscretions

in backbreaking numbers I shouldn't doubt."

"Isn't everyone guilty of the occasional, reckless impulse?"

"Not me."

"Yes you are." They both laughed and then she frowned. "Let's forget it, Danah. We're both grownups."

"We can't forget it. We have to get our stories straight."

"We're not appearing on the six o'clock news."

"It's worse than that—we're appearing in front of our respective spouses in a few hours."

"This has nothing to do with Holly. You and I have known each other for years. We've spent years and years of holidays together. We're practically family."

"Now that's really wrong." Paul laughed.

"You know what I mean. Life will go on. We know each other well enough to know what happened."

"There will be questions. We weren't even drunk. I really don't know how to explain it."

"No one is asking you to explain everything, Danah. The fact is, no one can explain everything. Things happen."

"Oh, but they don't! You have to make things happen.

Anyway, I like to know why things happen or why they don't. I get depressed if I can't explain things."

"I promise I won't allow you to kiss me again. How's that? Why? Because I realize it was upsetting to you and therefore wrong."

Danah suffered a pang of disappointment and attempted to survey the cedar siding. "Look, I don't plan to discuss this for three hours straight or anything, but, well things like this don't happen to me. I mean unexpected things don't happen to me. I take great care planning what I do. I live by deadlines. I know exactly when things will begin, how long they will take, and when something will end. I think before I do things. I never just do something. I'm more likely to be talking myself into doing something than actually doing something. I even question the very nature of action itself. Recently, I sat talking with Elsie about whether taking action is philosophically possible."

"I almost kissed you last Christmas. We were out in the garage, remember? I went out to get more wine, and you followed me."

"I'm not going to be drawn into a discussion of the absence of our sexual history, Paul."

"Well, I'm just saying that I did my thinking about kissing you last Christmas. Then, today I took action. That's all. It's quite simple."

"Simple?"

"I work hard at keeping things simple."

"Well, you've worked too hard at it. You're a little bit too simple, now, because this kiss has just complicated things horribly. Nothing is simple now. You just kissed your wife's best friend."

"Oh, Come on! It's not like we had . . ."

"No, no. Stop right there!"

"I'd better go," said Paul.

"No you don't. Tell me something. Did you come over here with the idea of stealing a kiss?"

"What difference does it make?"

"I don't know yet. Premeditated means something. It might help me understand what happened if I knew that it was premeditated on your part."

"I'm amazed to learn that life makes sense to you."

"What?"

"If one kiss from an old friend in a stable marriage throws

you, well . . . ."

"No, you're wrong. My life makes less and less sense. Not much sense at all, really . . . "

"That's more like it. Life does not make sense. So, this is just another confusing day."

"But what am I supposed to tell Holly?"

"Holly?"

"Holly your wife, *that* Holly."

"You're supposed to tell her nothing."

"I have to tell her. She's my best friend. We tell each other things like this."

"Has she told you things like this?"

"Paul, she's my best friend. I can't tell you that."

"OK, so what would be the point of telling her about this kiss?"

"I don't know, except we have a sort of unspoken code of honor. We tell each other everything that matters."

"Telling her about this would upset her. You know that. She wouldn't believe it happened the way it happened."

"Right. She'd never trust me again. Our friendship would

end. She'd go berserk. She'd yell at me. She'd yell at you. She'd be convinced that her marriage was over and that it was my fault."

"So, on balance, then, I'd say my idea is better. Let's keep quiet. It's an imperfect world, Danah, and we have very, very little, if any, control over anything."

"But that's not true. I can control myself."

"I beg to differ!" He smiled dangerously. She imagined him naked for two seconds.

"OK. You win. I won't say a word to anyone. You do the same."

"Agreed." They shook on it, then walked silently through the recreation room and out through the front door. He bounced back into his sports car and then was gone -- as if nothing had happened.

Given the right circumstances, we surprise ourselves.

14 OPENING NIGHT

"We're on I- 95, dear," said Vera on Bernard's cell phone.

"Mother, I -95 goes from Florida to, well, I don't know, beyond me. Can you be more specific?"

"We're hitting some traffic. Oh! I see the sign for the Long Wharf Theatre. We are in New Haven, Bernard says. Do you know what's playing at the Long Wharf?"

"Do you want me to find out?"

"Well, it might be nice."

"How long can you and Bernard stay?" Danah continued Windexing the entryway windows.

"I thought we'd just play it by ear this time." Danah rolled her eyes to heaven, and so did Bernard. "The signal is breaking down or up or wherever it goes, darling," said Vera. "We'll see you shortly."

Danah hung up and immediately berated herself for not having the guts needed to be straight with her mother about the length of their stay. Instinctively, she lifted the toilet seat of the downstairs half-bathroom and cleaned under the rim. What a pleasant slave am I! Another visit dodging the sniper's bullets. Would

Bernard dare wear his gun in our house, to Elsie's school, to a restaurant? Is that why he acts so invulnerable? How can I arm myself against an armed man? I am calling him on his bullshit this time. She slammed the toilet seat shut.

Twenty minutes later, while Danah sat on that same downstairs toilet, nursing a nervous stomach, Bernard's Lincoln Continental parked in the driveway. She heard Bernard's fist thumping the glass in the front door. You are not going to make me angry, Bernard. You are going to wait like a nice boy; and, unfortunately, waiting won't kill you. Danah rehearsed a smile in the bathroom mirror, before opening the front door.

"Everything looks marvelous, darling!" pronounced Vera, giving Danah a kiss and hug. Danah forced herself to look at Bernard over Vera's shoulder. She saw a short, overweight man with a limp. She stood still and watched him while he had his back to her. He coughed and spat something visible onto the pavers. It's landing sounded like a little slap in the face.

"Hello, Bernard. Are you ill?" asked Danah. He ignored her.

"Bernard will handle the bags," said Vera. "Show me around. I must say, darling, you've done wonders. I love this tile, and let me look at that deck." She walked up the half-flight of stairs and across the main room to the sliders. "So lovely! And that must be the office. What a difference that deck makes! And you designed it? How did you know what to do?"

"I just did what made sense every day, and I talked to the workmen a lot. They gave me ideas, and then, well, it's as if I learned the language of the house and the house pretty much told me what to do. I know that sounds strange, but, take the breezeway . . . When I sat here quietly one day, "listening" to the house, it became obvious that we needed to fill in the breezeway and create a room there. There was a gap in our home that no one talked about, a cold gap that made it impossible for everything to connect. Everyone has said how much that room adds to the house."

"But how did you know your ideas would work?"

"The town building inspector had to approve the plans and then they inspected the work at crucial stages. It was not as hard as everyone made out. Maybe I just got lucky."

Vera looked up at the exposed rafters in the office. "You make it sound very easy, Danah. Bob is a very lucky man to have you."

"It certainly did cut the cost to have me act as the general contractor."

"I can't wait to see the rec. room."

Danah led her mother back to the front door, down a step and through the glass door that used to be a wall. "Oh my!" said Vera. "It's huge and look how gorgeous: white, beige, and aqua! Is this the same tile as upstairs?"

"Same tile, slightly different color. So, this is where you're going to stay."

"Oh! I think this is a lovely addition. You've increased the value of the house, that's for sure. The window seat is like something from a play. I can't think which one. Maybe *Doll's House*."

The front door slammed and in came Bernard, puffing and blowing with two overnight bags.

"I thought you and mother could stay here. The couch folds out to a bed," offered Danah.

"I'm going to relax with a drink after all that driving. Want one?" he said to Vera.

"Not yet, dear, thank you. Hasn't Danah done wonders with the house?"

"I'm sure she has," he said, holding onto the doorframe and hoisting his right leg up the step. After he'd shuffled away, Danah asked her mother what was wrong with him.

"Now, don't start," replied Vera.

"No, I don't mean in general, I mean what's wrong with his leg?"

"Gout."

"Gout?"

"Yes."

"I thought that ended with Henry VIII."

"It's very painful and makes it hard for him to get around." Vera placed one bag on the window seat and unzipped it. "He has festering sores and swelling. It's very painful. That's why he needs a drink occasionally."

Danah took a deliberate breath, held it for a beat, and then blew it out. "Would you like a coffee, mom? I've found these amazing gourmet cookies from a new bakery called, You *Can* Take It With You When You Go!"

"Odd name for a bakery."

"I thought it was funny. They only do take-out."

"Oh, I see. Yes, I'd love a coffee. Your coffee is always so much better than anyone else's, I don't know why. How's Elsie? Is she excited? I'm so proud of her. I promised to take photos of her back to the girls at the beauty shop. I like your hair, by the way." They returned to the kitchen.

"Thanks. I've let it grow. I haven't had it done in ages. I like it, too." Danah untied a thin black ribbon on a red box of cookies.

"What a lovely little box," said Vera, hoisting herself onto a barstool with one hand on the back of the chair, as if she didn't trust the chair to be there for her. Danah popped a coconut cookie into her mouth and ground coffee beans. She glanced over at Bernard, who was now sitting at the dinner table, hunched over a tumbler of whiskey, still wearing his dirty, brown overcoat.

"Elsie will be home soon," said Danah, averting her eyes from him.

"You did pack my pills?" asked Bernard.

"You saw me do it," answered Vera. "I put them in your wash bag, remember?"

"Do you know, Elsie is slightly taller than me now?"

"I bought her some cute skirts and sweaters. I hope they fit."

"You have an uncanny knack for picking exactly the right size and style for her. She loved those T-shirts last summer." Danah gave her mother a panda mug of coffee.

"Where's *Trigger Happy?*" asked Bernard, staring at his drink.

"I thought you said you were putting in your own reading materials. You'll have to look, dear. I don't know if I put that in or not."

"I can't move," said Bernard.

Vera dutifully disappeared down to the rec. room to search the bags for his magazine of choice.

"It's as if you were afraid of my mother talking to me, Bernard. Are you?"

He unglued his eyes from the drink and stuck them on her. "I'm not afraid of you, Danah, if that's what you mean."

"No. That isn't what I meant. But it's interesting that you would take it that way." Vera returned, carrying the current edition of *Trigger Happy*. She plopped it down between his glass and the bottle.

"How could I possibly pose a threat to you, Bernard?"

"Danah!" cautioned Vera, on the brink of sipping coffee.

"No, seriously. I'm genuinely interested in why Bernard

would need to tell me he isn't afraid of me. Doesn't that strike you as a strange thing to tell one's host?"

"Drop it, Danah. You're not making any sense," said Vera, having successfully reestablished her position on the barstool.

"She's looking for trouble as usual," said Bernard, with a grin. Vera wrapped the black ribbon from the pastry box around and around her index finger.

"Me? You're the one who carries a gun, Bernard, not me." He also looked like the one who might spit bullets. He downed the whiskey remaining in the tumbler and poured himself another one. Instead of replacing the top on the bottle he began jabbing the air with it, in Vera's direction. The women stared at his performance. Danah could not imagine what possessed her mother to climb into bed with this monster every night.

"You told her that? You told her that?"

Vera looked flustered. "Was it a secret? I'm sorry, dear. I didn't know. I told her how well you did in the shoot-out. That's all."

"That's a very good question, mom. Was it supposed to be a secret, Bernard?"

He slammed the bottle down on the table as if he were about

to give an after-dinner speech in praise of alcoholics.

"Look, I didn't even want to come to this lousy play, so don't start with me."

"The cookies really are lovely!" said Vera, eating the last three in quick succession.

Danah caught sight of Elsie approaching the front door. She walked towards Bernard.

"Temper, temper!" she mouthed to him, with her back to Vera, and then in an upstage voice, added, "Elsie! Look who's here!" Vera slipped off the barstool and rushed towards her granddaughter.

"Look at you!" Elsie beamed at her grandmother. Vera gave Elsie one of those smothering hugs grandmothers are famous for giving. "I've got so much to tell you, Elsie, but I don't want to tire you out before your performance."

"Hello, Bernard," said Elsie, looking aghast at her disheveled step-grandfather. He waved two fingers on his right hand in small circles and gave a perfunctory smile.

"He can't get up just now. It's his leg. How did the dress rehearsal go this afternoon?"

"Terrible." Elsie peeled off her see-through backpack.

"Polonius farted behind the curtain, and everyone laughed. We never recovered."

"That's excellent. It really is. When a dress rehearsal goes too well, everyone relaxes and gets sloppy. You'll see. It'll go magically tonight."

"Do you want to see all the pictures I collected to help me prepare? You can look at my actor's notebook if you want to."

"You kept a notebook? That's a wonderful thing to do. Do you know, Elsie, I still have the one I put together when I played Rosalind. I'm going to give it to you later."

"Wow! Thanks, gran. You're the best!" Grandmother and granddaughter disappeared upstairs. Danah cleaned up the kitchen and noticed how easily Bernard made his way to the downstairs bathroom. Then she heard him piss like a horse. She noticed she was holding her breath. She ran upstairs to ask what Vera and Elsie wanted for a snack before the show.

"Mom, you know I can't eat before a show."

"I'll make her what I always used to eat before a show," said Vera. "Do we need to get dinner going now? What time must you be there, Elsie?" Vera squinted at her watch.

"Six fifteen. It's a seven o'clock curtain."

"Come and cook with me, Elsie. Do you have superstitions you have to follow before a show?"

"I don't know if it's a superstition exactly, but Mrs. V has given us a warm-up exercise to say: 'To sit in solemn silence at a dull, dark, desk, in a pestilential palace with you!'" Vera and Danah laughed.

"That's a great one! I've never heard that before, but it makes you speak crisply and it ends with a smile. Just the thing! I used to say this one: 'Mother is murdering Melinda. Father is fingering pheasants. And all the while, I am quite, quite lost.'"

Elsie immediately repeated Vera's warm-up routine, and by the time they got to the kitchen, they were saying it in unison with exaggerated melancholy followed by hysterical laughter.

"So what did you eat before going onstage, mother?"

"Chocolate sandwiches and milk."

"Oh! I want that! Have we got some chocolate, mom?"

"Does the Pope have a robe?" Danah reached behind the low-fat granola cereal boxes and produced a Hershey's 8-pack.

"Yay, mom!"

Vera was poking in cabinets. "At home, I have an electric grill, and I make this the way I make a grilled cheese sandwich. But you have a toaster. I can toast the bread and then put the chocolate and the toast in the microwave. That should do it."

"Can you have it ready for me after my shower, gran?" Elsie ran upstairs two at a time.

Danah ran out to pick up a bouquet for Elsie, and upon her return, she saw Bob had arrived with two pizzas and various tubs of ice cream. "Bob, the plan was to go out for a celebration dinner after the show."

Bob raised his eyebrows as if he were powerless to speak.

"Bob called from his car and spoke to Bernard, darling. It'll be all right. We can still go out for a drink afterwards."

Bob placed everything in front of Bernard on the dining table. Bernard helped himself and Danah turned her back on him, refusing to give him the satisfaction of seeing her derailed and upset.

"I'll get myself ready." Danah gave Bob a quick stare and a mind-message to join her in the bedroom. She felt tempted to take out her frustration with Bernard on Bob, but ever since the episode with Paul, she had been acutely aware of how good and trusting Bob was and she hadn't criticized a single thing he'd done or said.

"Was the pizza Bernard's idea?" she asked Bob, as he joined her in their master bathroom.

"Yes. When I asked about the dinner he said plans had changed. I've never seen him this drunk so early. Can't believe he'd just lie like that, though. It's not fair to Elsie." Bob spread too much toothpaste on his toothbrush.

"I don't think it's a conscious effort with him anymore. He lives in jerk-mode. By the way, avoid the downstairs bathroom for the duration. Bernard has marked it as his territory, if you know what I mean. He is so gross!"

"I'll sit next to him at the show and try to keep him in line."

"I'm going to be backstage with Elsie. I have to do her make-up and I'm the prompt." Danah put a black leather vest over a black polo neck.

"I didn't know. So, when should we leave?"

"Given the fact that Bernard will probably want to make a run to the liquor store on the way, we should leave now. Have you noticed how well he moves when he thinks no one is watching?"

"He'll be gone soon. It won't do any good cataloging his

faults."

"Until now I've always complained to you about him and then kept quiet. But this time I'm doing it different."

"Different*ly*."

"You see! You see how different it's going to be! I'm not even worried about adverbs."

"What's going to be different?"

"He's going to talk."

"You *want* him to talk to you?"

"No, what I want is for him to spill. I've got a very strong, well, call it a hunch. I think he's hiding something from me, something I have a right to know. I'm going to make him talk and I want you to do me a favor. When you sit next to him at the play, watch him like a hawk. Try to read his reactions. I bet you anything he'll walk out at some point. Tell me if he seems to react to particular parts, OK?" She sprayed perfume on her wrists and neck.

"OK. We'd better get going."

"Can you take the hairs off me? There's cat hair on everything." Danah handed Bob a lint roller. Danah had dressed in black so that she wouldn't be easily seen in the wings.

They rejoined the others downstairs. Elsie was hugging a Hamlet Bear, dressed in a puffy, Elizabethan black shirt and breeches that Vera had just given to her. Bernard was playing the martyr, and Vera was touching up her make up.

"Break a leg, Elsie! Let's go," said Bob, from the front door.

Bernard limped to the Lincoln Continental. Danah turned to Bob and said:

"Oh! I thought we'd all go in my van, there's so much room. It's silly to take two cars." Bernard installed himself in the Lincoln and shut the door. In a stage whisper, Vera said she'd join Bernard because he had a little errand to run. Bob walked over to Bernard's side of the car and gave him directions to a drug store and to the school.

While they were driving to the school Danah remembered she hadn't told Vera where she had made reservations after the play.

"What if Bernard comes up with a bunch of errands and they get there late and you don't even see them arrive? You must sit next to him." Danah felt a grenade of anger forming. She willed herself to breathe deep breaths. If I get that angry now, I'll go off at him, and I won't find out a thing.

"That's a cute bear gran found for you, Elsie," said Bob.

"The best!" replied Elsie.

Upon arrival at the school, Danah established an island of solitude for Elsie in the corner of a classroom near the backstage area. The fetid smell of old school dinners clung to the air. Elsie looked at herself in a handheld mirror and said quietly: "I can do this. I am doing this. Mother is murdering Melinda. Father is fingering pheasants. And all the while, I am quite, quite lost."

Danah enjoyed combing Elsie's long hair into a perfectly smooth ponytail. She used a sponge to apply pale foundation to her face, as instructed by Mrs. V.

Girls came in and out to chat. There was squealing, laughter, and lots of rushed, high-pitched chatting. Erika told Elsie that Polonius might gas himself before she gets a chance to stab him, and what then? This sent them into giggles.

Mrs. V. popped her head in and called everyone to a warm-up session. The whole class gathered onstage, behind the curtain, and sent a squeeze around the circle. Ophelia squeezed Elsie's right hand, and she passed it on by squeezing Erika's hand. After a few more exercises, they chanted in unison: "Will we be good or will we be great? That is the question," many times, getting louder or softer depending on whether Mrs. V.'s hand was held high or low.

At six forty, the school's orchestra began to play music by Prokofiev called "The Ghost of Hamlet's Father," and Elsie slipped off to find a moment of peace by herself. Danah double-checked that she had her copy of *Hamlet* with Elsie's lines highlighted in grey even though she was everyone's prompt. She briefly chatted with other backstage parents.

The music stopped and the principal, Ms. Goodison, took center stage and welcomed everyone with her customary warmth and enthusiasm. Danah stood stage right and strained to see Bob, Vera, and Bernard in the tenth row. Mrs. V. snapped on the tape of howling wind, and the show began. Elsie stood in her mother's shadow. Danah did not look at Elsie or acknowledge her daughter in any way.

A boy, dressed as a soldier, wearing a plastic sword, marched up and down the stage. Marcellus, another soldier, and Hamlet's best friend, Horatio, brushed past Danah and onto the stage.

"Who's there?" demanded the first soldier, Barnardo.

"It is I, Marcellus. I've brought Horatio." The three actors stood together and held center stage.

"Well, has the ghost appeared again tonight?" asked Horatio.

"Horatio thinks we are imagining the ghost," said Marcellus. "That's why I brought him along. Maybe if he sees it, he'll believe it," His voice cracked on the word *ghost*, and Danah thought the lack of control over his voice actually added to the sense of vulnerability.

"It has appeared the past two nights, at precisely this time," stated Barnardo, excitedly, as if the ghost were a media celebrity.

Jack Thompson walked slowly onstage under a spotlight that followed him all the way downstage. Danah had learned his name from the program. He was a new kid.

"There it is!" exclaimed Marcellus, in an unwavering stage whisper.

"See!" said Barnardo. "It looks just like the dead King!" said Barnardo, genuinely thrilled that the ghost had shown up on cue.

"Exactly like Hamlet's father. It's terrifying," said Horatio, taking two steps back.

"Make it talk, Horatio!" said Marcellus. Danah was distracted from the performance by a gaggle of four kids, followed by parents, coming up behind her and joining Elsie in the wings.

Jack Thompson spread his arms, as if he were about to fly. Queen Gertrude, standing beside Danah, let out a blistering rooster crow, which signaled Jack to exit stage left.

"I know where to find Prince Hamlet this morning." said Marcellus. "Let's go!" and Danah's stomach lurched at the sound of Hamlet's name. King Claudius, Queen Gertrude, Polonius, Laertes, and Prince Hamlet gathered in a semi-circle of onstage positions.

"Hamlet, my nephew, and now my son, why does a dark cloud still hang over you?" said King Claudius. Danah held her breath until Elsie spoke in a loud and steady voice.

"It doesn't, my lord," said Elsie, with the kind of attitude she would get in trouble for at home.

"Hamlet, please stop wearing black clothes. We know you miss your father. But all things must die. Why do you seem to have taken his death so personally?" said Gertrude, rushing her lines.

"*Seem*, mother? Black clothes might *seem* excessive to you, but wearing black is the only action I can take. These clothes show my feelings." Danah hoped the local paper was here to witness her daughter. She is magnificent, thought Danah, tracking Elsie's every word and action closely. Horatio caught up with Hamlet and told him about seeing the ghost of his father and so Hamlet agreed to join the guards that night. Laertes warned his sister not to take Hamlet too seriously and then left for France. Then, on came Hamlet, Horatio, and Marcellus, waiting for the Ghost to appear.

"There it is!" said Horatio.

"Angels defend us! Do you come from heaven or hell? What does it mean when corpses revisit the earth dressed in full armor?" asked Elsie, walking tentatively towards the Ghost. The Ghost walked downstage left and signaled for Hamlet to follow him.

"Prince Hamlet, it wants to get you alone. Don't go!" cried Horatio. Elsie approached the Ghost.

"If it has come to this, something is rotten in the state of Denmark!" mumbled Marcellus. Danah thought it was a shame the line was mumbled because so many people know it and would have liked to have heard it.

"It looks so much like my father. I have to follow it." Horatio and Marcellus walked offstage backwards.

"Hear me. I am your father's spirit, doomed to walk the earth at night while I pay for my sins. If you ever loved me, you will revenge my foul murder." Danah looked out at the audience. The

Ghost's speeches had been pre-recorded to add to the ghostly effect.

"Murder!" gasped Elsie, as if she had cut her finger. The Ghost paced up and down while his taped voice described how his brother, Claudius, had murdered him by pouring a poisonous liquid in his ear when he had been asleep.

"Take revenge, my son, but do not hurt your mother. It is almost morning. I must go." He turned upstage to look at Elsie and the tape said, "Remember me." The Ghost exited stage left. Danah saw her daughter fill the stage and command the attention of the entire house.

"Yes, poor ghost, I promise to forget everything I ever learned, and remember only your commandment. Oh, what a vile woman! And my uncle! What a villain! A smiling villain! I must remember this: one may smile, and smile, and still be a villain." Danah imagined thunderous applause. Meanwhile, Hamlet played with Rosencrantz and Guildenstern, who were dressed in matching grey track suits.

Danah loosened her grip on the script a little by the time they reached Act Three. Her pride in Elsie as she delivered speech after speech with poise and emotion was inexpressible. My daughter has transformed herself as only actors can. Gertrude exited on Danah's side. Her crown was pulling her hair painfully, and her mother came rushing to re-pin it. King Claudius and Polonius hid in the shadows, and Hamlet entered for the speech Danah had heard countless times, and yet she understood it now for the very first time.

"To be or not to be. Is it more noble to tolerate life's problems, or to fight back by ending it all? What is death? Sleep? . . . But in that sleep of death, what dreams might come! That's the problem. We don't know. Who would suffer injustice, rejection, and all the pain of living if it weren't for the fear of the unknown? We'd rather put up with the problems we have than run to others we don't know. This makes cowards of us all. We think too much, and lose the power to act." There was a rousing round of applause: It was not in Danah's imagination. The audience spontaneously gave Elsie applause, and Danah cried. Erika's mother gave her a hug.

The next thing Danah registered was the Players' arrival at the castle. The royal household had gathered to watch a play. Queen Gertrude asked Elsie to sit next to her, but Elsie chose to sit next to Ophelia. Danah squinted out into the audience at the row of people she believed were her family members. It seemed that Bernard had the aisle seat.

"I realize someday I will die, and you should marry someone else," said Player One, dressed as a King.

"Oh don't talk like that! Second marriages at my age! Even if someone my age does remarry, it's only for practical reasons, not for love. The only women who gladly remarry at my age are the ones who killed their first husbands," replied Player Two, dressed as a Queen. A coughing fit in the audience obscured Elsie's aside. There were more disturbances from the audience. Danah ached to know if Bernard was the source.

"Lady, what do you think of that?" repeated Elsie, with the presence of mind to know that the audience needed to hear this challenge to Gertrude.

"I think the lady protests too much," replied Queen Gertrude.

"What is the play called?" inquired King Claudius.

"The Mousetrap," said Elsie quickly, as if springing one. "Oh, and here comes the King's nephew, Lucianus!"

"My thoughts are black. My hands are ready. The poison is strong. The time is right," said Player Three as he poured poison into the sleeping Player King's ear.

"Yes, This is where he kills the king. Hold on just a minute, and you'll see how he wins the love of the widowed queen!" said Hamlet. King Claudius stood up angrily. He waved the Players away. Polonius made sure the Players left quickly, and everyone exited except Hamlet and Horatio.

"Did you see that, Horatio?" Hamlet stood, pointing to where they had exited.

"Very clearly, my lord."

Danah was riveted. She knew every word of the script, and yet she watched the actors as if they were fortune tellers. Before she knew it, Claudius was on his knees, and Hamlet entered without being seen.

"Oh, my crime is so terrible, it smells to heaven. I want to pray for forgiveness, but I can't. How can I ask for forgiveness while I still enjoy the things I killed for? My crown, my queen . . ."

"There he is. I should kill him now," said Hamlet, crossing diagonally in front of him. "But look, he's praying. My father's ghost said that Claudius killed him before he had a chance to ask for forgiveness for his sins, and that's why my father is still suffering."

Elsie walked further downstage and sat down, hugging her knees. "Is it fair to kill Claudius now, when he's had a chance to ask for forgiveness? No. If I kill him now, he might go straight to heaven." She looked at the kneeling Claudius, silently mouthing prayers. "No, I'm going to kill him one night when he's drunk. That's the best way to take my revenge on Claudius." Elsie exited stage left, the opposite side from Danah.

"My words fly up, but my thoughts remain below. Words without thoughts never reach heaven," moaned Claudius, before dragging himself offstage.

The kid playing Polonius either really farted or faked it right before Elsie stabbed him. Whatever happened, it sent her into a fit of giggles. She could barely get through the line, "Too bad, old fool, I mistook you for a better sort of rat." She really seemed to be losing it. Danah stood by horrified until she saw Elsie turn the hysteria into anger against her onstage mother, Queen Gertrude. After that, Danah happily witnessed the play take its inevitable and catastrophic course.

Elsie's final words before she lay lifeless were: "Horatio, you know the whole story. You must live to tell the world what has happened here, so they will know who was innocent and who was evil. Fortinbras has my dying vote. The rest is silence."

"Let Hamlet be buried like a good King of Denmark. Fire the cannon in Hamlet's honor!" shouted Fortinbras. Mrs. V. played the recorded sound effect of a cannon being fired, and it was done.

Danah couldn't remember having ever been more moved by a performance. The audience cheered, and she cried hysterically in the wings. She wiped her face on her sleeves. She tried to snag Elsie after the curtain call, but Elsie couldn't stand still long enough to be hugged. Mrs. V. called a meeting onstage in which she gave high praise to the entire cast and reminded them they had to get a good night's sleep and prepare to do it all over again tomorrow night.

"Was I good?" Elsie asked her mother, finally.

"I'm so proud of you," Danah replied, holding her squarely by the shoulders. "You were totally amazing, completely phenomenal, entirely extraordinary, simply superb, and I'm as proud as can be of you, Elsie!" They hugged tightly, and Danah felt tears again. "I had no idea it was going to be that good. I mean, I knew it would be good, but not that good. I mean, it was the real thing. You got everyone going. Especially the bit when you started giggling!

What happened?"

"Polonius faked a fart. It was so loud! I thought everyone would hear it. I was so wound up. It made me laugh suddenly." Danah packed up their stuff into a black sports bag.

"But it came across as brilliant acting. No one heard the fart. We just saw you crack and start to lose it. It was really an amazing performance, Elsie."

"I can't wait to hear what gran says."

"Are you going to change out of costume?"

"No."

"OK. Let's go. What's this?" said Danah, looking at a potted plant on a desk near them. "Is this yours?" Elsie examined the plant, wrapped in purple foil, and found a gift tag on it.

"Oh my god!" said Elsie, no longer needing blusher. "It's from Jack. Look!" The card said: 'Forget-me-not. Jack.'

"Jack played the ghost of your father, didn't he?" asked Danah.

"Hamlet's father." They walked through the hallways and swing doors.

"The flowers he gave you are called Forget-me-nots. That's

what the ghost keeps telling Hamlet. That was very thoughtful of him. Maybe he likes you?"

"Me? No, no. I don't think so. He has a girlfriend."

"He does?" said Danah, rather shocked. They had reached the school's entrance hall.

"Dad!" screamed Elsie, spotting Bob in the lobby.

"Elsie, you were spectacular!" said Bob, hugging his daughter.

"Elsie, you were, well you are an absolute actress, my darling!" said Vera, giving her granddaughter a mighty hug.

"Where's Bernard?" Danah asked Bob.

"He had to leave," said Bob, quietly.

"Where did he go?" asked Danah.

"To The Sushi Place, I guess. I told him where we were going to meet after the show, and when he started the coughing fit, he walked out. I assume he went to the restaurant. The Lincoln's gone. I checked." Danah nodded three small nods to herself and rounded everyone up. She congratulated every cast member she saw and shepherded her mother into the van.

The restaurant parking lot was so full that Bob decided to drop everyone off at the door and find a space for the car by himself.

Danah instantly treasured the sight of her mother walking arm-in-arm with Elsie. The reception area in the restaurant was Elsie's favorite thing about the place. The wishing pond to the right of the door and the rocky wall behind it that supported several waterfalls and little nooks housing antique Japanese fishermen had caused many dear conversations between mother and daughter. Vera searched for change in her pocketbook. Armed with new pennies, the three of them held hands, closed their eyes, casting their pennies and wishes simultaneously. Danah wished she would learn the whole story about Stewart. The far wall of the reception area showcased layer upon layer of aquariums containing brightly colored fish with nowhere to go. Danah identified with the fish-in-bowl predicament. She peered around what she could see of the dining room to see if she could spot Bernard. When she didn't see him, she was relieved, but she knew her mother wouldn't be satisfied with the answer, "We can't find him. Oh well, what shall we eat?"

They finally received the signal to follow a waitress and were led to a large, round table out in the middle of the floor. Danah's favorite window and corner tables were all taken. Perhaps this is a good thing. Being on display might keep us on our best behavior, and then she saw Bernard stumbling over a barstool at the sushi bar on his way back from the toilet. Danah recognized the drunken, vengeful look in his mud-pool eyes, his face a mask made of human flesh. A young woman quickly righted the barstool. He showcased the walking-stick walk across the restaurant floor and nodded at the customer who had picked up after him.

Danah gave herself a mental talking-to and promised herself to behave well. Vera scuttled after Bernard. Bob and Elsie sat down next to each other and talked about the performance. Bob was telling Elsie about Kevin Kline's version of Hamlet and how he thought they had the video of it somewhere. Danah stared at the Forget-me-nots, which Elsie had placed in the center of the table, and was reminded of Stewart.

Bernard shuffled to the table as if, moments ago, he'd just been discharged from an intensive care unit. He settled in between Vera and Bob. Everyone studied the menu in silence, as if a test would follow. Bernard soon waved down a young waitress.

"Can I get something American to eat in here?"

"What you like, sir?"

"Steak, potatoes, gravy. That sort of thing. And I need a

scotch. Anyone else need a drink?" No one at the table spoke.

"Yes. I bring that for you." The waitress escaped.

"So, Elsie, what will you have?" asked Danah.

"Sashimi dinner and a salmon hand roll, please"

"I'll have what you're having, dear," Vera said to Elsie, closing the menu.

"I'd like a sushi dinner with a salad," said Danah, adding, "So, Bernard, what happened? You left during the Dumb Show, I hear." He laughed.

"It wasn't that bad! You don't have to be rude about it!" he said.

"I'm not being rude. I'm honestly curious why you left."

"The show wasn't that dumb," repeated Bernard, vaguely amused.

"No, dear. You see, that part in the play, when you were coughing, well, the actors were miming how the King died. It's called the Dumb Show. I think it's called the Mousetrap, too." The waitress delivered a scotch to Bernard. He picked up the glass so quickly that it appeared to bounce off the table and land at his open mouth. He spoke to Elsie directly for the first time since his arrival.

"I'm sorry I missed the play, Elsie. But you looked cute up there."

"Cute?" repeated Vera, Danah, and Elsie in unison.

"There's nothing 'cute' about Hamlet, Bernard," snarled Danah.

He shrugged. "She did good. What do you want me to say?"

"Thanks," said Elsie.

"Well now, where's that great waitress of ours?" asked Bob.

"You should smile more," said Bernard, looking at Danah.

"'One may smile and smile and be a villain,'" quoted Elsie, smiling at her mother.

"Who are you calling a villain, Elsie?" said Danah, smiling back at her daughter.

"There's really a Shakespeare quote for every occasion, isn't there!" offered Vera.

During dinner, Elsie confessed that she had a crush on the ghost of her father. Bob told Vera about the time he played a gravedigger in High School.

Bob was paying the bill with a credit card when the talk turned to food and cooking. "The funny thing about Danah is . . ."

said Bob.

"Only one funny thing about me?" teased Danah, feeling expansive because Bernard had been quiet for some time.

"*One* of the funny things about Danah is that she likes to make meals from movies. Recently, she made *Dinner With Friends'* lemon polenta cake. When she wants to make Italian food, she rents *Big Night*."

"Do you remember that great risotto I made after Big *Night?*"

"You've got to worry when she rents *Jaws*, then," said Vera.

"No, seriously, mother. Do you think it's a saleable book idea? *Film Food? Movies with Menus?* I can see beautiful stills from the movies alongside mouth-watering photographs of the dishes. And there could be menus for dinner parties *before* watching specific movies, templates for invitations, and ideas for table decorations. What do you think?" They had all stood up and were ready to leave.

"I think that's a really good idea, Danah. You should talk to someone," said Vera.

"Maybe I *should* take it seriously. I'd like to break out of the work I do."

"So now you have two book ideas: that and *The History of the*

Kiss. That's two book proposals to write now," teased Bob.

Danah smiled, but she couldn't meet Bob's eyes. She remembered kissing Paul, and it frightened her to realize she would see Paul and Holly at the performance tomorrow.

Upon her return to the house, the men disappeared; Elsie went to bed well pleased with her evening; and Vera and Danah sat by a non-existent fire with one more glass of wine.

After some talk about how very talented Elsie was, Danah said: "Can you see how annoying he is? I mean, what he said to Elsie about being a cute Hamlet. I wanted to slap him."

"I can see he annoys you, dear. Actually, what I really think is that you two are too similar to get along."

"Similar? You've got to be kidding. I'd never walk out on a kid's performance and then call her work 'cute!'"

"He didn't mean anything by it."

"Well, it's high time he *did* mean something, especially when a child is listening. By the way, I saw one of Stewart's movies the other day: *Dark Stranger.* He was good, very funny. I hadn't expected him to make me laugh."

Vera looked as though she had heard news about an old

lover, not a dead ex-husband. "Where did you see it?"

"A teacher from Bob's school had a copy. We copied it. The packaging has his name on it. Do you want to see it?"

"Not now, dear."

"No, I mean, do you want to see the packaging?"

"Not now."

Danah swirled an inch of wine around the bottom of her glass. "When you and Bernard got married in London, did you visit Stewart?"

"Yes," said Vera, emptying her glass. They sat quietly on the couch for a moment. Danah watched a small spider walk across the back of her hand. Then she killed it. "Are you upset about something, Danah?"

"I was stressed out about Elsie's performance," said Danah, with other questions on her mind: What was my father doing fifteen years ago? Was he healthy, or was he dying? Which month did he die? When did you marry Bernard exactly? "Well, I hope you and Bernard have everything you need," she said, finally. "I'll check on Elsie. Good night!" Danah went upstairs. Vera went downstairs.

Hamlet Bear showered in the umbrella of light falling from

Elsie's bedside lamp. Her daughter's face, pale with stage makeup and sleep, appeared in profile. Her long waves of blonde hair stretched across the pillow. Elsie's beauty echoed that of a young bride from an old photograph, and yet she lay beside Scooby Doo. Danah turned out the bedside lamp and carefully closed the door behind her. The jumping light from the master bedroom meant Bob was watching television, probably the news. Danah hovered in the hallway, uncertain where to go, when she overheard Vera and Bernard talking. For once, Vera did not sound conciliatory. Danah stepped lightly down the hallway, straining to hear as much as she could. Crouching at the top of the stairs and looking between the wooden steps, she saw the door to the recreation room hanging open.

"We saw him because you insisted on it," said Bernard. Their voices carried like actors with hidden microphones.

"Well, what could I have said? I was at home when the hospice called. I was officially still his wife, you know. They said he was fatally ill, in-and-out of consciousness. What was I supposed to do?" Vera's voice carried with all the articulation of an actress.

"How the hell they got our number, I'd like to know. And then, when we got to that god-awful place, they said he might live for years. Linger. That's what they said, linger."

"They saw me as his wife, dear. They were doing their best to give me some good news. They assumed I wanted him to live."

"And they were right, weren't they?" Bernard said, bitterly.

Danah spied Vera busily folding and refolding a cardigan.

"I certainly never wished him dead, Bernard, if that's what you're getting at."

"He was in a hospice for impoverished actors, for Chrissakes. What good was he to anyone, really?"

Danah couldn't see Bernard. She figured he was already in the pullout bed. I could have helped my father. Did he have his favorite books with him? Did he long for a favorite food? Could he have gone for a walk if there was someone to take him? We could have rented a movie or gone to a local theater together.

"I did go there to ask for a divorce, you might remember. I did do that. But when we saw him, well, even before we saw him . . . the broken flagstones leading to the door, the stinging nettles in the front garden, and how damp it was, how cold, even in June. I had to turn on that electric heater to keep from shivering. And then there was that sweet woman a few beds down from him in the ward, the other side of that curtain. What was her name? Her daughter had made something of herself. I can't remember her name. Anyway, she smiled at us, and she could hear everything we said, and, well, I hadn't the heart to ask him. He was so happy to see me. It was like giving chocolate. You can't be mean afterwards. He didn't know who you were."

"If you'd served him papers the way I told you to none of that would have been necessary."

"I'm glad I saw him. I don't regret that one bit." Danah saw her mother sit down on the edge of the pull-out bed, with her back to Bernard, hands on her lap. "I've never asked you this, Bernard, but I'm asking you now: Why did you need time alone with Stewart that day? What did you say to him?" Danah held her breath. She strained to hear Bernard's response, but she heard nothing. Vera continued: "He died the very next day. That's what bothers me. He died the very next day after our visit, the next morning, actually. We got a call at the hotel right before lunch.

"I didn't do anything. He pissed me off, that's all."

"A dying man pissed you off?" She smoothed out the wrinkles in her lap.

"I explained our situation to him. We just wanted to be married, for God's sake. It wasn't a crime. Why couldn't he have just signed the damn papers?"

"He wanted to die married to me," Vera said with dignity.

"He started gasping for breath, heaving sort of, trying to get up on an elbow and reach for something. How did I know what he wanted?"

"I don't like the sound of this, Bernard. I'm telling you that right now."

"His face came over strange. He sort of erupted and then fell quiet. I left him and found you talking to a nurse."

"That's terrible! Awful! I didn't know that. Why didn't you tell the nurse? That was an emergency."

"Didn't look like he was dying to me. No buzzer went off. Wasn't he hooked up to something? And they told us he was on the edge. He was about to die anyway, that's the point. Remember that old hospice woman who said it was a matter of weeks?"

"Well, you had to prove her wrong, didn't you. You went and speeded the whole thing up."

"You make it sound like pre-meditated murder, for God's

sake. We had a man-to-man talk. He had started dying all by himself."

"Well, we're all going to die, aren't we, dear." With that she swung into bed with him.

Danah walked silently into Elsie's bathroom to think. She balanced on the edge of the tub. She struggled to pull out the facts one by one from the emotional rubble surrounding her. My father died in a hospice for impoverished actors. He saw Vera and Bernard the day before he died. My stepfather had a talk with him: a healthy-man-to-dying-man talk. So, for all those years, Vera had refused to divorce Stewart and yet she went to London to marry Bernard. Then, Bernard worked my father up so he could barely breathe and left him alone to die. Danah stood up and walked calmly towards the bedroom, relieved to have the facts at last. Vera believes Stewart wanted to die married. Stewart sort of *erupted* shortly after Vera left the room. Maybe he knew how close to death he was and wanted Vera back in the room? Danah got into bed and snuggled behind Bob, who faced the window. Is this what Stewart has been trying to tell me? I know now that when my father died, he was married to my mother. My father was married to my mother until he died. This is not the story I grew up on.

15 AN ACT WITHOUT A NAME

"So which movie has a cooked English breakfast in it?" asked Bob, looking up from the newspaper.

"Actually, I don't think I've ever seen an English breakfast in a movie," said Danah, "Isn't that odd? Someone should put that right." Danah marveled at how she and Vera were able to act as if this breakfast scene followed straight on after the restaurant scene last night, and as if there had been no interlude in which Bernard practically confessed to murdering Stewart. What do you call an act or scene like this where one character is about to burst but pretends all is normal? It is probably the Third Act: the climax has been reached but it will not end this way. Deciding to revenge my father's murder sounds right, and yet we talk of breakfast.

"I love the way you squish tomato into the fried bread, mom. I remember you making this for me before big tests at school," said Danah. Vera smiled.

To the sound of a flushing cistern, Bernard presented himself, wearing misshapen sweatpants and a white undershirt. He walked towards the dining table, where Bob sat reading a section of

The Sunday New York Times. The bulk of the paper made a centerpiece on the table. Bernard tugged at a section of the paper with thumb and index finger and Vera swiftly delivered a mug of hot tea to him.

"Are you ready for some bacon and eggs, Bernard?" asked Danah.

"Already eaten," he said, without looking at her.

"He always has a McDonald's breakfast. He went out earlier. Don't you worry about him," said Vera, and Danah wished it were as easy as that. Vera continued to cut thin slices of tomato, and Danah set the table. Elsie joined them, wearing tartan pajamas.

"We have to stay late tonight, mom, to strike the set. Can I go home with Erika?" asked Elsie, taking a piece of crispy bacon from a paper towel.

"Sure. Has she invited you?"

"She will."

"Holly and Paul are coming to see you tonight as well as all of us."

"No. We're leaving," said Bernard. Danah looked at Vera, who seemed to be hearing this for the first time also.

"Why is that, dear?"

"We're catching an earlier flight."

"That's all very well, Bernard, but you drove here, remember?" said Danah. Bernard stood up.

"I'll pack my things," he said to Vera. They watched him hobble across the living area and down to the recreation room. When he had shut the door, Danah said: "I thought you wanted to see Elsie's show again."

"Of course I do. I'd love to," said Vera. "But he's been suffering from cluster migraines and when one gets triggered, he needs to run for cover. He didn't sleep well, and that puts pressure on him. He's been having diarrhea for a few days. To tell you the truth, we nearly didn't come."

"He could stay here while we go to the play," suggested Bob. "It would be quieter for him here than driving a car."

"I'd really like you to meet Holly, mum. She wants to meet you. You've come all this way."

"Next time. I'll meet Holly next time."

"Why are you giving in to him like this?"

"Believe it or not, darling, sometimes he gives in to me. I've won a few battles in my time, don't you worry." Vera put an arm around Elsie.

"And what about Elsie?"

"Can you tape the show tonight, Dad? Then we can send a copy to gran."

"That's a great idea, Elsie. Yes, I can do that. I'll have to charge up the battery."

Vera and Danah served steaming plates of eggs, bacon, sausages, mushrooms, and fried bread with tomatoes. Danah no longer had an appetite, but she sat at the table.

"Will driving for hours on the highway relieve Bernard's stress, then?" asked Danah.

"If he thinks it will, it probably will. We'll break the journey. I think he wants to visit some car dealers on the way back. We'll take our time." Danah felt that, as usual, Bernard had won.

After breakfast, Vera and Elsie cleaned up the kitchen together, Bob went in search of the video camera, and Danah felt she had the power of a mismatched sock. She checked e-mail. She had twenty-six, but shut down the computer, leaving them unread. She heard noises coming from the driveway and looked out of the master bathroom window. Bernard was slinging bags into the Lincoln.

It was now or never: She flew downstairs and grabbed her new pruning shears from the garage. She went out back, beyond the fence that surrounded the pool. It was land she had avoided since last summer, when she had disturbed a nest of black snakes. She had been petrified as she watched two large snakes and a smaller one emerge from a green tarpaulin and glide past her into the marshland. Snakes had encroached on her dreams for the next several weeks. In the most vivid moment, she stepped out from a shower and watched a snake ooze through the top of the doorjamb. She had forced her dream-self to open the door slowly, hoping like hell the thing didn't fall on her, and she managed to save herself. That was the last of the snake dreams.

The little old bridge over the salt marshes to the south of her house was out. Two cranes had stood there all weekend, hanging their heads. Men had been working on it for a week. Traffic had been rerouted, and so, on this particular Saturday morning, with the tide in, Danah listened to the waves from out behind the pool with no interference from cars. The rhythmic slapping and squishing sounds of water running back and forth over the rocky beach soothed her.

Danah liked her pruning shears' willingness to redefine the

landscape without regret. Vines on the edges of the marshland reached for her white fence, grabbing and winding themselves around the uprights. One shoot had spiraled around a square post from the bottom to the top, every rotation equidistant. The weed had done its best to appear ornamental. This same weed, upon reaching the fence top, had continued to grow and now hungered in an arc above the forty-eight inch fence like an Apatosaurus, looking for more. The indifference of the white fence impressed Danah. Despite the fact that a living creature had invaded, the fence maintained its integrity and position.

A laugh forced itself up through Danah's throat. *And here I stand, in the forty-sixth year of my life, receiving wisdom from a fence post.* She raised the shears and chopped at the dignified weed.

The Lincoln's boot slammed shut. Danah drew shallow breaths through her teeth. *I will not allow him to get away without hearing from me,* she decided. *I may not have the wherewithal to say everything, but I can say something to the bastard who was unconcerned about upsetting my father as he lay on his deathbed. There must be something I can say to the man who was willing to do that.*

She entered the windowless garage from the pool deck through a back door. Bernard stood between a rake and a cultivator, smoking a cigarette. The garage was cluttered with things normally found in a basement.

Danah knew her way around and skirted the garden furniture. "What are you doing, Bernard?" He seemed smaller in the half-light, almost adolescent in his awkwardness at being found smoking.

"What have you been doing?" he replied, mocking her tone.

"I've been cutting down suckers and prickers. Funny you should ask," she replied.

"Don't get fresh with me, Little Missy."

"And don't you talk down to me. I am not, nor ever have I ever been, your Little Missy, Bernard." Bernard inhaled and exhaled smoke like an invisible dragon. Danah stood her ground as her eyes grew accustomed to the semi-darkness. She focused on the ax hanging above his head and wondered how secure it was. She walked quickly to the opposite corner from Bernard and pressed the little grey button that released the garage door: It squealed like a farmyard of Thanksgiving turkeys as it dropped, eliminating the daylight.

"Know when you've been beaten, you stupid," said Danah,

shaking with anger. She suddenly felt a sharp pain in her stomach as if the grenade of compacted venom she had carried for years had finally burst.

"Cut out the bullshit. Open the door!"

"What are you afraid of, Bernard?"

"I don't have time for your damn drama. Open the door, dammit!"

"No." It sounded as if he stumbled backwards. She heard the clang of metal and a stick falling, then silence.

"You could always hurt yourself, Bernard."

"Is this your idea of fun?"

"Yes. Must be. I am having fun. Thank you for pointing that out. Sometimes you get so caught up in a moment that you don't fully appreciate all the fun you are having."

"You don't know who you're dealing with. Now open the door."

"Meaning what exactly, that you have your handgun at the ready?" She could see him trying to light a second cigarette from the first. "You see, that's where you are very wrong. It's precisely because I do know you for the heartless bastard you are, one who would threaten gun violence, that I have called you here today."

"Right, very amusing, you middle-aged nobody. Now get the hell out of my way and open that garage door." Bernard was thrashing around, trying to move out of his corner, but he kept meeting with invisible obstacles.

"If you carry on like that just maybe something heavy and sharp will land smack bang in the middle of your head, and what would that do for your migraines, I wonder?" She saw the small fire on his cigarette suddenly advance towards her.

"Oh, that's good coming from the one who doesn't threaten violence. You don't believe in guns, but if you should corner someone into a space below an ax, and that ax should accidentally fall, that's OK? Yes, I saw the ax, asshole."

"Ooh! Survival skills kicking in are they, Bernard? I'm doing better than I thought!"

"What do you want, Danah?"

"Now that's a good question, Bernard. Score one for Bernard. This is what I'd like: I'd like to see you stop controlling my mother. You have her so that today, for example, she's going to spend time waiting for you in some sleazy lounge of a car dealership

311

rather than watching her one and only grandchild play Hamlet." No response. "Why don't you like her connecting with the theater, Bernard? Afraid that you might seem rather dull by comparison?" His cigarette end made a sudden leap towards her and then zigzagged to the ground as he fell over something. "Oh that must have been the blue recycling bin you hit. Good instincts. You do need to be reformatted somehow, but I can't for the life of me imagine how you could be re-configured so that anyone would ever want you around."

"You bitch! You want control so badly. So pathetic," sneered Bernard from the damp cement floor.

"Wrong, but revealing. You would see this as a control issue, wouldn't you? Control and the lack of it is all you know. Believe it or not, Bernard, I want Vera to be an important part of my daughter's life. They happen to have a lot in common, a love for the theater. And that's what really pisses you off. That's why you say you have a migraine today."

"Maybe your mother just doesn't give a shit about you or your precious, Princess Elsie. Maybe she's happier with me. Did you ever think of that? She chose me, today. Maybe she's about as sick of your highfalutin, judgmental ways as I am. Maybe she just can't stand to be around you more than a day at a time." Danah wiped tears from her face and was careful to control her breathing so that Bernard would never know how he had wounded her. She did doubt her mother's love for her. Tears covered her hands and face. Her heart was draining like a battery. The blaming, the name-calling had exhausted her. Her defenses had dissolved. Left to her own devices, she might have stayed in the darkened garage indefinitely.

"OK, cut the crap. Do you want your mother to find us like this? Do you want to explain why I'm lying on a concrete floor? Do you?" Bernard's voice worked like jumper cables, and she was back.

"How's this for cutting the crap then? I think the play upset you, sent you off-balance. I think it got you real worried to see one man kill another and promptly marry the dead man's wife. It upset you to see that acted out, and you knew it would make my mother think of Stewart, and how he died while still married to her. The two of you have played out your own version of that little scenario, haven't you, Bernard, and it doesn't sit quite as well with Vera as it does with you, because you are a selfish little runt."

"You eavesdropped."

"And you had the fucking nerve to upset my dad as he lay

dying – and those crimes aren't exactly equal, are they?"

"Save that shit for your therapist."

"And so, in answer to your earlier question about what I really want, Bernard, I have some answers for you now. I want you to cut me a whole lot of slack, Bernard. I don't want you monitoring phone calls, or insulting my daughter, or cutting short the time my mother schedules with us in the future. And I don't want your hissy fits spoiling every fucking visit. You can have my mother all to yourself about three hundred and fifty days a year. Back off for about fifteen. That's it. That's what I want."

She didn't wait for a response. It wasn't a negotiation. She immediately pressed the electric button controlling the hefty, double garage door and pressed it and watched the wide door lift like a curtain on a Broadway stage, marking the opening of the second act. She turned to look at Bernard and could hardly believe the transformation: an old man sprawled on the garage floor, one knee bent, one outstretched, with his walking stick out of reach. They locked eyes to see what they could see in each other and she felt the stirrings of pity. She bent down to get his stick and gave it to him. She watched to see if he could get back up on his feet. He needed help. The leg with gout was not responsive. She reached out an arm and he took it.

"I'll give you what you want if you do one thing for me."

"What?"

"Don't tell Vera what you overheard. Don't talk to her about how Stewart died. What's done is done. There's no point going over it again. It will only upset your mother. She is a very sweet lady."

"Yes. She is. Very sweet."

They heard the family approaching from inside the rec. room.

"OK. Deal."

As if on cue, Vera burst through the door, stage right. "Darling, I've been looking for you everywhere!" Bernard and Danah looked at each other and smiled.

"She meant me, Bernard." All three of them laughed.

"Well I am glad to see you getting along so well, but if we're going we had better go."

The family gathered beside the Lincoln. "Elsie! I nearly forgot," said Vera, holding out a black book with a leather cover. "The notebook I kept when I played Rosalind. I want you to have it, darling. You're probably the only soul on earth who could make any sense out of it!" Elsie took the book as if it were the key to a kingdom.

"Oh cool!" There are real reviews in here!" said Elsie, who had flipped to the back first.

"I remember I had a terrible crush on Touchstone, the country clown. I think there's a picture of him in there somewhere. Anyway, enjoy it, dear. You are an absolutely marvelous Hamlet, an absolute actress. I shall never forget what I saw. And you'll be marvelous again tonight. I'm so proud of you."

"Break a leg, Elsie!," said Bernard.

"Well, thanks, guys, for coming up. Have a good journey back." Bob hugged Vera and shook Bernard's hand.

"I hope you feel better, Bernard. Call us when you get home so we know you are both safe," said Danah. He nodded and gave her a wink. "Goodbye, mom," she added, holding her mother tightly.

"Thanks for everything, Danah. We'll stay longer next time. I promise," said Vera.

Bob and Danah stood on the driveway, each with an arm around Elsie, who stood between them. The trio watched Bernard's Lincoln reverse up the driveway and disappear. They walked back into the house and it was too quiet. As usual, they gravitated to the kitchen island. And there, on the granite countertop, was an enormous gift basket full of English candy, fresh fruit, and chocolates. A tag hung from the handle. Elsie read it aloud. It said: "Sweets to the sweet! Farewell."

16 THE WHOLE STORY?

"I haven't seen that dress before," said Elsie, coming up behind Danah.

"I've had it a while. Do you like it? Or is it too much?" They both studied the reflection of Danah wearing a neon pink dress with a fitted, buttoned bodice, white polka dots, full skirt, and pockets.

Elsie's head tilted to the right. "You can get away with it," she said, which pleased Danah then depressed her. She wondered exactly how long she could get away with it for. "Why are you wearing a new dress tonight?"

"I just want to look good for your play, that's all. So I'm OK?"

"You're OK."

"Now are *you* OK? Everything packed and ready? Remember, Mrs. V. is the prompt tonight, and another mother is running the sound effects. I'll be there to do your makeup." Danah bit off an uneven nail.

"I know."

"You're so great, Elsie. You are truly great. So unafraid and deliberate. So willing to take things on."

"Thanks, mom," said Elsie. They hugged.

"I can hardly believe . . ."

"OK, mom, I'm cutting you off right there." Danah smiled at her daughter.

"Tell daddy I'll be down in five minutes. Elsie left, and Danah sat on the bed to pull on her black ankle boots. With the boots giving her height and being tightly zipped up she felt ready to face Paul and Holly, neither of whom had she seen since the kiss. She glanced around the bedroom, saw a brown envelope, and put it in her handbag.

On her way downstairs, Danah dipped into Elsie's room to pick up her bag. She checked the contents. Everything was there, including Hamlet Bear.

"Let's go, darling!" said Bob. She couldn't meet his eyes.

"Ready. You look nice. Come on, Elsie. Let's go." Bob wore a blue linen suit and a red tie. Danah remembered Paul the way had looked that day: casual and Italian. "So, we're meeting them there?" Bob continued, locking the front door. "Two cars? The parking is so limited at that school."

"Yes," said Danah, knowing that under normal circumstances, she would have called to organize a car pool. "Yes, I know," she said, managing not to tell Bob about the Morgan. She wished she'd hammered out this sort of detail with Paul. She hadn't mentioned Paul's visit to anyone, but she realized now that it was a tactical error, because Paul must have told Holly what he thought of the renovation.

"Are you OK?" said Bob, looking at her as she stood, seemingly fascinated by the surface of the driveway.

"Yes, yes!"

On the way, Danah strained to remember her last conversation with Paul in detail. It seemed so horribly inappropriate now, driving with her husband and daughter to a school play.

The school parking lot was alive with cars. As they pulled into a spot, a car slid in next to them, making it feel as though they were still moving after they had stopped.

"What were the chances of that?" shouted Paul, bounding out of the Morgan.

"That yours?" asked Bob.

"Would I steal a car to come to Elsie's play?" everyone

laughed, and Paul took the opportunity to meet eyes with Danah.

The men talked cars all the way to their seats and beyond. Danah learned that Bob had owned a British sports car in his early twenties, an MG of some sort. Holly asked Danah how the visit with her parents went, how Elsie did last night, and what she thought of middle-aged men who bought flashy sports cars. Danah gave perfunctory answers and then excused herself to go backstage to do Elsie's makeup.

The backstage energy was a welcome distraction for Danah. The usual suspects were being rowdy. A group of boys teased Polonius about farting so loud that he would gas Hamlet. She spotted Elsie talking to the ghost of her father and hung back. Danah picked up a program and checked the cast list for his name. Jack Thompson played the Ghost of Hamlet's father. She had just decided to look for Jack's mother when she saw Jack leave. Elsie came running towards her looking as if she had either been named prom queen, or had a spiking fever.

"He asked me out!"

"Who? Who asked you out? Jack?"

"Yes, Jack! We're going out after the play tonight!"

"But you said Jack had a girlfriend already."

"They broke up."

"Do you want to go out with him?"

"Me and every girl in the class!"

"Where does he want to take you?"

"He doesn't *take me*, mother. We just go somewhere together. Probably the pizza place. He has a to-die-for older brother. Oh my god! Selwyn!"

"Selwyn?"

"Selwyn has a car. He'll be driving Jack and me downtown after the show for pizza. Oh my god! I can't believe this. Where is Erika? I have to tell Erika!" Elsie ran out of the classroom into the riptide of kids in the hall.

"Wait! Honey, we have to discuss this!"

Danah worried Elsie had lost focus for the performance and would forget her lines. Then, she worried about Elsie having a boyfriend with a to-die-for older brother. Then she worried about a kid driving her child around at night. Meanwhile, she set up foundation, blush, sponges, mascara, hairbrush, and mirror on the desk.

"Mom! My makeup!" said Elsie, suddenly reappearing with Erika. Danah began by brushing Elsie's hair into a sleek ponytail.

"So, is Elsie staying with you tonight?"

"Can I, Erika? Selwyn can drop me at your house."

"Fine."

"Can't Erika go with you to the pizza place?"

"I can't push it mom, not on a first date."

"I need to know where you are, Elsie. Jack seems like a nice boy, but you never know. Call me when you get back to Erika's."

"You know Jack's mother. She's running the sound effects."

"I've *seen* her. I don't *know* her. Listen, call daddy's cell when you get to the pizza place. I mean it. Call from the bathroom if you don't want Jack to hear." Danah finished sponging Elsie's face. She didn't need much blush.

"Onstage warm-up!" shouted Mrs. V. from the doorway.

"Break a leg!" said Danah before making her way back to the audience. She sat between Holly and Bob and immediately whispered the dating information to Bob, expecting him to object.

"So, you're fine with this?" said Danah.

"Nice boy. I know the mother. Nice woman. She's active in

the high school PTO."

"Oh well, that's good then, I suppose," said Danah. "Jack is a good-looking boy. I'll say that for him."

"I can't believe we'll be going through all this with Harry, one day!" said Holly, who had been unusually quiet.

"And with Alice or Alex," added Paul, looking at his wife from his seat the other side of Bob.

"Alice or Alex? You're not what I think you are, are you?" said Danah.

"It's very early. I only found out this morning, although I've been feeling exhausted all week, but that's nothing new! But we said we weren't going to say anything to anyone, Paul!"

Danah hugged Holly and tears came to her eyes.

"We can tell these people anything!" Paul said. Bob shook Paul's hand and got up to kiss Holly.

"I'm so happy for you guys," said Danah. "Elsie can babysit for you!"

The chamber orchestra played Prokofiev. Danah patted her friend's belly and smiled. Holly having a baby made everything simple again in Danah's eyes. It felt as if the world were suddenly solving its own problems and that all would be well. The house lights faded as spotlights came up on the Danish soldiers on guard. Danah noticed different aspects of the play this time.

"Take revenge, my son, but do not hurt your mother," said Jack Thompson, and Danah couldn't help liking him for saying that.

"The purpose of theater is to hold a mirror up to nature," said Hamlet. Danah felt that Elsie's date with Jack was making her rush the lines, but that the gushing added an interesting intensity, a manic edge. Nevertheless, Danah sat there trying to will Elsie to slow down, and after a while, Elsie did slow down.

The fifth act had never before struck Danah as anything more than a series of dreadful mishaps requiring excellent choreography. Tonight, her heart went out to Hamlet. He survived the treachery of his so-called friends only to arrive home for Ophelia's funeral. He had bravely decided to return home to face his demons and it was heartbreaking that the world hadn't stood still while he was away in England. Instead, Claudius had continued to plot against him. Hamlet was in no position to carry out his own agenda. He coped as best he could with his heartless stepfather. He remained loyal to his real friends, and, while looking evil in the face, he continued to care about the world. When Elsie said: "You must live to tell the world what has happened here, so they will know who was innocent, and who was evil," she was moved to tears of pity and didn't care who saw it. Holly passed her a tissue.

The cast took an extensive curtain call to a standing ovation. Bob, Holly, and Paul followed Danah backstage. Elsie looked radiant, and relieved that it was over. Danah caught Elsie's attention by waving, and she came running over to hug everyone.

"I never understood the play until tonight! You were great, Elsie!" said Paul. Danah thought she saw Elsie look to see if Jack was watching her talk to this handsome adult man.

"You are a miracle, Elsie!" said Bob, "And I've got the video to prove it," He tapped the video camera dangling from his left shoulder.

"Can I see some, Dad? Play the end back on the little screen." A group of kids spontaneously appeared and squeezed together to watch the end.

"That's awesome, Mr. Blanko," said Horatio, who seemed more interested in the technology than the performance. He engaged Bob in a conversation about the capabilities of the next generation of video cameras. Meanwhile, Danah tried to have a private word with the ecstatic Elsie about the evening ahead.

"OK, people! You are all needed onstage. We have a set to strike!" shouted Mrs. V., and Elsie was gone. Danah looked at Bob with her mouth open.

"She'll be fine," said Bob. "Come on, let's get dinner."

"Want to ride in the Morgan?" Paul asked Bob.

"Can I drive?" said Bob. The men walked ahead of the women, and Danah was glad of it.

"Creative Eats, right?" said Bob, over his shoulder.

"Yes. See you there. The reservation is at eight," said Danah.

"We'll never see them again!" said Holly. "They are kids with a new toy. They'll lose track of time."

Creative Eats was an eclectic restaurant in an old New England farmhouse two towns over. The men walked in soon after the women, and they were promptly shown to their round table to the right of a fieldstone fireplace lit with silver candles. Bob ordered champagne, and they got down to the business of working through the wordy menu.

"Swedish-cured barbecue pork loin sounds good to me," said

Paul.

"Cured? You want to eat something that's been cured?" asked Danah, staring at her menu.

"What? You prefer the word *recovered* or *healthy* or something?" said Paul.

"Well, frankly, if I have to eat something that's had problems, well I'd rather not. Is there a Danish-healed salad in here somewhere?"

"I thought you liked this place," said Bob. The champagne arrived. "To Alex or Alice and Elsie, not forgetting Harry!" They all chinked glasses.

"I might eat something in recovery," said Bob, almost to himself. "Bernard really was a handful this time," he added, looking up from the menu.

"Oh yes, how were your folks?" asked Holly.

"Mom was great. She and Elsie get along so well. She loved the play. She gave Elsie a Hamlet Bear dressed in black!"

"And then there was Bernard," said Bob, shaking his head.

"Why aren't they here tonight?" asked Paul.

"It's a long story," said Danah. She sipped champagne.

"Actually, he was better this time. I made him listen to me."

"Really?" asked Bob.

"Don't you guys ever talk to each other?" said Holly.

"No. No, we stopped that long ago," said Danah.

"Oh, you!" said Bob. "Paul, back me up here, don't you think women exaggerate about us not talking?" Paul gave a silent shrug, which made them all laugh.

"Even when he tries to write me a note, which isn't often, he manages to find the tiniest piece of paper in creation, and then he writes like a native Chinaman struggling with a literal translation. Like this: *Back late. Day good. So tired now.* And we probably communicate more than most couples! Wasn't it Erma Bombeck who said men have a vocabulary of about twenty words, which they use sparingly?"

"Think of men like high-level government officials. The more they know about something, the less they are at liberty to discuss it," said Bob.

"But, see, this is what we don't get," said Holly. "Why don't you like talking? Women like talking. It's how we find out what's going on and how we get over things." said Holly.

"Perhaps it's because we know *you* know what's going on, and we don't have anything to get over?" said Paul, looking directly at Danah.

"Men like talking. They talk about important stuff," said Bob.

"Well, my feeling, and I'm speaking as a wife," said Danah, "is that if the husband can repeat what he's saying to anyone else, it doesn't qualify as *talking*. I can hear that kind of talk on CNN or ESPN."

Holly laughed all by herself.

The waiter came. Danah ordered salmon in ginger, soy, and rice vinegar. Holly had bream with anchovies, thyme, and chickpeas. Paul had the cured pork. Bob had Vietnamese chicken and mint salad. White wine arrived. After a sip of wine, Danah leant down and picked up her black leather purse. She pulled out the brown envelope and held it up as if it contained Oscar results for Best Picture.

"Now, inside this envelope is something I wouldn't talk to anyone about except you guys. It's a photo. You've seen it Bob, but I've never had the heart to talk about it." Danah took a big gulp of wine. "I only found it recently. It's a photo of my father, mother, and me when I was a baby. Elsie playing Hamlet and talking about the ghost of her father has made, I don't know, made me feel like my own father is a sort of ghost. Now, the thing is," Danah paused to pull the picture out of the envelope. "The thing is, this is the only picture of us together, so I sort of have to get a lot out of it. I was wondering if you'd all take a turn looking at it and tell me what you see." Two waiters brought various dishes. "Do you want to do this, or is it stupid? There will never be a right time. After seeing Hamlet seemed like as good a time as I'd get," said Danah.

"Of course we want to help you, Danah," said Holly, taking hold of photo. "Well, you know, what this says to me, the way you two are leaning in to each other and touching noses, well, it shows your connection. He knew you existed, even if you doubted him all these years. Maybe he even knew at the time of this picture that he might be absent from your life? It's interesting how your mother is holding your hand so you can't touch him. There was a whole lot beyond your control. You were literally a baby the last time you saw him." She passed it to Bob.

"I don't remember seeing this before," said Bob, taking off his glasses to get a better look. "Where was this taken?"

"I don't know. London, I suppose."

"Because what strikes me is that this is a color photo of a

black-and-white picture. It's as if it were photographed from an album, laid on the grass."

"What?" said Danah, feeling her world exploding in slow motion.

"You can see the black-and-white photo was mounted in a photograph album. I didn't see the grass at first, but it's there," said Bob. Danah put her hand out across the table and Bob returned the photo to her.

"You're right. That's exactly what happened, isn't it? But I didn't take that picture."

"Would Vera have taken it?" asked Paul.

"Why would she? I recognize the background, now. It's taken from one of her old show business scrapbooks. I haven't seen them for years. Bernard hates them. He hates everything to do with her life in the theater and with my father, Stewart. That's really strange. A few months ago, it crossed my mind that I should ask Vera to give those books to Elsie. I wouldn't put it past Bernard to throw them away." Danah passed the picture to Paul.

Bob said, "Well, someone took that scrapbook outside for good light and took that picture. If Vera didn't, and you didn't, who did?"

"The only other person in the picture?" said Danah, earnestly. The men laughed. Holly gave her a sidelong glance intended to warn Danah she was edging into dangerous territory. Danah passed the photo to Paul.

"Where did you find it?" asked Holly, knowing the answer perfectly well.

"On the floor of my walk-in closet," said Danah, grateful to Holly for reeling her in.

"This picture was staged, Danah," Paul said, quietly. "It's a posed shot."

"How do you know?" asked Danah.

"There's a photographer's arc light reflected in the window behind your dad, see?" Paul held the photo up for everyone to see.

"You're right!" said Danah. "It must have been a photo shoot for the newspapers, for publicity. It was just one more publicity shot. Isn't it ironic he'd be playing peek-a-boo with me?"

"This does not mean the connection between you and your dad was fake. You know that, right?" said Holly.

"I have a hard time knowing anything when it comes to him.

Maybe you're right. Often, the only place an actor is fully alive is onstage or with an audience of some kind. Actors connect with their feelings, even dangerous ones, onstage or in front of a camera, when they know it's for a limited time only."

"Your mother might not have been comfortable with him around when there weren't cameras around," said Bob.

"Maybe."

"Because they got divorced when you were a baby, didn't they?" asked Bob. Danah smiled and ate for a moment.

"No. They didn't. You see, that's the thing! During this past visit, I found out some stuff. I overheard Vera and Bernard talking. My father stayed married to my mother until he died. She wouldn't serve him papers! He died fifteen years ago."

"Wow! That's a different story," said Bob.

"Exactly. That's why I found it so touching tonight when Elsie said to Horatio, 'You know the whole story.' It's so rare that we know the whole story."

"How do we ever know if really we do know the whole story?" said Holly.

"I think you know. Your insides stop aching, for one. And

then all the stories you've been told about your life make more sense. I understand my mother more now."

"Did you overhear anything else last night?" asked Paul.

"Plenty. Vera and Bernard went to London fifteen years ago to beg him for a divorce as he lay dying in a hospice. My mother left Bernard alone with Stewart briefly. I heard Bernard admit to my mother that he upset my dad so much that he was gasping for air. Bernard saw him gasping, told no one, and walked away. Stewart died soon after that."

"Oh my god!" said Holly.

"Your instincts were right about that man," said Paul.

"So, I got Bernard alone this morning. I told him I knew what he did."

"That's what you were doing right before they left? Vera was looking everywhere for him. Where were you?" said Bob.

"In the garage . . . We have an understanding now. Things are going to be better." They all ate in silence for a moment. "I love you, guys," said Danah.

"Well, in the spirit of full-disclosure . . ." said Paul, looking at Holly. "I think we should tell you about our plans to expand the health club." Paul explained how he had hired an architect, approved his plans, and sent them out to the building department for permits.

"It's a dream we share. We've always dreamed of a business promoting health and having two healthy kids," said Holly.

The evening continued with an extended eulogy from Bob about the Morgan. Holly talked about how she imagined a second child would change things. They said goodnight around eleven.

Once home, Danah suddenly remembered to check her phone messages. The first message was from Elsie, who had made it back to Erika's and had a blissful evening with Jack and Selwyn. The second message was from Vera:

"Darling! Darling! Are you there? Please pick up if you're there. Perhaps you're out at dinner? I'm calling from North Carolina, from our hotel room. I'm all right. It's Bernard. He's not good. He has severe lower back pain and cramps. I think it's his kidneys. He won't do anything about it. If it keeps up like this, he'll have to check into the hospital at home. I wish I could drive. He's asleep now. But he said something about you two having a fight, and that you turned out the lights on him in the garage, which made him fall. And you just left him there and laughed at him? You refused to help him? Is that really true? I told him I didn't believe you would do such a thing. It doesn't seem like you're there. I'll call again tomorrow. Goodnight."

Danah joined Bob in the kitchen He was pouring them each a glass of iced water from the fridge.

"Elsie called. She had a good time. She's at Erika's now. And my mum called. Bernard is ill, possibly dying. Mom and he are in a hotel in North Carolina and I can't say I care."

"That's terrible. I thought you two had come to an understanding. What happened to that?"

"Apparently, there was no understanding. He twisted everything and told Vera all sorts of shit that makes me sound pretty bad. The strong implication in her message is that I deliberately made him fall."

"That's ridiculous."

"Instead of telling her how I tried to be straight with him and bridge the gap between us, he has made it sound like I simply attacked him and, as a direct result, he now has some kind of kidney trouble. He has refused to go to a doctor."

"Where did you get the idea he's dying?"

"Call it a hunch. And I know I shouldn't think this, or say it, but it would be a hell of a relief to me if he did die."

"Do you really want him dead?"

"Dead would do nicely."

"You don't even believe in capital punishment!"

"I honestly believe Bernard has done this to himself. He's been sending out bad energy, creating bad karma for decades. He's a nasty man. He's nasty to children. He was content to let an infant die of a fever, unmoved by seeing a dying man gasp for breath. You know how nasty he is, Bob, I shouldn't have to explain this to you." Danah's eyes searched the pantry for the perfect snack for a moment like this. She found salt and vinegar potato chips. "Sometimes it takes hundreds of years for karmic justice to take place. Come on, Bob! He's evil, and I'm sick of him. I did my best with him and I've just had enough. I've had thirty years of his petty bullshit."

"He makes your mother happy, but I don't like the way he tries to turn your mother against you."

"My point, exactly." Danah stood behind Bob, who had sat on a stool, and she massaged the space between his shoulder blades with her thumbs.

"You know what I mean. I don't like him either, but I don't think it's right to be talking the way you're talking. I don't agree with it," Bob turned around to look at her.

"Look! A horrible old man is very ill," Bob made a cautionary face at her. She continued, "OK. OK. Maybe he'll come awfully close to death, see what a selfish jerk he's been his whole life, and reform."

"We don't even know what's wrong with him."

"Oh, I know what's wrong with him. I've known that all along. The question is, what's the cure. He's rotten. That's it. He's rotten. There's been something rotten about him all along."

17 LOVE HAPPENS

"I'm here, mother!" said Danah, having run from the bathroom to the landline phone on the wall in the kitchen. "How's Bernard?" Danah wrapped her dressing gown tightly around her and struggled to tie the soft belt with one hand.

"I'm at the hospital now. An ambulance brought us here. I don't honestly know where we are, darling. What time is it?"

"Just after seven in the morning. How's Bernard, mom?"

"He had watery diarrhea first thing this morning and cramps all through the night, well, I thought he was going to die right there on the bedpan."

"So, is he a bit better now?"

"Not really. They've given him an IV and now the diarrhea is bloody, which is not a good sign at all. Oh my god, Danah, it's awful here. We had to wait for them to treat people with gunshot wounds. I saw two young men wheeled past me, well, I can't even begin to tell you what they looked like. Can you imagine?"

"What are they saying about Bernard? Do they know what's wrong with him?"

"We're waiting for test results. They don't tell you anything. I don't know what to do. I can't even drive, of course. I don't know what to do without him."

"Do you want me to drive down and be with you?"

"Oh! Thank you, darling, but no. It may be nothing."

"Bernard is tough. He'll fight this. Waiting to hear the diagnosis is the worst part, and that's nearly over. You have done all anyone can do."

"They've given him a sedative."

"That's good. He needs some rest to heal. Can you get some magazines and go to the cafeteria?"

"Yes, yes, I could do that but I'm not sure where," she sucked in a breath. "I'm not sure where anything is." Vera erupted into huge, frightened sobs. For a moment, Danah felt she had failed her mother, that if only she had been a better daughter, none of this would have happened. She willed herself to remain present.

"I'm sorry. I mustn't do this. I know better," spluttered Vera.

"It's OK. It is very scary. Bernard is an important part of you. I get that now."

"Yes. I love you, Danah."

"Can you call me back in two hours? Call me at nine. You'll probably have the results by then. People will help you find everything. Just ask for help. Go and get something to eat, mom."

"Yes. That's right. That's it. Thank you, darling."

Danah walked out onto her deck and stared at the marshland until she saw a yellow canoe silently cutting through the haze. I don't want my mother's world to fall apart, and Bernard, for better or worse, is her world. I could confront him about the way he accused me of causing all this, but it would be just another argument, which is pointless. She puzzled over the symptoms her mother had described. It sounded like food poisoning or colon cancer to her. She ran ahead of herself wondering about the living arrangements if Bernard had to be institutionalized. There was a hospice in the next town, and her mother could live here. Bob would go down and arrange the sale of the car dealership and the house.

And, from nowhere, the word *grateful* appeared to Danah. She felt the word in the air, like a leaf swept up in the swirl of a April wind. My father, Stewart, is grateful to me for taking care of Vera, she said with the certainty people have about arithmetic.

Danah reentered the house. She went on a cleaning spree by

way of gaining some control of her world. Precisely two hours later the phone rang.

"Danah?" said Vera.

"What is it?"

"Not good, dear. Not good at the moment, you know."

"We'll deal with it, OK? Can you tell me what they told you?"

"E. coli. They said, E. coli. I have to stay here. I have to tell them if I start getting diarrhea. They have him on an IV, and they keep asking me where we ate in the last ten days, and I can't remember anything about the last ten days, except how wonderful Elsie was as Hamlet. I have told everyone about her performance." Her mother remembered Elsie, even in the midst of this crisis.

"How is E. coli spread, apart from uncooked hamburger?"

"They're worried about someone with it cooking or touching you without washing their hands."

"But he didn't do any cooking," said Danah, mightily relieved. "Did he eat hamburgers on the way back?"

"Yes, yes, he did."

"Where?"

"I feel so stupid, Danah. I'm not used to questions. Bernard always answers. He knows what we do. We ate in New York somewhere. No, it was before that bridge. It must have been New Jersey, off the highway. If I drove there again, I might remember. He had a hamburger. I had a salad."

"Bernard will remember, mom. He'll tell you when he wakes up. He just needs some rest. I'm sure you're OK if you didn't eat any of his hamburger."

"I didn't. Yes. That's right. I should stay in his room and ask him when he wakes up. They've put him in intensive care. They moved him. I hated seeing him so white on that gurney. They talked about complications. The young doctor, the good-looking one, used the word *syndrome*. What a horrible word."

"I think we should come down, mom."

"No. No, I'm sure he's getting better. They're treating him. They know what it is. It takes a few days for these things to work themselves out. He should be OK in a few days."

"Where are you going to sleep?"

"In his room. One of the nurses put up a cot for me. She reminded me of a friend you used to have, Jeannie or Jenny something, remember her?"

"Jenny, yes. We were good friends in 5th grade. Are you sure it's not her?" They laughed. "Do you remember the sleepovers we used to have?"

"I remember your bedroom in that condo we had then. You kept everything so neat and tidy. I remember looking in on you at night, even the books on your nightstand were alphabetized, and I thought somehow this natural order that surrounded you would protect us both. Your life was so clean and tidy. I wanted it to be that way forever. That's why I never told you very much about your father, darling. I didn't want him and his knack for chaos to infect your life. Unfortunately, you can't alphabetize life and set it on a shelf: Adolescence, Bankruptcy, oh, I don't know, Children, Disease, E. coli. It does not work that way. Life can only be tamed in rare moments, in the middle of the night, when you watch a sleeping child."

"I remember that room. I had a ballerina lamp with a pretty pink shade like a tutu. It was little-girl heaven, and everything was where I wanted it to be. I spent hours arranging my dolls on the third shelf of the bookcase. I had a notebook with facts about every doll: her birthday, what she ate, who she liked, and what she wanted to be when she grew up. Are you there?"

"I'm right here, darling."

"And I imagined all those dolls leaving me one day and having perfect houses of their own. Do you remember Ming Lee? I loved that doll in her red silk pants and Chinese embroidered jacket. She was the strongest doll I had. She was the only one who could cry and still look perfect afterwards. She cried a lot. She missed China. She liked rice, and she was determined to have an important job. You know, I think it's OK to try for perfection, to try to alphabetize scary stuff in the hopes of getting some power. And it's OK to settle, to compromise. Isn't that the human game: Aim high and accept what happens? I've always been really, really good at the aiming high part."

"I know you have. It takes a long, long time to learn to live with what is, my darling, and to simply enjoy being. I've just remembered something about Stewart I think you should hear. He tried to enlist in the army during the war. Well, they wouldn't have him because of his health. This is before I knew him. His sister told me this story. So, he decided his war effort would be to keep a London theater open every night, all through the Blitz. He was good at being in the moment and making people laugh. I think it must have been the Windmill Theater. You could probably look it up in old newspapers. I always thought that was a wonderful thing to do."

"It *was* a wonderful thing to do. I'll tell Elsie that story. She'll appreciate that."

"I don't know how I'm going to get through this, Danah."

"Well, look, mom, we have to accept the way things are with Bernard right now. That's how we'll get through this. Did you eat anything today?"

"A muffin. I think I'll go back and sit with Bernard now. When he wakes up, I can ask him where we ate. There's a nice little garden I can see from his window. There are azaleas in full bloom and benches, even children running around."

"Azaleas, benches, and children? A, 'b,' and 'c!'" You see, when we least expect it, order and purpose return. We can still alphabetize the world, mom!"

"Just don't let me see 'd' for dead. That's all I ask."

Danah smiled. "I know, I know. Think of something else for 'd.'"

"I can't."

"We will. Go back to his room, look out the window, and see

something else for 'd.'"

"I'll call you tonight, dear. I'm sure you have other things to do today than sit by the phone."

Hearing these words, Danah decided to get out of the house for a while and go to a mall—for the first time in over a year. I'll get some baby things for Holly, she thought, pleased with the unexpectedness of the errand.

"Did you hear from Vera?" said Bob, taking his breakfast plate to the sink.

"Bernard's got E. coli. My mother's pretty worried, but she's coping."

"Should we go down there?" Bob put the paper on the island counter.

"No. She's calling tonight. She'll know more then. She's optimistic. He's on an IV. That's all you can do, I guess."

"Coffee?"

"No thanks. I feel like getting out of the house for a while. I want to blow a few hours at the mall. I never do that! The play is over. The workmen have gone. I need a break."

"OK, well, later today, Elsie and I are seeing that action

movie she talked about. Do you want to join us?"

"No thanks. I so rarely get the impulse to go to a mall. I don't know when I'll be back."

Danah chose the fast lane. We are each one of us, in our own little time capsules, speeding along until we come up side-by-side with another. At this moment, Danah was cheek-to-jowl with another minivan. She pulled ahead of it in what felt like slow motion. The highway divided. She curved to the left and was alone on the road—no one ahead, no one in the rear view mirror. Elsie's last line from Hamlet arrived in her head. 'And the rest is silence.' She smiled to herself. Silence had always made Danah anxious. Silence meant someone wasn't telling her the whole story. Silence meant a failure to find the right words. But what if, somehow, from now on, silence was a comfortable part of life?

Parking next to a mammoth metal pole labeled D4, Danah wondered what her mother had come up with for 'd.' and realized that she herself was a 'd.' She pushed through the double glass doors into Sears. A wall of TV screens confronted her, and she compared the color tones and clarity of images of a soap opera that they were all tuned to. A red banner running across the bottom of the screens announced breaking news: a two-car crash on the highway. She moved close enough to hear that both men had died. She saw Paul's car. The Morgan had been crushed. And now she watched a crane pull a truck out of a ditch. Traffic was backed up for four miles. Both men were dead on arrival at the hospital.

Danah found a backless, wooden bench. Paul, the Paul she had kissed, had died this morning. She fixated on a child eating a cone piled high with chocolate ice cream and covered with every color of sprinkle. This child is enjoying a treat. Paul is dead. That's the way it is right now. The child smiled at her even as she dialed Holly's number. Harry picked up.

"Hey sweetheart! This is Auntie Danah. Is mommy there, Harry?"

"Mommy's sad, Auntie."

"I know, Harry. She is sad. She had some bad news. Can you tell her Auntie Danah wants to . . ."

"Hello?" said Holly.

"Is anyone there with you, Holly?"

"Harry's here, aren't you, honey!"

"I'm so sorry, Holly. My god! It's awful. I don't know what to say."

"Yes, yes, of course. Are you coming over? Now?"

"I'm on my way."

Danah took to the highway like a kite to the wind. She flew. Her heart took a few dives, and she recovered. She held steady.

"Don't say a word!" said Holly, opening the door to her house. She looked older than last night. The two women hugged tightly. "Harry has been playing with his trucks all morning." Holly shook her head emphatically, signaling to Danah that Harry didn't know yet.

"What's your favorite movie, Harry?" Danah asked. Harry immediately ran to the den.

"I'll get him settled down and come back," she told Holly. Harry handed Danah a DVD about large vehicles.

"It can't be true, right? It's not true, right?" said Holly as Danah poured two large glasses of wine. Holly reached out for her glass and downed it like water after a run. She pointed at a glass in the sink. "I mean, that's the glass he drank from this morning. He held that glass a few hours ago. That's what I know, what I'm sure of, you see."

"How did you hear?"

"The police. Maybe an hour ago, I don't know. Something about, 'Your husband was in a fatal accident.' I think they're sending someone over here. I must go to the hospital, but not with Harry. I have to go, if it's really true. Is it true? Can things change like this?"

"Things can change, yes. Bob and Elsie can take Harry out for the day. I'll go with you to the hospital."

"Will you stay with me, Danah? Don't tell Harry. Don't let Bob or Elsie tell him. I want him to live as long as he can thinking that his dad is alive and coming home."

Danah went outside to call Bob so that Harry wouldn't hear. Holly, meanwhile, wandered around unplugging things and closing curtains.

The women visited the hospital in a dreamlike state. Holly told someone in white: "We never talked about our funerals. We just didn't. It wasn't something we planned on having. My husband was very fit . . . until he died." Then she broke into hysteria, repeating 'very fit until he died, that's very funny.' Danah reassured Holly she could go home and think about how she wanted to handle things.

Danah sat on a metal chair against a white wall in the room

where Paul lay dead and Holly's heart broke wide open. Danah had never been in a room with a dead person. She did not cry. She stared at her slip-on suede shoes and imagined the room where her father had been taken after he died. The tears she had never cried for him finally fell. She ached from trying to imagine his face, his eyes, and any look they might have exchanged and she realized that she loved her father in spite of everything. She stood up abruptly and joined Holly. She looked at Paul's face and hair—miraculously unspoiled.

"He was a gorgeous man. I mean it. A truly gorgeous man in every way." Danah kept staring at him. Holly looked at Danah. Then, their eyes met and they laughed in grief and profound connection.

"Really?" replied Holly, studying Paul's face, and wiping away tears with the back of her hands. "I always thought you found him too pretty."

"He was gorgeous, as few men are."

Holly crumpled onto the linoleum floor in a semi-faint. Her mouth transformed into the shape of misery and she moaned, "What am I going to do?" until she couldn't say it any more. Meanwhile, Danah removed every wrinkle from the pale blue blanket covering Paul's body. When Holly fell silent, Danah crouched beside her, took her hand, and insisted she stand up.

"I'm going outside now. You can talk to Paul. I think he'll tell you what you're going to do. He will. He will tell you." While pacing the hallway floor, Danah called Bob, who told her that Vera had called. Bernard was recovering. The doctors expected him to make a full recovery. Danah felt relief, happy that her mother's world remained intact and some gratitude toward Bernard for pulling through.

Holly emerged from the room looking peaceful. In the privacy of Danah's car, she confided that Paul had indeed spoken to her.

"He said I'm going to have our baby and continue to be a great mother." They smiled at each other through tears and love.

"Yes. You're having a baby. That's exactly what you're doing!"

A week later, Paul was celebrated at a memorial service. Bob gave a speech. People stood up and spoke spontaneously. Many people testified to Paul's sense of humor, his kindness, his ability to do what he wanted to do, and his talent for being happy.

The following week, Danah arranged to meet Holly at the

health club. It was the first time Holly had returned there since Paul's death. The two staff members on duty said how pleased they were to see her. Holly nodded while looking up at the high ceiling and the industrial light fixtures. After entering Paul's office and closing his door, Holly said: "The last time I was in this room, he was alive. He was showing me plans. Where are they? Here. Look. These are the blueprints for the extension. This is the new playroom, with its own bathroom. Here's the number of the guy he was going to hire to do this work for us." She handed Danah a scrap of paper with Paul's writing on it.

"Anthony Del Vecchio?"

"Yes." Holly swung around in Paul's chair.

"I'll call him."

"Why?"

"Because Paul liked him, and he won't wait forever."

"Wait? For what?"

"A commitment, a date. He'll have other jobs. We've got to get on his schedule. Pass me the phone." Holly pushed the white phone towards Danah, who set up a meeting for later that day. Anthony had heard about Paul's death and wanted to make the job a priority.

"Today?" said Holly with a dash of excitement.

"He sounds like a nice guy. We'll get a schedule together and make these plans fly, OK?"

"This is probably a good idea. OK, do what has to be done. Paul would have consulted with you anyway. What can I do?"

"Your job is to show your kids how dreams come true," said Danah. Holly nodded. "Shit happens, Holly, and so does love. We have to continue to be present and to be . . . ourselves."

Danah threw herself into the role of general contractor on Paul's behalf. One day, not long into the process, she found herself watching the workmen from the top of a twelve-foot aluminum ladder. Two men measured, cut, and carried two-by-fours to the corner where two other men framed the new playroom. Danah watched Norm. He stood beside a pair of sawhorses dotted with aqua paint from her recreation room. While she scrutinized the workmen like a theatrical director checking blocking, she fingered an antique, silver chain around her neck. It had belonged to her grandmother. Danah had received it from Vera a few days ago in the mail. She tugged at the chain until an antique, silver locket emerged from under her red sweatshirt. She slid her thumbnail into the crack on its side, and the locket popped open. It held a black-and-white photo. She smiled. After she snapped the locket shut, she held it a moment between thumb and forefinger, with eyes closed, drawing comfort from the warmth it had absorbed from her body. Then she slipped it back under her sweatshirt secure in the knowledge that she had everything she needed, even if it wasn't always in plain sight. No matter what changes in my life I know that I love and I am loved.

ABOUT THE AUTHOR

Annabelle has been published steadily over the last 30 years. She has written many plays for children. *The New York Times* and *The International Herald Tribune* ran articles about her proprietary educational theater series, Classic Theatre for Schools. Born in Edinburgh, Scotland, Annabelle lived in London, England, until she met her future husband and this led her to live in New York City. Annabelle now lives in Connecticut. She is very active on Google Plus and thoroughly enjoys connecting with people via that platform.

45471235R00205

Made in the USA
Charleston, SC
22 August 2015